"Go get some gear on," Bridget ordered.

"Seriously?"

"Chicken?" she asked.

Mike laughed. He felt like a seven-year-old being dared.

"So what position am I supposed to play?"

"I thought you were a goalie," she taunted.

Challenge accepted. He wasn't sure what she thought she was trying to prove, but he could handle a girl in road hockey, even if his game had been off lately.

"So what are the rules?" he asked once they'd strapped on their pads. He tapped his stick on the pavement.

"I'm going to score. You're going to try to stop me. Play to five?"

"We'll need to stop before that. You're not going to score."

She was good. He had to give her that. Much better than he'd expected. Mike, however, was better than good. He was one of the best. He was soon in his zone, watching her every move and expression. She didn't score, though she came close.

After fifteen furious minutes, Bridget called time. "I guess I owe you an apology."

Mike looked down at her. "It's okay. I admit to provoking you. And this was actually a lot of fun. You're not bad—for a girl." He grinned at her.

"You're not bad, either—for a...for a guy from Quebec."

Dear Reader,

I'm so excited you've joined me for my first Harlequin romance!

The sports world offers compelling stories. There's the athletes' dedication and the amazing things they can accomplish. There are the fans who live and die with their teams, a loyalty that transcends geography and success or failure. It doesn't hurt that athletes are by necessity in top physical condition. Combine all that and you get some great settings for romance.

In this story, Mike Reimer is a successful hockey goalie, but past experience has convinced him that his commitment to his sport makes relationships untenable. Since he's dealing with a crisis of confidence in his play, that has to be his first priority. Still, he can't help but notice Bridget O'Reilly when she dives into his life...and falls in love with his car. Bridget is a former competitive swimmer now channeling that drive into coaching. She understands the passion it takes to win because she shares it. As Mike gets back to his championship form, his future is leading him out of Toronto. Bridget, however, has her family and her own dreams in the city. Is either of them willing to risk it all for the other?

To share your own love of sports, the people who play them and the stories they generate, please find me at kimfindlay.ca, on Facebook at kimfindlayauthor or on Twitter, @missheyer74.

Kim

HEARTWARMING

Crossing the Goal Line

—

Kim Findlay

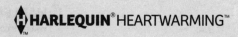

Recycling programs
for this product may
not exist in your area.

ISBN-13: 978-1-335-63356-9

Crossing the Goal Line

Copyright © 2018 by Kim Findlay

Printed in U.S.A.

Kim Findlay lives in Toronto, Canada, with her husband, two sons and the world's cutest dog. When she can get time away from her accounting business, she can be found sailing, reading or writing, depending on the season, time of day and her energy level. You can find her at kimfindlay.ca, @missheyer74 or on Facebook.

For my parents and sister, who let me read,
and my husband and sons, who let me write.

CHAPTER ONE

NOT EVERYONE WHO had red hair was short tempered. That was just a cliché. Bridget knew she was pretty even tempered, despite having bright red hair. Of course, she wasn't perfect. There were a couple of things that could set her off. One of those things was Wally the Weasel, and he'd done it again.

Bridget shoved open the door out of the pool area and stalked down the hallway with all the authority one could muster in a swimsuit and flip-flops. She reached the Weasel's office at the far end and, of course, he wasn't there. Bridget shoved her glasses back up her nose with her finger, and huffed a breath. She had no doubt he'd carefully timed his morning activities to miss her. She'd have loved to stay and wait him out, but she had her own timetable.

She glared at his desk, and then turned and stomped out. Fortunately, this was the quiet time of day at the exclusive athletic club, so she didn't meet anyone. Making nice to the members was never her strongest suit, and was close to impossible when she was angry.

Once she returned to the pool, she began to relax. She was back in her world. It might feel claustrophobic to some, but she was perfectly comfortable here. The chlorine-infused air was moist and the place echoed with the slightest sounds of the water's movement in the pool. But in this world, she was confident, and one of the best at what she did.

Tad, the pool assistant, had finished setting up the lane swim markers that had sparked Bridget's fit of temper, and was sitting on a bench, looking at his phone. She'd swear that kid would expire without that gadget. He was living dangerously: water would destroy it. She never had her phone in the pool area for that very reason. One had only to lose a couple, or five, and the lesson sank in.

"Tad, get the boys," she called across the pool. Tad looked up guiltily, nodded and scurried into the men's changing room. Bridget went into the women's room, and found her four female charges. They were small, and very nervous. Bridget squatted down to look at them at their level.

"Hey, there, I'm glad to see you all got into

your swimsuits. We can come out to the pool now, but you can be near the water only when there's an adult around, okay?"

They nodded, but no one started moving. They were a little hesitant, which wasn't surprising. She smiled reassuringly, grabbed two little hands, and led the way.

Tad had brought out four little boys. Three were looking at her apprehensively, while one was staring around like he owned the place. It had been years since Bridget taught beginners, but she recognized the signs. He was going to be one of those.

Bridget noticed someone swimming in the lane Tad had set up, but that was not her focus now. These eight kids were. The pool was supposed to be used only by her for the next forty-five minutes, so the Weasel, snob that he was, was up to something. He'd been opposed to the idea of this class from the beginning.

She had the kids sit on one of the benches, and again squatted in front of them so she could look at them eye to eye.

"I'm Bridget, and I'm going to be teaching you to swim. Has anyone here taken swimming lessons before?"

Bridget knew they hadn't. She'd helped

with the selection process and these eight had been chosen for the pilot project because they had no exposure to swimming instruction. But it was a good way to get started. Seven little heads shook, while one kid shrugged, like it was no big thing.

"I think it's important that everyone knows how to swim. We live in a country with a lot of lakes and rivers, and lots of swimming pools. Also, swimming is fun. It's really good exercise. It's a sport, too. Have you seen it in the Olympics? I used to compete for Canada, and I'm now coaching the swim team at the club here to race in swim meets. Maybe someday one of you can represent Canada as a swimmer."

Bridget wanted to inspire them if she could. She'd loved competing, and she thought it taught a lot of life lessons.

"Were you any good?" It was that boy. Bridget mentally reviewed the attendance sheet in her mind. Ah, yes. His name was Tony. He'd apparently decided to challenge her from the start.

Bridget looked him in the eyes. "Did you have a specific lap time in mind?" There was a pause. Tony wasn't sure how to respond to that. "I won a lot of races," Bridget continued, "but I was never good enough to make the Olympic team. However, I'm pretty sure I can still swim faster than anyone you know." Bridget wasn't boasting. She knew what she could do.

Tony crossed his arms. "You can't beat a guy. My dad says girls can't beat guys."

And just like that, Tony had pushed Bridget's biggest button. She had spent her entire life trying to prove that girls could do everything guys could do. It was a never-ending task. "I think your dad is mistaken, Tony." Bridget indicated the man swimming in the lane. "He's swimming pretty well. You think I can take him?"

Tony hesitated. He hadn't expected that. He wanted to save face, but wasn't sure what to do.

The other kids were impressed. "Can you really swim faster than him?"

Bridget assessed the swimmer. Adult male, tall, good physical shape, but yeah, she could take him.

Bridget called to Tad to look after the class. She pulled off her heavy glasses, bane of her life, pulled on her swimming goggles, and strode over to the end of the pool. The goggles didn't help much with her vision, but she knew this place like the back of her hand, and she could navigate blindfolded.

The man in the lane may have been swimming pretty well, but he wasn't a racer. There was wasted movement: technique issues she could see even without her glasses.

He was about halfway up the lane, swimming away from her, and she paused, caught her breath and pushed off in her starting dive.

The pool was Bridget's element. When she was a kid, she had wanted to be a professional hockey player just like her brothers had, but her poor vision messed with her depth perception and limited her ability to play a fast-moving game on the ice. Instead, she'd channeled that drive into swimming, and she'd excelled.

She surfaced, having picked up half the distance the other swimmer had on her. She started her smooth, sure stroke, slicing through the water with precision and power. She was within a couple of body lengths by the time he hit the wall, and she knew she had him.

Recreational swimmers don't train on turns, and she had.

She came out of her turn another length ahead of him. She could sense he'd become aware that this was a race, and increased the tempo of his strokes, but she made it to the end of the pool with lengths to spare.

She hoped her temper hadn't led her astray. In her experience, men could get upset if a woman beat them. Her focus was supposed to be on her class, but maybe she'd earned some respect from her students, especially Tony. That should make him willing to listen to her. She wanted to continue with that momentum, so she lifted herself out of the pool, no longer aware of the other swimmer, until he spoke.

"That was impressive. Do you take private students?"

Bridget had pulled off her goggles, and when she turned, the man was a blur. She looked at him fuzzily.

"Sorry, no. I didn't mean to disturb you. I was making a point for my class." She nodded her head toward the blurs that were her students. Perhaps the hardest part of this job, other than the Weasel, was being nice to members who were not always nice themselves. She added a perfunctory smile. At least he hadn't pitched a fit about losing to her.

And the rest of the class did go smoothly.

Tony was silenced, and the other students were suitably impressed. It wasn't until all the kids had been returned to the changing rooms that she became aware that the lane swimmer had finished and left. She shrugged. She wasn't sure if she'd see him again. Her plans for the Weasel included terminating the lane swimming during her class, so she hoped she wouldn't.

Bridget's position as swim coach involved being at the club early for morning practice, and again after the kids were done school for fitness training and more practice. Weekends would often involve traveling to swim meets. Since they were in Toronto, the traveling was often just across town, but at times she was gone for entire weekends.

Her hours were irregular, but she loved her job and didn't mind that her time off was out of sync with most people's. She was determined to get to the Olympics, this time as a coach. She had a couple of swimmers who had tons of talent, and she found helping them was becoming as fulfilling as racing herself.

She was teaching this swim class in what should have been her free time. She got her charges safely off to the teacher's aide who was returning them to school, and changed into shorts and a T-shirt to do her own training. One of the perks of the job was using the facilities, and midmorning there was no one using the machines in the weight room. She liked to keep almost as fit as she required her swimmers to be.

After she'd had a shower she would make another attempt to track down Wally.

SHE DIDN'T FIND him until just before her afternoon practice. When she appeared in his doorway, he flinched.

"Hello, Wall-*ter*," Bridget corrected herself. He insisted on being called by his full name, and Bridget was sure it wouldn't be wise to let him know her nickname for him. He'd freak out over Wally, let alone Weasel.

"I don't know why you have so much trouble with my name," he responded peevishly.

Bridget ignored his comment. "I've got a question for you."

"I'm very busy."

"Oh, this will take only a moment. You see, the pool is booked at nine for a class I'm teaching, but somehow there was a lane swimmer there this morning."

Wally shuffled some stuff around his desk. "Yes, well, it's like this…the management committee asked if I could make that arrangement for this new, ah, associate member.""

Associate member? Bridget thought. That was a new one. But if the request came from the management committee...

"Perhaps you could have notified me?" she asked.

"Ah, sorry, I thought I had." They both knew better.

"Are you expecting any more 'associate members' to be wanting the pool at nine a.m.? Maybe enough to take up the entire pool?" Nine had been chosen specifically because it was after the morning swim training and lap swims for those going to work or school, and before the water aerobics classes began. It was the quietest time in the pool, except after closing.

Nobody was being put out by her beginner class, except Wally, who didn't like having these "freeloader" kids in his precious club. He was more concerned about maintaining the club's reputation than any of the members were.

Bridget and Wally were at cross-purposes in respect to this class.

Wally seemed to be enjoying a little joke.

"No, I don't think we'll have any other members like him."

"If any others should come up, please let me know and make sure I actually respond. Otherwise..." Bridget left the threat hanging, partly because she wasn't sure just what she'd do, and partly so that Wally could imagine the worst.

Bridget headed out to change for her afternoon coaching. There was something funny about this, but she had places to be, and couldn't take the time to shake Wally down any further.

SOMETHING WASN'T QUITE RIGHT. Mike was sure of it. He'd done his second morning lane swim, and the instructor who'd raced him the first day was there with her class. She hadn't raced him this morning. Instead, she had ignored him. He was getting the feeling that she wasn't happy with him being there.

He'd been getting that feeling a lot in Toronto.

Hockey fans weren't happy with him, and he couldn't blame them. He was one of the best-paid goalies in the league, and when he arrived last spring he was supposed to make the team better. Instead, he'd played badly; as badly as he'd ever played as a professional.

Although Mike hadn't been thrilled at the trade to Toronto, he had pride, and he was not happy with his performance. He hoped that he could bring the fans around by playing up to his level this year, but training camp had just begun. His time to prove himself hadn't arrived, so he was still living with last year's reputation.

The hockey team wasn't happy with him, either. After a "prank" had damaged his watch while he was swimming laps at the team facility, he'd come up with this alternative. Swim here first, then practice with the team.

The athletic club management committee had been welcoming, and the club manager almost too welcoming, but now that he was here, he realized something was going on. So after he'd showered and dressed, he stopped by the office of the club manager, "Call me Walter," to check.

Mike knocked on the door frame.

He thought he saw a wary look on the manager that was replaced by a worried one once Walter recognized him.

"Come in, come in!"

Mike stayed in the doorway. The office wasn't that big, and he didn't plan to be there long. "Are you sure there's no problem with my using the pool for laps in the morning?" he asked.

Walter paused for just a moment. "Of course not! We're so pleased to have you here. And, of course, normally there's nothing going on in the pool at that time."

"There seems to be a class."

"Oh, that's just Bridget's special project." With a sudden suspicious glance, Walter asked, "Has she said something to you? Has she done anything?"

Mike wondered if Walter was afraid of the redhead, Bridget.

"No. Is she likely to?" he asked in amusement. Did Walter think she could hurt him somehow?

The other man sighed. "She has a temper, and she's a little obsessive over that class."

So it was this class, not all of her classes, Mike thought.

"What's so special about that class?" he asked aloud.

Walter shook his head sadly. "Those kids aren't members, and their parents certainly aren't. They're from the local school. As you can tell, the neighborhood around the club went downhill sometime after the club was established, and, well, the locals aren't the kinds of people we'd accept as members. Bridget thought this class bringing in neighborhood kids would help with community relations. Not that we have problems, I assure you. Just a little graffiti, and honestly, these days, who doesn't?" Walter smiled ingratiatingly. "If you have any problems with Bridget, any at all, just let me know."

Mike had the strong impression that Walter was hoping he'd find some.

"Bridget is a swimming instructor?" he asked. She was obviously good. Maybe he could hire her for a couple of lessons. It was frustrating to have someone beat him that easily. He hated losing.

"No, not exactly. She's the coach for our swim team." Walter sighed, obviously not happy to have to sing her praises. "She was a competitive swimmer, and yes, there has been improvement with the team so far,"

Walter didn't seem to hope or want that to continue, but he cleared his throat, adding, "She's not really one of us. She came up with this crazy idea about building community relations by teaching local kids to swim and got some of the members all excited about it, but I'm just waiting for those kids to cause a problem. They don't know how to behave in a place like this, and they're not likely to become members in the future. They're going to start thinking they're entitled to use our resources, and it's going to cause trouble down the line."

Mike kept his expression neutral. "Not really one of us" meant not rich. Mike had grown up close to the poverty line, so he didn't feel quite like "one of us," even though he now had enough money to make him welcome almost anywhere. When he was young, he would have been one of "those kids."

He felt warmer about this Bridget. If she'd swum competitively, well, that would explain how she was able to beat him. And he liked her motive for starting this class, whether or not it would work out.

He also understood a little better why she might not appreciate his swimming during her class time. The pool was plenty big, so they could coexist, but Walter was obviously opposed to the idea of the class and would be pleased to squeeze it out. This must look like a first step.

"Thank you, Walter. I just wanted to understand. Since I'm new here, I don't know the protocol. Didn't want to ruffle any feathers."

Walter assured him that no feathers worth worrying about were being ruffled.

He smiled and tried not to dwell on the fact that Walter had a very punchable face.

Mike thought he'd like to make a gesture to indicate that he would support the class, and decided to think that over.

He had no idea that the gesture would result in his being kidnapped.

BRIDGET FOUND THE gesture in an envelope addressed to her a couple of days later. In the envelope were ten tickets to a preseason Blaze game. There was a printed note, apologizing for the intrusion into her class space, and indicating that these tickets were in appreciation. There was a scrawl at the bottom that was presumably a signature, but it was illegible.

Bridget understood it was from the lap swimmer, and even for a preseason game, these hockey tickets were hard to come by. She cynically thought that money could solve a lot of problems. The lap swimmer must have a lot of cash. He was probably some business type, of which the club had many.

She'd never been to the new arena built for the expansion team ten years ago, and had never seen a professional game live in her life, even though her whole family had been hockey fans from birth.

Canadians loved hockey, so the new team, the Toronto Blaze, had quickly gained fans and sold out the same as the sister team. Her brothers would be very envious. That was the good part.

Taking eight kids along would certainly limit how intently she could watch the game. Or maybe prevent her from watching it at all. Bridget had nephews and nieces so she knew what she was in for.

The club had a van to take the swim team to meets, and Bridget was able to book it for Saturday. Tad was happy to come along when there was an opportunity to see a hockey game.

As expected, the outing wasn't a walk in the park. The kids weren't really bad. Tony of course had to question everything Bridget told him, but eight kids were a handful. She and Tad finally corralled them in their seats. Then Bridget had to prevent Tony from finding a better view by climbing over the seats in front of him. Seats that were occupied.

Bridget would have gladly watched the play on the ice, even if it was mostly prospects playing, but the kids started to get bored. Popcorn and drinks helped distract them for a bit, and then the trips to the bathroom began.

During the break between the first and second periods, Bridget and Tad split the children up and took them around the arena. Bridget started to wonder if this had been worthwhile. It would be nice to have the chance to explore the arena but these kids didn't want to look at hockey memorabilia; they wanted to run.

Then, at the end of the second period, someone appeared at the end of their row.

Bridget had taken the aisle seat so that no one—Tony—could get out without her knowledge. Because of that she was the first to realize he was there, and she recognized him at once. The man was tall, six-four according to the newspapers, and Bridget thought that looked right. He was wearing a suit, minus the jacket, and wasn't bad looking, especially for a hockey player. He had all his own teeth and hair, for starters. His nose had a distinctive bend from a previous break, but he wore it well. His hair was dark, his eyes a light gray.

This was Mike Reimer, the expensive goalie Toronto had acquired in a trade last year from Quebec City. The goalie who'd won three Cups in Quebec and then bombed out in Toronto.

He was standing at the end of the row, holding a handful of team hats. For a moment Bridget stared, wondering why he was there. Had their benefactor set up a meeting with a member of the team? Or…but no…

Then Tony said, "It's that rotten swimmer from the pool!" And Bridget closed her eyes, wanting to strangle Tony.

Now she understood the preferential treatment her lane swimmer had been given by the management committee at the club, and the tickets for her class. She felt stupid. Anyone but a blind swimmer would have realized… but she had to open her eyes and deal with this. As briefly as possible.

MIKE HAD NOT been enjoying the hockey game.

He was in the luxury box with the rest of the players who weren't playing that afternoon, but no one from the team had been talking to him. He got it. He really did. He knew he'd let them down during the last playoffs, and he hadn't been forgiven. He was naturally a reserved guy, and had spent his entire career with one team. Learning to make nice with new guys wasn't his forte.

It didn't help that Mike's backup was a popular guy. When the team's starting goalie had retired after an injury last year, many thought that Turchenko would get his chance. Turchenko thought so, too. He was a gregarious guy who spoke in fractured English, and his mangled phrases were often quoted. He was blond and blue-eyed and looked good in photos. He was also undisciplined and lazy, not making the most of his natural talent. Mike found him immature.

But Turchenko was playing today, and doing well. So Mike "overheard" a lot of comments about how good the kid was doing, and he had to bite his tongue. Nothing was going to change unless he, Mike, went out and played like a top goalie, and there were still a couple of games before he'd be back in net. So, he grabbed the hats he'd picked up for the kids and took them over to see how things were going.

The redheaded instructor was there, this time in jeans and a jersey (not his of course) looking a little frazzled. He felt some satisfaction from that. It still smarted that she'd beat him in swimming.

"Everyone having fun?" he asked.

Bridget turned to the row of kids and asked, "Having fun?"

The response was positive. Mike passed down the red-yellow-and-black hats, which each kid immediately put on. Good, Mike thought. He was making progress with someone.

Bridget turned to her charges. "What would you like to say to Mr. Reimer?" she asked.

A chorus of thank-yous came back, with something that sounded like "bad swimmer." Mike thought that was a little unfair. He reserved his talents for frozen water.

"Thank you very much, Mr. Reimer," Bridget added.

He blinked. Bridget turned back to the kids, dismissing him. This was a new low.

Before he could ask what her problem was, he heard a cough behind him.

"Mike Reimer? Could I take a picture?"

Mike turned. Part of being on the team was public relations, and he'd always honored that. So he signed what was put in front of him, smiled for pictures, ignored the comments made behind his back and left as the third period started without speaking further to the swimming class.

BRIDGET HADN'T PLANNED on kidnapping anyone. She'd dropped off the eight kids, with sticky faces, stories and hats, in front of their local school. Parents and caregivers were waiting, and Bridget thought, after reviewing the outing, that there wasn't much in the stories that would worry any responsible adult.

Of course, with Tony, all bets were off.

She drove back to the club and dropped Tad at the front door. After parking the van, she'd taken the keys in and filled out the form that Wally the Weasel required. She made sure to note that there was no damage, since Wally seemed to expect these kids to act like wild animals. She'd stopped by her desk (a cubby off the pool room) to catch up her notes on the swim team, and then, finally, had been ready to head home.

She was still a little irritable, but she was free, and was looking forward to a relaxing evening. Now that the hockey preseason had begun, there were sure to be some of her brothers and friends at the house to watch a hockey game, and her mother would have prepared an incredible amount of food. Bridget rented the apartment in the basement of her parents' place, so she decided she might as well join them. She sent a text to see who was around.

She slipped out the back door to get her car from the parking lot, and beside her fifteen-year-old Mazda was a man leaning on a car.

Not just any man, and not just any car.

MIKE SAW THE back door open, and then the red hair. He crossed his arms and waited. He wasn't exactly sure why he'd come back to the athletic facility. He didn't have friends here to make plans with on a Saturday night. He could have gone to a bar or club. He knew he'd have heard some insults, but a well-known athlete whose salary was published in the media could find companionship.

He'd grown tired of that scenario long ago, though. Puck-bunnies and sycophants weren't what he wanted. He just wanted to hang with someone.

The redhead—Bridget—had been a little testy at the game, but he wasn't sure if that was the kids, or him, or maybe she just didn't like hockey. He decided he was going to find out.

He'd heard of love at first sight, but this was the first time he'd seen it happen, right in front of him. Bridget had come out, checking her phone, not even noticing him. Then when she'd looked up, she seemed annoyed. But as he'd waited, her expression softened, a small smile turned up the corners of her mouth and she moved forward as if drawn by an irresistible force.

Mike watched as she closed in on him… and then passed him…staring at his car. She brought one hand up, as if to touch it, then dropped it again.

She shook her head, and looked back at him. "A P1?"

Mike raised his eyebrows in surprise. "Yes."

He watched as she completed her circuit of his car. Not everyone would recognize a McLaren, or know which one he had. He'd impressed people with this car, mostly when they realized what it cost, but he'd never been ignored for it. He didn't like that. It was a nice car, even a beautiful one, but still it was just a car. Maybe he'd been spoiled. People noticed him. They might think he was slime crawling out from under a rock, or they might think he was a hockey god, but they didn't ignore him.

With a sigh, she finally tore her gaze away, and saw him standing there, waiting.

"If I won a lottery…" she said dreamily. "Brian wants an Aston Martin, and Patrick a Ferrari, but this—she's exactly what I'd choose."

Mike didn't know who Brian and Patrick were, and he didn't much care. He'd decided this had been a mistake, so he'd ask about the kids and the game and get out of there. If he wanted his ego stepped on further, he could just walk down Yonge Street.

"So, the kids all got home safely?" he asked.

Her eyes narrowed. "Yes," she answered tersely.

What was her problem?

"I hope everyone enjoyed it," he persisted.

"I think the kids enjoyed the hats and the popcorn more than the game. There weren't that many players they knew." She paused for just a moment. "Turchenko seemed to be doing well."

Mike was tired of hearing how well Turchenko was doing. The guy had played well for the half of the game he'd been in. He also hadn't been challenged that much. Mike knew, though, that a lot of people, including most of his teammates and the fans in Toronto, hoped he'd win the starting job and leave Mike to warm the bench.

He was determined that wasn't going to happen. So his response was not very diplomatic.

"Of course, everyone likes Turchenko. He's blond and blue-eyed and flirts with—"

"Right, because I care only about the way he looks. I couldn't possibly understand hockey with my poor female brain," Bridget spit out.

Mike hadn't meant that. He'd been raised by a strong woman who'd used her brains and hard work to deal with being pregnant and stranded at sixteen. He'd been going to say that Turchenko flirted with the press, not women, but Bridget had reacted like an angry cat. Her eyes were flashing, her freckles almost obscured by her heated cheeks, and he could swear her very hair was vibrating with anger. It was fascinating.

Walter had said she had a temper, and Mike was obviously getting a look at it. He was tired and irritated, and glad he wasn't the only one out of sorts. Instead of answering diplomatically, he decided to poke the bear.

"A lot of people think they understand hockey, but it's different when you're actually playing it."

Yep, Mike thought. *Her hair is vibrating.*

"Okay, come with me," she snarled. She stomped over to the Mazda. She unlocked the door and looked back. "Get in, hot shot."

"In that?" Mike responded, looking from his pride and joy to the car Bridget was halfway into.

"Afraid of a girl?"

The bear was well and fully poked. Those eyes were almost lasering through him. With a shrug, he swung himself around the car and opened the passenger door. He'd barely folded himself in when a blast of rap music assailed his ears and Bridget tore out of the parking lot.

Mike propped his hand against the roof of the little car to keep from falling on Bridget as she down shifted for the turn. He should have known that anyone who fell for his car the way she had would drive a stick. And skillfully, too, though she was going a little too fast for safety.

"Okay, now that you've got me, where are we going?" he yelled over the music.

"To play hockey!"

Mike wedged himself against the door. He didn't know what she had in mind, but this was more fun than he'd had in a while.

CHAPTER TWO

SHE OBVIOUSLY KNEW the way well, and as she took another side street, he realized he was lost. But they finally pulled up in front of a brick two-story on a dead-end street. Bridget pulled out the keys, and Mike welcomed the sudden silence as the "music" stopped in mid-phrase. She slammed out of the car and stalked up the driveway before unlocking the garage door and sliding it open.

Inside was hockey gear. A moment passed. Then he realized that when she said they were going to play hockey, she hadn't meant on a screen or table. She wanted to play road hockey. He almost laughed. Sure, she was a good swimmer, but did she really think she could take on a professional hockey player?

Apparently, she did. She was dragging a net down the driveway. Mike opened the door and got out of the car. As she set up the net on the street, he noticed that the block was perfect for playing road ball. Originally, the plan must have been for the street to extend further; the pavement stretched out another fifty feet then dead-ended at a chain-link fence and an abandoned parking lot. There were pink and blue lines marked in chalk. This was a well-used space for road hockey. He'd have loved access to something like this when he was growing up.

"Go get some gear on," she ordered.

"Seriously?"

"Chicken?" she asked.

Mike laughed. He felt like a seven-year-old being dared.

"So what position am I supposed to play?"

"I thought you were a goalie," she taunted.

Challenge accepted, Mike thought. He wasn't sure what she thought she was trying to prove, but he could handle a girl in road ball, even if his game had been off lately. He'd better be able to…

He followed her back to the garage where there was an impressive amount of gear for both road and ice hockey. She pointed to a pile of goalie equipment, and he picked through for the largest pads he could find, then tested a couple of sticks before settling on one. She tossed him a helmet, and he put it on. It wasn't anything like his own, but if she managed to fire a ball at his face, he was sure there'd be a lot of force behind it.

Bridget was holding a couple of tennis balls and what was obviously her own helmet and stick. Both showed signs of wear. Mike wasn't surprised. While he was confident he was better than she was, she was obviously athletic, practiced at road hockey and highly motivated. So was he.

"So what are the rules?" he asked once they were back on the road. He knocked the sidebars of the net with the stick to check its size and stability. Then he tapped the stick on the road a couple of times and turned to see what she was planning. He could see her focus through the thick glasses.

"I'm going to score. You're going to try to stop me. Play to five?"

"We'll need to stop before that. You're not going to score."

Eyes blazing, she started.

SHE WAS GOOD. He had to give her that. Much better than he'd expected. She occasionally whiffed completely, but she was fast, smart and very determined. She could place the ball exactly where she wanted, and with a lot of force.

Mike, however, was better than good. He was one of the best. He'd grown up playing road hockey and it wasn't a difficult transition from the ice back to the pavement. He had lightning-fast reflexes and could read a player's intentions from their body language and expression. He was soon in his zone, watching her every move and glance. She didn't score. She did come close, tested him pretty well, but he was just as determined as she was, and this time, it was his element, not hers.

After fifteen furious minutes, Bridget called time. Pulling up her face guard, she looked at Mike. He stood up to his full height, shoving up his face guard as well.

"I guess I owe you an apology," Bridget said after a pause, her previous anger clearly dissipated.

Mike looked down at her. "It's okay. I admit to provoking you. And this was actually a lot of fun. You're not bad—for a girl." He grinned at her.

"You're not bad, either—for a…for a guy from Quebec," she countered. "But I should probably get you back now—"

A car had pulled up on the street behind hers. She turned, and stiffened. A man got out of the car. He was older than Mike and had flaming red hair that matched Bridget's. Not old enough to be her father—a brother? Uncle? Another car followed, and two more guys got out, neither with the red hair.

"Hold on, Bridge! We'll join you in a minute," said the red-haired man.

He jogged up to the house and went in the front door. The two non-redheads were pulling gear out of their trunk. Bridget sighed and turned to Mike.

"Sorry, that's my brother Patrick."

"I'd guessed that."

"And two of Cormack's friends." She gestured toward the other men who had now opened the garage and were grabbing another net.

"Cormack must have told them we were playing. They think they're joining us. If you want to get in the car, I'll throw this stuff in the garage and we can get you out of here."

The sound of the front door closing interrupted her. "Three on three?" Patrick hollered. "Who's your guy, anyway?"

"Put your mask back down. I'll tell them we're done and get rid of them."

Mike thought for a moment. He had no place to go except his hotel, and he'd seen more than enough of that. Maybe it would be fun.

"Or we could play. Think we can take them?" he offered.

Bridget whipped back to face him, eyes sparkling. "Really? You have no idea how much I would like to take them down a notch, or ten."

Mike had to smile at the way her face lit up. "Sure. I'm having fun. Are you going to tell them who I am?"

"Are you nuts?" she asked and waved at his mask.

Mike put the face guard back down. He had no idea where this was going, but it was certainly more interesting than watching hockey on TV alone at the hotel. Playing on the road, no stakes beyond pride: this was what it was like growing up, when he always played goalie because he was the smallest. He wasn't the smallest anymore. He thought he had at least four inches on any of the others, but that flash of joy he'd felt back then was here.

CORMACK, ANOTHER REDHEAD, came out the front door dressed up in goalie pads while his two buddies set up the second net. Mike wondered what the family was like when all the redheads' tempers flared.

Bridget crossed her arms as the four men came down the driveway. "You know, we were just having a bit of fun here. I don't think Mike wants to play anymore."

Mike stood, arms resting on his goalie stick, waiting to see what was coming next. Had she changed her mind?

"Ah, come on, Bridgie. I'm sure Mike won't mind a few more minutes. Just a bit of fun," said the older redhead, Patrick.

Patrick smiled at Mike. It was a charming smile, meant to sell: either Patrick himself or whatever goods he had on hand. Mike had seen smiles like that, and it put him on his guard. Behind the smile, the eyes were assessing. Assessing him as a player, or as someone spending time with his sister?

Mike shrugged, leaving Bridget to take the initiative.

"I'm kind of tired," she said.

"I thought you were at the game today?" Cormack asked, a note of resentment in his voice.

"I was at the game with eight kids," Bridget corrected him. "That's not exactly a day at the spa. And no, before you ask, I didn't get much chance to watch the new guys."

"Well, Bridgie—" Patrick began.

"Don't call me Bridgie," she interrupted.

"We could make it interesting."

"Interesting how?" she asked, head tilted oh, so, casually. Mike thought he'd be wary if he were Patrick. Surely he knew his sister by now.

"A little wager. I've got some leaves that need raking."

Bridget considered. "My car could use a cleaning."

"First to five?"

"Or whoever is ahead after half an hour. Are you okay with that, Mike?" she asked, turning to look at him.

Mike nodded.

"So who's playing with Mike and me?"

One of Cormack's friends, Bernie, was chosen.

Patrick stopped near Mike and asked casually, "So where did you two meet?"

Mike looked at Cormack and saw that he was waiting for that answer as well. Bernie also seemed pretty interested. So, the assessment was from a brother, not a player.

"He's the guy who got the tickets for the game today," Bridget answered.

She was either unaware of the proprietary attitude of her brothers or so used to it that she didn't react. Mike was a little surprised. He'd expected her to get upset about that, and he wanted to see her hair vibrate again.

"Oh, you're the lane swimmer. Bridget yell at you about that yet?"

Apparently Bridget hadn't known who he was then, so neither did these men. That would explain the odd expression on her face when he'd shown up at the game. He filed that away for future consideration.

"It turns out it isn't Mike's fault. It's Wally the Weasel," Bridget answered.

Mike bit his lip. The name was perfect. Maybe that was Wally's problem with Bridget: he'd heard that nickname.

"Are we playing or talking?" Cormack asked.

Mike wasn't sure how this would go. He didn't doubt that he was going to be better than Cormack, but Patrick was a big guy, and Bridget was a woman, and his sister. Then there was Bernie on their team, and his improbably named friend Bert: two unknowns. Mike was competitive, and he assessed the men's potential as players. Would the guys be chivalrous with Bridget, or did the redheads all have that same need to win?

Patrick, it turned out, was competitive but fair. He had size and speed, and he didn't have the whiffing issue his sister did. But he didn't have that same drive Mike had, and again, Mike was better. Bert and Bernie were competent at most. Cormack was willing to cut corners, but gave his sister no slack. Bridget didn't back down from anything, which was what he'd come to expect from her. She took and gave hits, and talked as much smack as the guys.

And Mike was finding the sheer enjoyment of playing this game, whether on ice with his team or on a street with a woman he barely knew, was still the best feeling he'd known.

The game was called when another car arrived and pulled into the driveway. Bridget and Mike (and Bernie) were up three to zip. An older man stepped out of the car, red hair threaded with gray. Obviously the father. He paused for a minute, then headed to the street. Mike wondered how many redheads were going to end up playing. Then an older woman, red hair making it obvious she was the matriarch of the clan, leaned out the door.

"Dinner's ready! And no, we're not waiting on the end of your game."

"Okay, Mom! We'll just clean up," Patrick answered.

Mom apparently had clout. The others started gathering balls and the nets. Mike stood up from his defensive stance, not sure what to do now. It was time for him to leave, but he had no vehicle. He'd been kidnapped, so was Bridget planning to take him back? Should he call a cab?

The others were talking about the game. Bridget was stressing how very clean she needed her car to be, since she'd won the bet, thanks to Mike. Mike moved slowly to remove his pads, waiting for Bridget to remember him...

"Nice game, Mike. You've got some good moves there. Do you play much?" asked Patrick.

"Stop it, Patrick," said Bridget.

Mike looked from Patrick to Bridget.

"I just said..." Patrick had that selling smile going again.

"I know, but you're not going to recruit Mike for your beer league team."

"Bridgie, it's not up to you. If he wants to play, he could. He's pretty good."

Mike was glad someone was finally happy with his performance. But he guessed from Cormack's frown that the other man didn't like being shown up. He wasn't sure if knowing who had outplayed him would make it better or worse.

Cormack grumbled. "Maybe the Blaze should recruit him. He's as good as that overpriced—"

"Shut up, Cormack," Bridget interrupted.

"Oh, I know, you don't like Turchenko—"

Mike decided it was time to show himself. He pulled off his helmet and grabbed the net with one hand, ready to do his share and return it to the garage.

"—but you're just prejudiced. Turchenko played really well today..." Cormack trailed off. He'd seen the others staring, and turned, recognizing Mike at last.

Bridget looked from her brothers to Mike. She grinned at Patrick. "I don't think he's going to play on your team, Patty, he's already booked."

Mike braced himself. Cormack was obviously a Turchenko fan, and Mike had heard from a lot of them. The whole family, apart from Bridget, might feel the same. They were obviously hockey mad, and Mike hadn't been hearing anything good from Toronto fans.

There was a pause, and then Cormack muttered, "Sorry." Throwing a stink eye at Bridget, he continued, "Didn't know who you were."

Mike tossed the net onto his shoulder. "Don't sweat it. I've heard a lot worse. And not always to my face."

PATRICK RECOVERED WELL. He grinned and held out his hand. "Nice to meet you, Mike Reimer. I'm Patrick O'Reilly. But what happened in those playoffs last year? You cost me my hockey pool! And now I've got to clean Bridge's car."

Mike shook his hand, and the awkward moment passed. As the rest of the guys dragged the hockey gear up the driveway, Mike turned to Bridget. "Why don't I just call a cab?" he said.

She shook her head. "No, the least I can do is take you back."

"But if your family is having dinner now…"

"Hey, Mike," Patrick interrupted. "Come meet my dad. He won't believe who Bridget had playing road hockey with her."

Mike looked at Bridget, who shrugged. Patrick grabbed Mike's shoulder and swept him toward the senior redhead.

After that it was an impossibility for Mike to avoid dinner. Bridget tried to give him an opt out, but once he admitted that he had no plans, Bridget's mom starting setting him a place at the table. Mike had to admit that he didn't fight very hard. It had been a while since he'd had a home-cooked meal, and Bridget's family reminded him of the neighbors he'd grown up with. He hadn't seen them lately. And again, there was that empty hotel room.

He found one big difference from the childhood dinners he'd known with his old neighbors, the Sawatzkys. Mrs. O'Reilly was devoted to her family, and having a large one made that a time-consuming job. She was a calm and placid center to this lively group. However, she had certain rules, and one of those rules was to not talk hockey at the table.

The boys tried, but a look from their mother (honorary mother, in Bernie and Bert's case) stopped them in their tracks.

Bridget, who was beside Mike, explained, "Only topics of general interest at the table."

Mike looked at the people gathered around in the large dining room. Since Bridget's dad had grilled him on the last playoffs as soon as they were introduced, he had to assume Bridget's mother was the only non-hockey fan sitting there. He decided he liked this family rule. He was sick of talking about his poor performance in the last playoffs anyway.

"So, Mr. Reimer," said Mrs. O'Reilly, passing around the first bowl.

"Mike, please," he said, with a smile.

She nodded her head. "Mike, then. Where did you meet Bridget?"

"In the pool at the athletic club. I unwittingly took up some of the pool when she has her morning class."

Mrs. O'Reilly smiled. "So you're the one who provided the hockey tickets for the class. That was very nice of you. I'm sure the kids had a lovely time."

"I hope so," Mike said, noticing that Bridget was biting her lip.

"Are you new to Toronto?" Mrs. O'Reilly continued.

Mike could see Cormack across the table rolling his eyes. Mrs. O'Reilly was definitely not a hockey fan.

"Relatively new. I arrived here late last winter, but was away most of the summer. I've been back here only a couple of weeks."

Mike knew this wasn't news to the rest of the people around the table.

Mrs. Reilly looked at him with concern. "That must be hard on your family."

"No family here, ma'am." Mike wondered if Mrs. O'Reilly was also assessing him as someone who wanted to spend time with her daughter. Bridget seemed to be well protected.

Meanwhile, her mother looked at him with concern. "Your parents?"

"My mother's in Arizona. No siblings. My father isn't in the picture." Mike braced himself. This was a part of his past he didn't like to delve into.

"Mom," Bridget interrupted. "Mike plays for the Toronto Blaze. He's a professional hockey player. He's taken care of."

"Well, I know as a hockey player they're probably taking good care of you, but a friend of Bridget's is always welcome. Or Cormack's," she added, smiling at Bernie and Bert.

BRIDGET DECIDED IT was time to divert the conversation before Mike thought the family was grilling him as a potential date.

"I saw Mike's car at the club. Guess what he drives?" she threw out.

That immediately caught the attention of everyone but her mother.

"Ferrari!"

"Lambo!"

"Hummer!"

Bridget turned to Mike, letting him give the news.

He shrugged. "It's a McLaren."

He wasn't surprised to find that the family knew what this meant. Bridget hadn't picked up her car knowledge in a void, and he soon learned that her father was a mechanic, Cormack worked for him, Patrick sold cars and Bernie and Bert shared in this family passion, too.

"What year?" Patrick asked.

"What's the top speed?" Cormack wanted to know.

Bernie asked the color. Mike enjoyed talking about his car, and was happy to answer questions.

"Did you drive it?" Bernie asked Bridget.

There was a pause. Mike shuddered at the thought of his dream car being driven by the woman who'd whipped him over here as if driving for NASCAR.

"I'm the only one who drives it." Mike explained, noticing Bridget eying him speculatively. He was relieved when the conversation moved on.

After an excellent meal of shepherd's pie and homemade chocolate cake, everyone gathered their plates and took them into the kitchen. Mike went to follow, but Bridget grabbed his plate.

"I've got it. I have to help Mom clean up, then I can give you a lift back. You okay for a few minutes?"

"No problem. Are you sure I can't help?"

"No, Mom would never allow it. I'll be as quick as I can." So Mike followed the other men into the family room.

IT DROVE BRIDGET nuts that her mother wouldn't let the guys clean up, but she knew from years of arguing that her mother wasn't going to change. Her mother had conventional ideas about the household division of labor. Bridget wasn't home for meals that often anymore, but when she was, she always wound up in the kitchen. Bridget had to defer to her mother, but let Cormack try to make her do his housework and he'd be walking funny for a while. Her mother looked around the spotless kitchen.

"Well, that should do it," she said. "Why don't you see if they need anything?"

Bridget sighed.

"'Cause they're already full of food, and if they want anything else, they can get it, Mom. They're more than capable of taking care of themselves."

"Mike might be too polite to ask for something. He did seem a nice young man."

"Okay, I'll ask him, but I was about to drive him back. And we're not dating, Mom. I don't think he'll be around again." She couldn't imagine this becoming a regular thing. Mike moved in much different circles: probably lots of dinners and benefits and gorgeous women to take to fancy events when he wasn't playing hockey and traveling. She'd lived in Toronto her whole life and had spotted a hockey player only once or twice. They would merely be crossing paths in the pool from here on out.

IN THE FAMILY ROOM, she found the men watching a hockey game on TV. The Winnipeg Whiteouts were playing Minnesota. At least it wasn't Quebec. That was Mike's former team, the one he'd played so poorly against in the playoffs after being traded here to Toronto, and she was sure he didn't really want to discuss it. She could see that they'd passed around some beers. Mike's looked mostly untouched. He was also more absorbed in the game than the others, responding only to direct questions—which sometimes had to be repeated.

She perched on the arm of her father's recliner.

"I don't think he's really with us, do you?" she whispered, indicating Mike.

Her dad nodded. "I can understand why he's one of the ones who made it. He's focused. Your brothers were never that serious about it."

"Yeah, he was like that playing road ball, even. I thought I'd be able to get at least one past him, but…"

"He takes it seriously. So, where'd you find him again?" her father asked.

"He was the lane swimmer I told you about."

Her dad looked at her. "That doesn't explain how he ended up playing road ball with you."

Bridget looked a little sheepish. "Well, he stopped by the club after the game and, uh—"

"And…what?"

"All right, I lost my temper. He said something about me not knowing how to play hockey, and I was already irritated by the kids, and…" Bridget trailed off.

Her dad smiled. "I get it. Someday you're going to get in trouble with that temper. It's your mother's fault—her red hair, you know." He winked.

Bridget leaned over and kissed his cheek. "I know, 'cause you never get mad," she teased.

BRIDGET FOUND HERSELF a seat and waited to get Mike's attention. She thought he'd be eager to leave, but he ended up staying for the entire game. Her brothers, Bert, and Bernie, all wanted to talk hockey with him during the first intermission. She'd caught his gaze, raised her brows and nodded to the door, but Cormack had asked a question, then Bert, then her dad. Mike had shrugged, so…she'd planned to watch the game anyway, so she sat back and enjoyed the evening.

It wasn't easy to drag Mike away from the postgame family room analysis. Cormack wanted to continue discussing the move the Whiteouts' goalie had made that almost led to a goal.

"You gotta be aggressive. Get out there and

challenge the skater," Cormack said, for about the fifth time. Bridget knew from playing with the boys that Cormack liked that move a lot.

Mike shrugged. It was obvious he didn't agree, and that Cormack was hoping to grind him down.

Her dad interjected. "Son, you've got a man here who's won three Cups. I think you should listen to him."

Bridget could see Cormack badly wanted to bring up how Mike had played last spring, but a look from their father kept his mouth closed…for now. He'd probably grumble about it for the next week.

Bridget led the way to the door. Patrick shook Mike's hand for a second time.

"If you ever get the urge to play road ball again, stop by. We have a game going most weekends."

Mike thanked him, and followed Bridget out to the street without making any further commitments to the O'Reillys. She had to admire his public relations game. That was something she was lacking herself, and needed to work on.

Once in the car, she'd been quick to turn the

volume down on the music. She drove more calmly through the darkness, temper gone.

Bridget broke the silence. "I just wanted to apologize again for, let's see, kidnapping you, making you play road ball, inflicting my family on you and taking over your evening."

Mike laughed, a warm sound in the dark. "I had fun, believe it or not. I had no plans for the evening, and you have a nice family."

Bridget shifted gears. "That's right, you said no siblings."

"True," he answered sounding puzzled.

"Only children always love my family. My best friend was an only child. She loved to hang at our place. She ended up marrying my brother."

"Patrick?" Mike hazarded.

"Seriously? No, he's way too old for her. He's my oldest brother. He's married to Nancy and already has three kids."

"Cormack, then?" he asked, surprised.

"No, Brian. He is the best of my brothers, so—"

"Brian? You have three brothers? All older?"

Bridget laughed. "No, I have five brothers, all older."

Mike was silent.

"Yes, tonight could have been so much worse," Bridget continued. "When we're all together, we're our own hockey team."

Mike leaned back. "I was an only child, but I hung out with the Sawatzkys upstairs from us. They had four boys. As an only kid of a single mom, it used to be nice to feel like part of that big family."

Bridget didn't respond. As the youngest of six, she'd loved visiting her only-child friends in their nice, quiet houses, where they had their own things and didn't have to fight for them. *The grass is always greener*, she thought.

They pulled in to the club. She rolled down her window and waved her pass to open the gate.

BRIDGET PULLED THE car to a stop beside Mike's McLaren. He noticed her eyes linger on it for a moment. He hoped she wouldn't ask to drive it since he didn't want to upset her, now that they were getting along. And he was curious about something.

She turned, ready to say polite farewells, when he spoke. "May I ask you a serious question?"

She cocked an eyebrow as she turned off the ignition.

The car was immediately thrown into darkness. Mike could barely make out her pale skin, but he could tell she was still looking at him.

"You were…not a professional swimmer, but as close as that gets, right?"

He could tell she nodded in the darkness before she said, "You could put it that way, yes."

"What made you decide to move to coaching?"

"I wasn't fast enough." Her answer came immediately, either a familiar response or so obvious she didn't need to think.

He paused, considering the sentence, then asked, "That was it?"

"There's so much that training and conditioning and sheer will can do. But I wasn't getting PRs anymore."

"PRs?" Mike echoed.

"Personal records. When you go faster than you've gone before. Even when I stretched myself, it wasn't making that fractional difference that would separate between first and fourth place. I competed to win. When that wasn't happening, I was frustrated and couldn't enjoy myself anymore. New swimmers were coming up, and they were starting to pass me. I wasn't helping the swim team, and I wasn't winning, so I retired."

The *R* word, Mike thought.

"So, why coaching? You didn't want to leave the sport?"

She considered before saying, "It wasn't so much that I realized I wasn't fast enough and therefore decided coaching was the next best thing. I'd been a swimming instructor when I was in high school, and took all the jock courses at college. As I became one of the older team members, I found myself helping the coach out. When I announced that I was retiring, he asked if I'd stay on as his assistant. Then, when this opening came up at the club, it seemed like a good opportunity to become a head coach. It was less of a career plan than a natural evolution."

"You like it? You don't miss competing?"

Bridget laughed. "Oh, I still compete. With you the other day in the pool, and then this afternoon. With my brothers, over almost anything. With a guy at the stoplight who thinks his little souped-up toy with a spoiler can beat me from the line. I compete." More seriously, she continued, "I do still miss racing, but less than I used to. I'm starting to feel that when my kids win, I win. And that's pretty good."

The dark encouraged confidences. There was a moment of silence, then Bridget blurted, "Are you thinking of retiring?"

Mike was. He hadn't mentioned it to anyone but his college coach. After the disastrous playoffs, he had vanished as soon as possible and gone to see his former coach. They'd had a relationship that was closer to father and son, and Mike trusted him more than anyone else, outside of his mother. That was the only time he'd mentioned the *R* word.

Mike wasn't ready to retire. Hockey was his life. He had no plans for what would happen after hockey. He'd just turned thirty and he should have years yet to play. But something had changed with the way he'd played, and he didn't know if that meant the end of his career. He wasn't ready to share that, though, especially with an almost complete stranger.

"I'm sorry," Bridget said, breaking the silence. "That's none of my business. I tend to speak first and think later."

Mike smiled to himself. He'd learned that already. But he had been asking her some personal questions, and after playing hockey with her, and spending time with her and her family, he thought he knew a bit about her. She wasn't a braggart; he'd learned about her swimming only from Wally the Weasel (that name was very catchy) and her father. And she understood competing.

So instead of freezing her out, he said, "No, don't apologize. I may not have a choice about retiring, depending on how I play this year. I wondered how I'd know when it's time."

"What worked for me isn't necessarily what will happen for you," Bridget responded. "I was never a top-level swimmer. At international meets, I'd sometimes have a PR, but I could never beat the Americans and Aussies. But you, you're a top goalie. Even if you slow down a bit, you're going to be better than most of the others out there. And you have a tough job with a limited time span. You have only a few years to make your big money."

Yes, that was true, but he had enough money now. More would be good: growing up poor meant he wanted as much financial security as he could get, but he wasn't hurting anymore. At least, not for money.

"I think those are the kindest words I've heard from a Toronto fan since I've been here," he responded.

"I don't think Toronto fans are known for

being kind. Crazy, yes, masochistic, sure, but not really kind. And they're tough on goalies. You're replacing a popular guy, and Turchenko has a lot of fans here, so they're going to be rough on you."

"You're not a Turchenko fan?" Mike asked, remembering her brother's comment.

"I think he's got a lot of skill, but he's not working hard enough. He makes spectacular saves, so you know he can do it, but he shouldn't have to. He pulls a lot of boneheaded moves."

Mike smiled again. This woman was obviously smart, and he agreed with her about Turchenko. But he'd revealed enough.

"I should let you go. You work in the morning?"

"Don't worry about the time. It's my own fault for abducting you like that. I do appreciate your being such a good sport about it."

Mike unfolded himself from the car. "Honestly, I enjoyed myself. I like your family and—" he paused and leaned in "—you couldn't score on me."

With a grin, he slammed the door shut on her sputtering.

BRIDGET DIDN'T SEE Mike the next morning. She reprimanded herself for noticing. He was a big-time professional athlete. He had been very nice last night, but he was from a different world. He wasn't interested in her, and she wasn't looking for a guy now anyway. Coaching may not have been her first career choice, but now that she was doing it, she had serious plans.

She had a good workout and then headed home to get ready to spend some time with Jee. They'd been best friends growing up, and they still shared almost everything. Bridget couldn't really be her friend's confidant on marital issues since Jee had married her brother Brian—even if Brian was her favorite brother. Bridget didn't think Jee had issues with her in-laws, but then, she'd known what she was getting into. Jee had spent most of her free time at Bridget's.

Everyone in the family knew that Jee and Brian had been trying to start a family for more than a year now. But Bridget knew the details that the others didn't. She felt for her friend's troubles, but all she could do was provide a shoulder to cry on and an ear to listen.

Bridget could tell when they met that Jee had had bad news again, so they went on a shopping spree. Bridget shopped only in athletic stores or online, but she was happy to keep Jee company and to compliment her choices. Jee would roll her eyes at some of her comments, but by the time they were done, Jee was looking a little more cheerful.

They stopped at a neighborhood restaurant to have dinner. Jee wanted to hear about Mike. The family news network had been working with its usual speediness.

"There's not much to tell. I bet you heard everything that happened and some that didn't."

"What's he like? He's good-looking, right?" Jee asked, perking up a little.

Bridget focused on the first question. "He was nice enough not to raise a stink about me kidnapping him."

"Kidnapping? Nancy didn't mention anything about that." Jee sounded shocked.

"Patrick couldn't tell her what he didn't know. I didn't share that with the family. You know he was the lane swimmer, right?"

Jee nodded. Bridget had complained to her about the lane swimmer. She recapped the events of the day for her friend but didn't mention the conversation in the car. She didn't think Mike wanted public speculation about his possible retirement. In Toronto, that would cause an uproar. Maybe she'd read too much into it anyway.

"So is he cute in person?" Jee asked.

Bridget thought. "Not really cute. He's big—taller than any of the boys, and he's fit, obviously. He's got a bend in his nose, but otherwise he's pretty undamaged for a hockey player." Bridget thought about the gray eyes, smiling at her, daring her to try to score on him. He had a nice voice, too, and well, he wasn't ugly.

"No," she continued. "Cute is not the right word, but he's okay-looking."

"You mean he's no Connor Treadwell," Jee said, an edge to her voice.

Bridget blushed. Jee was the only member of her family who knew all about the crush she'd had on Connor Treadwell. Connor was a champion American swimmer. He was retired now, but Bridget had run into him at meets over her career, and since he was now coaching, she'd met him at competitions and conferences, too. He had blond hair, bright blue eyes and an incredible body that a swimsuit exposed to admiration. Bridget had gone out with him a couple of times, but they hadn't parted on good terms. Jee thought he was a jerk, but Bridget knew she was partly to blame herself.

"You should be happy about that," Bridget responded. "But except for running into him at the club, I doubt I'll have anything to do with Mike Reimer again."

CHAPTER THREE

MIKE HAD NO plans to spend time with Bridget. His focus was on hockey, and he'd learned the hard way that hockey and relationships didn't mix for him. The road ball game had been fun, but that wasn't going to make him the best again. Still, it had reminded him of why he played. It would be a nice touch, and reflect well on his upbringing, if he made some kind of thank-you gesture to the O'Reillys. He could send Mrs. O'Reilly some flowers, but he didn't know their address, and he wasn't going to have them delivered to Bridget at the pool. He'd picked up on the fact that the family was hockey mad, which was something he could work with. Once the regular season games began in October, he thought it was a good time to set something up. When he saw Bridget was teaching during his next lap swim, he came back to the pool after changing.

She was ushering the kids into the changing rooms. One kid was giving her a hard time. He thought it was the one who muttered at him at the game. When she finally shooed the boy into the changing room, Mike called her name. She started, then recognized him and walked over.

Her hair was standing up in spots, and her glasses looked heavy on her face. He wondered why she hadn't had her vision corrected. She was comfortable in a swimsuit, and she had a fit and trim figure. Her movements were sure and controlled. She might be a coach, but she was still an athlete.

"Mike?" she asked, sounding surprised.

"I should be able to get a couple tickets to tomorrow's game, if you think someone in your family might like to go? I'd like to thank them for the evening last week."

BRIDGET BLINKED. HE wanted to thank them? She thought she should be thanking him. As she'd told him in the car, he'd been an awfully good sport.

"Ah, sure. That would be great," she responded.

"I'll need to send you the details on how to pick up the tickets. What's your cell?"

Bridget recited her number. She held back

a grin. She'd have to tell Jee that she'd given her phone number to a hockey star.

"Okay, I'll set it up with the sales department."

"Thanks. You don't have to, you know," she assured him.

"Don't thank me until I know for sure I can get them for you," he said, busily typing.

Bridget shrugged and turned to go. She was busy, but her dad would be thrilled.

Sure enough, later that day Bridget got a text telling her where and how to pick up the tickets. Bridget saved the text and showed her dad that night when she got home. Her mother thought Bridget should go, since Mike was "her" friend. Cormack argued that she'd just been to a game. Since Bridget was working till after the game started, the problem was solved: her father went with Cormack. She knew Patrick would be irritated when he found out, but fortunately, the O'Reillys had had lots of experience with arguments among siblings.

MIKE SAW BRIDGET only briefly on occasional mornings. They'd nod, and that was about it. He was absorbed with work, where he'd won the starting goalie's job. Now he had to make sure he played well enough to keep it. His entire focus was on rebuilding his hockey skills and reputation. When he wasn't practicing, training or playing, he was watching tape and conferring with coaches. He still had to prove himself. His last playoff performance was fresh in everyone's mind so he overheard a lot of negative comments, but he kept up his cool front. He wasn't nicknamed Iceman for nothing.

October started well. There were a couple of shootout losses, some wins. Turchenko started in the second of a back-to-back pair of games and didn't do well. Yes, things were going almost exactly the way he wanted. And then, just as that first month was winding up, it happened.

Toronto was playing Philadelphia on *Hockey Night in Canada*, one game before the first meeting of the season against Quebec. Mike was playing like he wanted to, and feeling good about the next game against his former team.

There was a two-on-one breakaway in the third period. Mike was focused on the player with the puck, but kept his peripheral vision on the man's teammate, waiting for a possible pass. He could hear the crowd responding in the background over the scraping of skates on ice. Everyone was shouting, and suddenly his goalie crease was crowded with hockey players, one guy landing in the net. Mike was trying desperately to ignore everything but the puck when he felt a weight on his ankle through the pads, and a sharp pain. The whistle blew, and one by one the players stood up, all except for Mike.

Damn. He knew what that feeling was.

The coaches and trainers came out. Mike insisted on getting on his good foot to let one of the trainers pull him over to the bench upright, but that was just for pride's sake. He wasn't going to be playing the rest of this game, or quite a few after this. Turchenko put on his helmet to take over, while Mike finally surrendered and let the medics carry him away.

Mike had his ankle tended to by the team doctors. They fitted him with a soft, removable cast which meant he had to take more care not to reinjure himself, but overall recovery would be shorter. He was given a strict regimen to follow, including in-home therapy sessions with the team trainers. Then he was sent home to recover. And to wait. Wait to see if Turchenko would take his job.

"Home" was the solitary splendor of a hotel suite. Last season Mike had been traded at the trade deadline, so they'd put him up in a hotel for the remainder of the season. He'd been so angry with management—they'd asked him to waive his no-trade clause. He'd agreed to the deal but walked out in an icy fury before even finding out where they wanted him to go.

He hadn't even thought of listing his property in Quebec. Reality just hadn't sunk in yet. Quebec City had been his home for his entire hockey career. He was popular, had friends, fans. But management slanted the news so that it seemed he'd asked for the trade, and when his replacement had led Mike's former team to sweeping a playoff series over Mike and the Blaze, the fans back in Quebec had seemed to be happy he was gone. Suddenly he was no longer wanted at home in Quebec, but he had nowhere else to go. Toronto hadn't welcomed him. He'd been waiting to hear that another trade was in the works, but that hadn't happened. He'd finally listed his Quebec home when he'd come back to Toronto at the end of the summer, but he was still living at the hotel.

And he was once again quietly and impotently furious. Unlike the O'Reillys, his temper was slow-burning and stayed under the surface. His career was out of his hands, and it was infuriating.

Two days later he was able to watch Turchenko earn a win against Ottawa. He wanted to throw the remote at the television. That was supposed to be Mike's win. Mike didn't think Turchenko played well, but he was good enough, and the pundits were predicting Turchenko would take over the starting position permanently.

That would leave Mike playing backup until Toronto could find another team willing to take on his expensive contract. If he didn't bounce back from this injury, regain his form, there might never be another contract. That, he refused to think about.

The best-case scenario was that he'd recover and play at his previous top level. In that case, whether or not the Blaze kept him till the end of the season, neither Toronto team would be able to offer what he could ask for in free agency next summer. There wasn't a single scenario that left Mike living in Toronto, so this was a temporary stay. The impersonal hotel room underlined the impermanence of his future. When he wasn't winning, it turned out people didn't want to be with him. His mother had called, but she was busy in Phoenix. She'd come if he asked, but she'd raised him to be self-reliant.

Then he got the text.

THE O'REILLYS WERE watching the game when Mike went down. Bridget had been at a meet on the other side of the city, and had stopped in on the way to her basement suite. Her mother warmed up some food for her while she joined her dad and Cormack and Bernie and Bert.

Bridget's mom didn't follow hockey, but she liked Mike, and even though they hadn't seen him for a month, she picked up from their talk that the young man who had no family around had been hurt. A couple of days later when Bridget stopped by to catch up, she found that her mother had made up her mind.

Bridget and most of her brothers had inherited their father's temperament: they could fire up in anger, but it passed as quickly. Bridget's mother didn't have a temper, but she could be incredibly stubborn when she made up her mind. Mike's story had touched her, and she was concerned that he was injured, in a new city, with no family for support.

Bridget tried to explain that he was a highly paid professional athlete and could afford any care he needed, and that the team was invested in keeping him well. Her mother said that he had been very nice to the family, and that they should return the favor. When pressed, Bridget had to admit that she did have a way to contact Mike. She hated doing it. Mike hadn't reached out to them since he'd provided those tickets, so she felt she was crossing a boundary Mike had put in place. But as a result of her mother's insistence, she finally agreed to ask him if they could do anything for him.

She pulled up the number on her phone that Mike had given her and started typing.

This is Bridget O'Reilly. My mother was worried—

"Do you have to tell him who you are? Doesn't the phone number let him know that?" Her mother was reading over Bridget's shoulder.

"Mom, he sent me one message. I highly doubt I'm in his contacts. It's just going to pop up as a random number."

"And say we were all worried. You make me sound like a fusspot."

Bridget rolled her eyes, since her mother was behind her and out of view, but she deleted the second sentence.

This is Bridget O'Reilly. We hope you're doing well.

Bridget was not going to sound like she was up at night worrying about his injury.

Do you need any help?

"Ask if he'd like some soup. There's nothing better than homemade soup when you're not feeling well."

"He doesn't have a cold, Mom. He broke a bone." According to the papers, it was an ankle bone. He'd be out four to six weeks, which meant it would be December before he'd be playing again. She started her text over.

This is Bridget O'Reilly. We saw you go down and hope you're recuperating well. My mother has some homemade soup she thought you might like.

She hit Send before her mother came up with anything else.

Bridget knew Mike would think they were overstepping. He'd probably block her number, if he hadn't already. After all, they hadn't done anything but nod in passing for most of a month. He couldn't be close friends with every group of fans he interacted with.

Bridget was so convinced he wouldn't actually respond that when her phone pinged an hour later, she expected it to be Jee. Instead, the message read, I'd love some soup.

Bridget stared, as if the text was some kind of trick. Now her mother would be able to say she'd told her so.

Actually, that wasn't the worst part for Bridget. Her mom needed someone to take her to see Mike. She wouldn't drive downtown. Bridget, who had time off in the middle of the day, was the one who would have to chauffeur this trip. She expected an awkward meeting, but Mike had said yes for some unknown reason, so they pulled into the closest parking garage and carried a bag with soup, rolls and pie into the lobby of Mike's expensive hotel.

Mike had a suite on one of the top floors. Once the front desk let him know they'd arrived, a bellboy went up the elevator with them to let them into his suite. Bridget followed her mother down a hallway with a couple of bedrooms, and came out to the main room, with a combined seating, dining and kitchen area surrounded by windows with sweeping views of the lake. *Not bad*, Bridget thought.

"Mrs. O'Reilly, Bridget, thanks for coming. Sorry, I can't get up very well…"

Bridget finally got a good look at Mike.

He was stretched out on a couch with his cast resting on a pillow. He had a couple of remotes beside him, as if he'd just turned off the TV or video gaming system set up across the room from him. He looked tired, stressed and not very welcoming. *You didn't have to invite us*, Bridget thought. But then he smiled, a tired, but friendly smile.

"Please, have a seat."

There were several seats to choose from: the room was bigger than Bridget's whole apartment.

"I'll take this stuff over to the kitchen area," Bridget said, transporting the bags to the other side of the island.

Her mom put her coat on the edge of a chair. Then she crossed over to Mike and put a hand on his forehead. She adjusted a couple of cushions.

"How's that? Are you doing okay? Don't you have someone staying with you?"

"Much better, thank you. I'm doing as well as expected. I don't need an attendant, as long as I'm careful."

Her mother gave him a look she'd given to Bridget as well as her brothers many times.

"And of course you're careful?" she said, disbelievingly. "I could tell you about my kids…"

Bridget paused as she put the soup in the mostly empty refrigerator. Just what stories was her mother planning to share? Fortunately there were more stories about her brothers than herself. Her mom apparently didn't believe the broken arm she'd gotten in the superhero contest the boys had invented was very funny, but Bridget thought Mike was looking less gloomy. *Misery loves company.*

Bridget sat on the edge of the love seat that faced Mike's couch while her mother learned the details of the injury, and the resulting recovery process. She looked around. It was a nice suite, though rather corporate—bland and not at all homey. She noticed some weights, a bench, and a complicated home gym over near the windows. She was sure that wasn't part of the original hotel decor but it would explain the dining table pushed back against the wall. Mike must be working out here while he was recuperating. That made sense: she couldn't really picture him hobbling to the hotel gym. She tried to imagine how much a suite like this would cost, and couldn't even come up with a ballpark figure.

She came back to the conversation when she heard her name.

"Don't you, Bridget?" her mother was saying with a disapproving look.

"Don't I what?"

"You work out after your morning swim practices."

"Yeees…" Bridget agreed cautiously.

"Mike wants to fit in some additional workouts when the team people aren't around, so you could help Mike in the mornings. He has to be especially careful with that cast."

Bridget's mother cast a doubtful look at what was around Mike's ankle. As kids, they'd always had the familiar plaster casts, but while Bridget had been fortunate enough to keep her bones intact while competing, she'd seen these casts. This one was blue plastic, with inflatable padding, and could be removed as needed. Mike had left it open, probably anxious to avoid as much muscle atrophy as possible.

Bridget had helped teammates do their workouts with those soft casts, but that was a whole different thing than working out with Mike Reimer. Bridget opened her mouth to object. Mike beat her to the punch.

"I couldn't impose. I'm sure Bridget is too busy for that."

Bridget looked at her mother. She was giving Bridget that look, the "didn't I raise you properly?" look. What was her mother thinking? Mike could have all the help anyone needed, so why would he need her? She turned to look at Mike, and, for just a moment he looked—sad? Lonely?

"Don't you have people from the team coming in every day?" Bridget asked.

"Of course, if I want to do additional workouts, I'll be fine on my own. It's not like I haven't worked out before. I understand, you're busy."

Was he actually lonely, maybe bored here, all on his own? Where were the beautiful women coming to keep him company? His entourage? Did hockey players have those?

"And what are you eating? Do you only have access to hotel food?" Bridget's mom spoke as if she were referring to a school cafeteria rather than a starred restaurant. "I'd be happy to send you some. I always make too much."

Bridget knew her mother would be thrilled to have someone else to cook for. And she also knew who her mother would enlist to deliver the food. Well, if she was being pressed to come by anyway…she bit her lip. "Mike, it wouldn't be a horrific inconvenience to come over sometimes and work out with you. But I feel like we're imposing."

Mike sighed, and his shoulders dropped. "Honestly, it would be nice to see someone from time to time. I'm not a good patient. Too much time on my own and I get a little… restless."

Bridget's mother smiled. "I know what it's like. I raised six kids, and none of them were good at being sidelined. I can send some of the boys over in the evenings as well. Just till you're back on your feet. You tell them when you've had enough and I'll make sure they don't overstay their welcome. Now, I'll go warm up that soup for you."

Her mother headed over to the kitchen area.

An occasional mutter about the pots was all they heard from her for a while.

"Are you sure you don't mind?" Bridget asked, watching him closely.

Mike let his head rest against the back of the couch. "Really, I don't. Most of the day I have nothing to do but watch sports channels talk about whether Turchenko is going to be the permanent starter. If you could take pity on me, it would at least distract me for a while and I'd feel like I was doing something to keep my job."

"Then I guess you've got a spotter for the duration. And a food delivery service, if I know my mother. Cormack's the only one still living at home, so she has a lot of mothering not being used."

THE NEXT DAY Bridget stood in front of the suite doorway, backpack containing her post-workout clothing on her shoulders, and carrying a cooler with her mother's next installment of food. Her hair was still a little wet from the pool. Tony had been into splashing this morning. Bridget had restrained herself from drying her hair. She was only here to do a workout. How she looked didn't matter. Still, she'd made sure to wear her least ratty sweats.

She'd been provided with a key card to get in so that she didn't have to disturb the bell-boys or make Mike hobble down the hallway. She'd texted him to let him know she was at the hotel. She was nervous, even though Mike sounded as if he'd like some company. She'd worked out with many people, including men, so it wasn't like she didn't know what she was doing. Maybe it was because he was such a highly paid athlete. Or because guys could have real ego issues if they were challenged by a woman. That was all she was worried about, surely.

She made her way down the hall, taking in the view of the clouds obscuring the lake. She pulled off her jacket and saw that Mike had maneuvered himself to the bench. He was wearing only shorts—and his cast, of course. It shouldn't have been disconcerting. She'd worked out with swimmers in less. Yet some-how this felt more personal. She wasn't at a competition with a bunch of people around. She was alone with Mike in his home.

He smiled when he saw her. She smiled back, hesitantly. "So, what's the plan?"

"The trainers are taking care of my leg,

keeping the muscles working around the broken ankle. I need to do the upper body, and core work, maybe the rest of my leg work tomorrow. Since I can't do any cardio until I'm okayed to swim, it's just weights for now."

Bridget cast an eye over his equipment. It was comprehensive.

"Looks like you should have everything you need. I was going to fill up my water bottle—some for you too?"

He nodded, already concentrating on setting up the bar for his first reps. She got the water and grabbed some towels. They began.

Bridget stood over the bar, ready to spot in case Mike got in trouble. He had more weights on it than she used, but he was a big guy, and he had different goals for his conditioning than she did. He settled in place, told her how many reps he was intending, and they started.

Once she was in a familiar routine, Bridget found she was calmer. She was also more aware of Mike as a man. She'd seen him, somewhat vaguely, at the pool, and she'd seen him in jeans when they played road ball and in dress clothes at the rink. But now he was wearing only those shorts and she could get a good look at just how fit he was.

She worked with many fit swimmers. Mike was less lean and more powerful. His thighs were massive, and if a few days off had made them less toned, it wasn't apparent. His abs were spectacular. All that up and down in front of the net, she deduced. His arms, chest—he was an impressively fit athlete. She told herself not to stare.

They took turns lifting. Mike turned out to be a good workout partner. Some people you had to push through a workout, talk them into doing just a little bit more. Mike pushed himself; in fact, she had to make him stop. They were perfectly compatible that way, since she often pushed herself a little too far, and once during this workout, when she was in a zone, he actually grabbed the bar to stop her from going further than she should.

Before she left, Bridget brought up something she thought might be an issue. "Would you like me to stop my brothers and friends from coming over in the evening? Mom doesn't realize…"

Mike looked at her, puzzled. "Doesn't realize what? That Cormack is a Turchenko fan? There are a lot of them around. If he takes over the starter's job, I might as well get used to the gloating."

"No, I mean you might have someone else coming over," she offered.

He shrugged, telegraphing how few people were knocking on his door. "It's a big room."

"I mean, you might prefer not to have additional guests."

Mike looked at her for a moment and laughed. "Female guests, you mean? Don't worry. I'll put your brothers off myself if I get a hot date lined up."

Bridget was peeved. She was just trying to be helpful. He didn't need to laugh at her.

CORMACK AND THE two B's did go over, as did Patrick and Brian at different times. Bridget heard about it through Jee later. After a couple of games, Turchenko started to play poorly and was pulled for the backup goaltender. The backup didn't do much better, but not much was expected of him. So, while Cormack might be disappointed that his player was making his case to remain as a backup, and Blaze fans were enduring their usual beatdown, at Mike's there was an excellent spread, courtesy of the hotel's room service, and apparently a good time was had by all. Bridget wondered why no one else realized this was an odd situation. They were the blue-collar O'Reillys, and hanging out with a hockey superstar had never been part of their lifestyle. What was going to happen when Mike was done recuperating?

Bridget went most mornings to work out with Mike, but she had a swim meet on the weekend, so didn't see Mike again until Monday. It was a gray day in November, full of sleet; winter was making its first foray. The suite was gloomy and the sound of the icy pellets tapped on the big windows.

Mike was in a quiet mood. He wasn't a talkative guy most of the time, but his mind was definitely elsewhere. Bridget offered to leave him alone, but he just grunted and crutched to the workout machines. Bridget wasn't sure what was bothering him, but she followed his lead and kept the conversation limited to what was necessary. After showering and changing into street clothes, she started warming the soup her mom had sent over. Mike came back from his own shower, by now able to crutch dexterously down the hallway, wearing a pair of sweats cut off short on the leg with the cast and a long-sleeved Blaze T-shirt. The black shirt made his eyes look silver and emphasized his muscled build. Bridget told herself to smarten up.

"Thanks," Mike said, looking at the soup. Then, noticing that she'd set only the one place at the breakfast bar, looked up questioningly. "Gotta go?"

"I have things to do, and I don't think you want company now," Bridget answered honestly.

Mike paused for a moment. "Sorry. I've been distracted, so I'm not the best company. But I'd like you to stay. Unless, of course, you really need to go…"

Bridget could feel her mother nudging her to be helpful. She said, "It's nothing pressing, but I don't want to get in your way."

For a moment, she thought he wasn't going to respond. He was looking out the windows, though the sleet obscured the view, and then he finally spoke.

"It was on a day like this that my wife died. When I'm stuck inside like this, I can't avoid reliving it."

Bridget felt her mouth open. She quickly closed it. His wife? Dead?

Mike looked back at her shocked expression. "You don't know the story? I thought the headlines were everywhere."

Bridget shook her head.

"It was seven, almost eight years ago.

March, just before the start of the playoffs, not long before I was called up."

Bridget worked the math in her head. "We were on a tour in Australia that spring. I remember Toronto wasn't in the playoffs, so I'd mostly ignored the hockey news. Besides, Quebec won, so…oh. That would have been your first Cup."

Mike looked out the windows as the half ice, half rain pelted them, though Bridget doubted he really saw what was out there.

"The short version is that she was in a car accident. Bad weather, car went off the road. She was probably driving too fast and would have died on impact."

"I'm sorry. That's awful."

Mike had his crutches, but was mostly balanced on his one good foot.

"She was pregnant."

MIKE STARED OUT over where the lake would normally be. Back then there had been no spectacular view. He was a farm team goalie for the Rimouski Raiders, in Quebec. Their place was barely adequate, but Amber had worked hard to make the most of it. As she often complained, she didn't have anything else to do.

He found himself talking, mostly to himself.

"We met in college. I'd been drafted by Quebec when I was eighteen, but my mom insisted I had to get a degree. She'd never cared much for hockey and wanted me to have a backup plan. So instead of going directly to the farm team, I went to college on a hockey scholarship, and met Amber in a freshman English class. She knew nothing about hockey but came to every game and started learning rules like offside and icing." He smiled at the memory. "Her father was a professor there, and she'd grown up in that town. Lived in the same house her whole life. She'd had this storybook life that was so different than mine.

"We graduated the same year, and got married that summer. In the fall, I had to report to Rimouski."

He remembered the excitement of finally, finally being able to start his hockey career. But there had also been trepidation. What if he wasn't good enough? "Amber hated it. Most of the guys on the team were single, and she was positive they were taking me to strip clubs and that we were meeting women every time we were on the road. The married guys were older and had kids, so Amber didn't really fit in with their wives.

"She wanted me to quit. She'd tell me that the chances were that I'd never make it to the big show, and if I loved her I'd want her to be happy. She told me I was selfish, putting my dream above her. I argued that I'd thought it was our dream. I was young, and sure I was going to make it, if she'd just stick it out a bit longer. I didn't want to give it up."

His grip tightened on the crutch handles. That had been a bad period. He'd never dreamed that they would spend that much time fighting as newlyweds.

"We made the playoffs that year in Rimouski. I was playing well. I tried to convince her that it meant I would make it, that we would make it. We had a big fight. It was the night the team was going out to celebrate. I left, slamming the door. When I came back, she was gone. She'd packed up to go back to her parents.

"Then the police came to tell me she was dead. And that she was pregnant when she died. I don't even know if she knew that. She hadn't told me, in any case."

Mike still wondered if she'd known, and if

she had, if she had deliberately left without telling him. That fear could still hurt.

He turned from the window and saw Bridget watching him with those big eyes behind her glasses. He'd almost forgotten she was there. He hadn't revisited this memory in a long time. He wasn't sure why he had today, unless it was the weather, the frustration of being trapped in this room…or Bridget's undemanding attention.

MIKE PULLED BACK his shoulders. He obviously was carrying some major guilt on them.

"You thought it was your fault," Bridget said. She couldn't imagine how that would feel, grief and guilt wrapped up together.

Mike turned on his good leg and looked directly at her. "If she'd just waited out the season before giving up… Two weeks later, first round of the playoffs, the Quebec starting goalie was out with a concussion after a fluke play in the warmup for the first game. I was called up as the backup's backup. He fell apart, and I got to play. I took everything I had, grief and anger and guilt, and focused it on hockey to avoid thinking about Amber. That's when they started calling me Iceman, but it wasn't a lack of feeling that powered me through that.

"I got the starter's job the following season. Had a contract then, and I had it made. Amber could have had everything she wanted. We both could have."

There was silence, broken only by the snow and ice pelting on the panes. Bridget tried to imagine that conflict, between your dream and the person you loved. How would you choose? What would she do in that difficult situation?

"And you still feel guilty?" she asked.

Mike shrugged. "I always will. But I've talked it through with a counselor, so I'm supposed to be good. That anger is gone now, and that might have been what made me able to play at the level I'm used to. Maybe I really have lost it." His expression was bleak.

"No way," said Bridget.

"Thanks," Mike said dismissively.

Bridget straightened, her temper sparking. "Don't patronize me. I'm not just saying that. I don't know if you can still play well now or not, but I know it wasn't anger that kept you going for seven years."

Mike stared at her, eyebrows raised. "How would you know?"

"Because that's not what anger's like. I mean, I get it. When she first died, your anger and pain and guilt would make you want to play hockey all the time to blank out or numb how you felt. I get that. I'd probably have done the same in the pool. And I know I do anger differently than you do. I get fired up and say or do something rash. You go quiet and probably feel it longer. But anger is a fresh emotion. Unless you're going to your wife's grave to whip up that feeling all the time, it won't last. It'll change—become hate, or resentment or depression or guilt, but it won't still be anger. I believe you could feel guilty, but guilt doesn't make you do better. It eats away at whatever is good. You couldn't build a hockey career on that. I mean, I'm Catholic. I know guilt."

Mike didn't respond. Bridget realized she'd jumped in where not wanted. Again.

"Sorry, it's not my place. I was just reacting in coach mode. You don't need a lecture from me."

Mike raised his hand. "I'm not upset. I was feeling it out. I hadn't looked at it like that. Maybe I've been talking to the wrong people."

"Didn't you say anything about this to one of your coaches? Isn't this part of their job?"

"Once. He hemmed and hawed and the next day I was asked to waive my no-trade clause."

Bridget's mouth opened again. "You mean, that was last year? That's why you left Quebec?"

Mike crutched himself over to the couch, and dropped down, setting his bad ankle on a pillow. "Yes. I blew up when they asked me to sign the waiver. I didn't even find out where they were trading me. If the coach thought I was done, I didn't much care."

Bridget's eyes flashed. "And they made it a self-fulfilling prophecy. Way to blow someone's confidence. Those weasels! Everyone thought you wanted out! And that losing in the playoffs last spring was karma catching up with you."

Mike sighed. "We had a new coach. He wasn't a big fan of me. He was new, and I'd been there my whole career. The fans assumed wins were all mine and didn't give him any credit. He also had a young goalie he'd been working with at his last club. When I was gone, the kid was brought over and became the starter."

Bridget stared at him. "Why didn't you let anyone know? What they did to you was almost evil!"

Mike shrugged and poked at a cushion with his crutch. "I can do stupid things. I was too proud. I thought that I'd built up enough of a rep that someone would come to me to find out the other side of the story. After all, my teammates were supposed to be my friends. I also didn't want the story getting out that I was done."

Bridget nodded and considered him. "When you're back, you're going to have to show them. When do we play Quebec again?"

Mike smiled at her usage of the word *we*. "Next week."

Bridget sighed. "Turchenko."

She muttered the name as if it was a four-letter word. That warmed him. "Yep. Then we have a home-and-home against them in March. Turchenko did win the last game against them."

"Oh please," Bridget said scornfully. "Toronto won by one goal. Quebec hit the crossbar twice. That was all that saved him. That's not going to happen again. Well, you'll be playing in March. You can show them."

Mike didn't want to acknowledge how

much her confidence was helping him. "I'll do that. But first, I have to get back on the ice. And reclaim the starting position."

"You will. I have no confidence in Turchenko," said Bridget. "But Cormack will tell you I've never been a big 'Turd-chenko' fan."

Mike laughed out loud. "You do have a talent for nicknames. Should I ask what mine is?"

"You don't have one yet. You'll have to really get me mad before that happens. Are you good now? I should probably get some stuff done."

"I'm good. Thanks for letting me vent."

Bridget left, and Mike sat in the chair, reviewing their conversation while his lunch went cold. He had been crediting his old anger and guilt with elevating his play, somewhere deep down. Now that the grief was mostly gone, leaving a small ache, he'd wondered if he could still play as well. Sure, he'd played horribly last spring, but his confidence had taken a major hit. If Bridget was right, then maybe he *could* play just on skill. Age was going to stop him at some point. But he might not be there yet.

Bridget must be a good coach. She was a great workout partner and knew her stuff when it came to fitness. And he was learning that she had a good handle on the mental part of sports, which played a big part. She was fit as well. He couldn't help noticing that she looked good in her workout gear— really good—even when sweaty. He appreciated that she dealt with him as a real person. A lot of people saw him only as a goalie, or couldn't get past his status or money. And it was fun when she got mad. He'd like to see more of that. He wondered again why she'd never had her vision corrected. Those heavy glasses seemed to have impeded her. They did make her look like she was listening intently, though.

He looked around, realizing that the weather was calming and his soup was cold. He shrugged and ate it anyway, turning on the TV to the sports channel most obsessed with the Blaze. Might as well see what he was up against. He noticed that for the first time, he could feel a little sprout of hope.

CHAPTER FOUR

"WHOA THERE!" BRIDGET SAID. "Keep that up and you'll injure yourself again!"

Mike grinned at her over the bar. He knew he was pushing himself, but he had good reason. Turchenko had continued to struggle. Mike didn't enjoy his team losing, but knowing he had a reason to stay fit was definitely aiding in his recovery. The team trainers were pleased with his progress, and now they needed Mike back with the team. He'd been asked if he'd start coming in to the team facility to do all of his workouts, now that he was ready to resume cardio exercise. They'd provide transportation and assistance, but they wanted him with the team.

Mike hadn't mentioned this to Bridget yet. He'd been keeping things deliberately light. He wasn't quite sure why he'd told her about his wife. Or why, that first evening, he'd gotten so close to discussing retirement. He was the Iceman. He was quiet and reserved, and didn't talk about himself. He didn't know what it was about Bridget. Perhaps she was just an excellent coach, since he was confiding in her the way he should have been able to with his own coaches. He didn't want to dig any deeper into that. He knew from experience that hockey required his primary attention, and people had a hard time accepting that. It was one of the reasons his social circle was almost exclusively limited to hockey people: when there was a choice, he always chose hockey.

He wondered if working out with a female partner was always better, or if it was just working out with Bridget. He wanted to thank her for her help.

Management had also invited him to watch a game from the owner's box. The team offered a driver and assistant. Mike had another idea. The O'Reillys were all hockey crazy, as he'd learned. The one game he'd been able to give Bridget tickets to had been a preseason game with eight kids to watch. The other game, her father and brother attended. He thought he could thank her, and let her know he was moving over to working out with the team at the same time. Bridget was wiping down the equipment after their workout before leaving.

"Want to come to the Nashville game tomorrow?" he asked her from the kitchen where he was cutting up fruit for a smoothie.

"You're going to a game?" she asked, surprised, since he hadn't since his accident.

"I was asked to come."

Bridget raised her eyebrows. "Perhaps with Turchenko playing like crap they want to suck up to you."

"Yeah, maybe. Watching games live is much better than on TV, so I'm happy to go."

"Okay, I'm in. Should I wear my Turchenko jersey?"

"I'll have security chuck you out if you do," he answered, with a smile.

She asked if she should pick him up. Mike grinned at the thought of trying to get into her vehicle with his crutches, let alone what the ride would be like. He responded that he'd arrange for her to park her car at the hotel and they'd take his vehicle, which had a pass to get into player parking at the arena.

Bridget arrived in good time, almost quivering with excitement. Mike knew he was being a little cruel, but he kept a straight face as the valet at the hotel entrance pulled up in an old-school Land Rover.

Bridget looked confused. "Where's your McLaren?"

"It's a summer car," he responded innocently.

Her eyes flashed. "I should leave you to get yourself to the arena."

"That's a scary threat. If only they had drivers and cars you could hire to take people places."

She snorted. "You're just afraid of women drivers," she said. "It would serve you right to get a female cab driver." She paused and looked at the Land Rover. He could see the emotions passing over her face. The Rover was still a pretty cool vehicle. "Okay," she said. "I'll drive you."

"Thanks. Since you can drive a stick, this is roomier and safer. If you hit anything, I've got some protection."

He tried to keep his face straight as he maneuvered into the Rover with the anxious assistance of the valet. Bridget was still sputtering as she got behind the wheel. When she saw his smile she stopped.

"Okay, smarty-pants. It would serve you right if someone did hit us."

She got over her snit and asked him questions about the Rover, and why he'd picked it. He admitted that while he didn't need all its capabilities, winters in Quebec were icier and snowier than Toronto, and he'd liked knowing he could handle any weather thrown at him. Plus, he thought the Rover was cool.

Bridget looked at him out of the corner of her eyes. "Well, at least it's not a Hummer."

Mike was about to reply indignantly when he noticed the grin she was trying to hide. "Next one," he promised.

MIKE DIRECTED HER into the area for player parking. Bridget felt like she was getting the handshake to enter some super secret club. Security was tight. The team had provided a couple of assistants to take them up to the owner's box, complete with a wheelchair for Mike. Bridget wondered what brain trust had thought he would agree to that. Didn't they deal with male egos all the time? Mike turned down the wheelchair and sent the gophers away.

Bridget had been to the arena for that preseason game in October, but this was different. Mike might play behind a mask, but his face was recognized. He was asked to sign things, people snapped pictures, asked about his ankle and on occasion offered advice about everything from foot rubs to stopping pucks. Mike was obviously familiar with fan behavior and handled it easily. Bridget was an invisible sidekick, happy not to be in the pictures. She'd occasionally hold his crutches, or snap a photo for those who weren't into taking selfies. She'd decided not to wear her Giguère jersey, opting for a fairly generic Blaze long-sleeved T, and she guessed that most of the people swarming around Mike thought she was with the team, escorting him.

A few people expressed a wish for Mike's quick return, and it made Bridget feel good. Mike had been winning some games before the injury, and with the way Turchenko was playing, people were starting to realize Mike was the better option as the Blaze's starting goalie.

The luxury box was intimidating. Top management people were there, people with money and power. Bridget didn't know how one was supposed to deal with them. It was revealing that Mike did. She guessed he'd been interacting with people like this for years now, and with his résumé, which boasted Cups and numerous other awards, he probably was a power person himself. Mike introduced her by name but didn't specify their relationship. Bridget wondered just what you would call it. Workout buddy? Friend? Driver? She was happy to stay in the background since she knew from experience that she had a pretty stellar talent for putting her foot in her mouth. Mike looked for her as the teams cleared the ice to start the game and waved her into the seat beside him.

There were definite perks to being in a box. No lining up for food, drinks or bathrooms, and the seats were much more comfortable. Watching the game with Mike was new, too. She had thought he was focused when watching TV. Watching in person, he was completely oblivious to everything around him. She could sense the tension in his body. Everyone was tense; it wasn't a pretty game. Both teams scored numerous times, but it was easy to see that Mike wasn't very happy with Turchenko's play. She watched Turchenko instead of the defense this time, considering, trying to be objective. He made some great saves, and then let in a soft goal. Mike seemed to feel pain with each bad goal. He wanted to be out there badly. She hoped the team doctors would check his ankle carefully.

She wasn't sure he could be trusted not to rush back to the ice before he should.

The power people gathered in groups toward the back of the box, discussing the game. Bridget turned to Mike, waiting to see what he wanted to do.

"I hate this," Mike said. He lifted his head and looked around. He caught her glance, and smiled.

"It's okay, I'll survive. I've got to get back out there." He nodded toward the ice.

"You also have to let your bone heal."

"Yes, Dr. O'Reilly," Mike teased. "And now you need to get home for your beauty sleep. Me, too."

THEY TOOK A back way to the player's parking garage. The other players were still cooling down, showering, changing and giving interviews, so there was no one else there. Bridget didn't envy them. She'd been spectacularly bad at giving interviews. She was either on her guard and answered in monosyllables, or said too much, and found her comments were pulled out of context, making her look like an idiot. She was still working on that. It was going to be part of her coaching life, though her least favorite.

Bridget thought she was doing quite well with the Land Rover, but there was so much congestion with postgame traffic that they weren't going anywhere fast. Mike was quiet, still dwelling on the game, she expected.

She decided to distract him. "So, if you'd still had the McLaren on the road, would you have let me drive?"

It took a moment for the words to work their way into Mike's head. He looked at her and said, "No."

"Hey, I'm a good driver. And I would kill to drive her."

"I'm the one you'd kill. You're much too aggressive. And anyway, I can't get into my McLaren with crutches."

Bridget glared at him. "I am not too aggressive. My car likes to be driven that way. And you can't say I'm driving aggressively now."

"You're not driving aggressively now because we're stuck in gridlock." There were thousands of people all leaving the arena at the same time.

"What if I promise to drive like someone's grandmother. Just once…" Bridget wheedled.

Mike looked at her with amusement. "The

day you score a goal on me is the day I let you drive her."

Bridget privately thought that day could be a long time away. But she wouldn't admit it.

"I think you have a problem with women drivers," she reiterated.

"I have a problem with anyone driving my car. I'm not letting you, and I'm not letting your brothers. My car, I drive."

"Until I score on you."

"Yeah, till then. Good luck."

Bridget chewed on her bottom lip. This was a challenge, and she'd always responded to challenges. She wanted to do it; wanted it badly. Driving the car would be nice, but making Mike eat his words would be nicer. She looked over at him and found he was looking at her with misgiving.

"I just made a big mistake," Mike said.

Bridget quickly switched to concern. Had the outing been too much? "You shouldn't have come tonight. I could tell it was tough for you to watch. Mind you, unless you were a Nashville fan, it was tough to watch for anyone."

"Nice try, Bridget, but I'm not worried about the game—at least, I'm over it now. The mistake was daring you."

Bridget laughed. "Too late."

"I don't know," he said, musingly.

"You can't back out on the deal now!" Bridget protested, pulling through the intersection on a very late yellow light.

"I can if you're going to run a red!" he yelled.

"That wasn't red. And I think I need to get you home, since you're an invalid and it's making you cranky."

"If you get in an accident, the deal is off. I can't risk that with my car."

"Of course not. I'd never hurt anything as beautiful as that!"

Mike had seen her falling for his car, so he knew she would intend to take great care. But he also knew what it felt like when you got behind the wheel of a vehicle with that kind of power and responsiveness. He'd taken a few risks himself. He looked at Bridget and was sure he saw gears turning in her brain.

"You can't sneak into the suite in the middle of the night, put a net behind the bed and shoot a puck at it. You have to score fairly."

"Of course," she answered, seeming offended. "But maybe we should clarify what you think is fair. You have to be awake, apparently. What if you're drunk?"

Mike laughed out loud. "That's only good if you're drunk, too."

"Noted. But I'm not giving up. Still, it'll be fair. I'm not too bad, really, and if you were having a bad day…"

"That scares me more than what Turchenko was doing out there."

Bridget stuck her tongue out at him. "I'm a good driver," she said, as she cut someone off to change lanes.

"My poor car."

"See? You're already accepting the inevitable. How long do I get to drive it? Do I get extra chances if I score more than once?"

Mike was happy that they'd finally arrived at the hotel. This conversation was going nowhere good.

Bridget pulled to a stop in front of the hotel. A valet appeared, opened Mike's door and helped him with the crutches. Another opened the door for Bridget, and she passed him the keys.

"When you take down the Rover, could you bring up the car that's in its spot? Ms. O'Reilly needs to get home."

"Of course, sir."

"Why don't you go head up? You don't

need to wait for me," she offered, and he noticed she sounded a bit distant.

"No, I'm fine. I'll wait for your car to arrive. I wanted to say something anyway." Mike wasn't sure just how to put it.

Bridget crossed her arms. "I can't drive your car no matter what," she guessed.

Mike smiled. "No, I won't be that mean. I'll just hope for the best. I was asked by the team if I'd start coming in to practices in the mornings. They'd like me to help with Turchenko."

"Help him take over your job, you mean?"

"No, I think everyone is sure I'll be the starter again, but there are times, like back-to-back games, where he'll need to play. They think I can help."

Bridget nodded. "That makes sense. You're almost out of the cast anyway, aren't you?"

"I wanted to let you know. It means we won't be working out here anymore. I'll be heading in to the team facility every day. I hope you don't mind."

Bridget's cheeks flushed.

"No problem. I was glad to help the team, but I'm quite happy to get back to the club. I do have my own things to do," she said coolly.

There was something in her tone of voice—Mike knew something had gone wrong with the conversation, but the valet showed up with her car. She thanked him for the game, and took no time to get into her vehicle and start off. The speed of her exit made him cringe for the fate of his car.

He hadn't handled this well. He'd upset her, and he wasn't sure exactly how. He was more than grateful to the whole O'Reilly family, but especially to Bridget. This convalescence had been a tough time. They'd helped him get through. They'd stuck with him when he was struggling. He wanted to find a way to express his appreciation, but right now, he was tired from his first outing in weeks, and he needed to rest.

MIKE WAS WELCOMED back to the team more warmly than he'd expected, but he missed the workouts with Bridget—also more than he'd expected. Though they'd just exercised together, for the most part, they had talked seriously once. That had unlocked something in his brain. He was considering that instead of being the bastard who'd used his wife's death to give himself the career he'd always wanted, maybe hockey had just helped him get over losing Amber. Maybe, he could even try again, sometime after he was done with hockey. To find someone else. Have another chance to have his own kid. He'd spent time with the O'Reilly family, and before that, the Sawatzkys. He would like that kind of family someday. Not while he was playing, he wouldn't make that mistake again, but later, in that scary future when there was no more hockey to play.

Two weeks later he was able to lose the cast permanently. He no longer needed to swim at the club; the pranks were over. He started some on-ice workouts. Once again, hockey was taking up all his time and energy, mental and physical.

He didn't forget the O'Reillys and the debt he owed them, but they were on the back burner for the time being. This was why hockey didn't mix with relationships. He couldn't allow himself to get distracted from playing, and people usually had a hard time accepting that.

CHAPTER FIVE

BRIDGET SNIFFED. SHE wasn't one to cry, but she was sad to be finished with her special class. The kids had all done well. For the last class, they'd played games in the water, and then she'd given them each a certificate and a hug. Even Tony looked sad to say good-bye. She overheard him admit that one of the girls was actually the best swimmer of the group, which Bridget considered to be a major breakthrough. The program was a success, much to the dismay of Wally the Weasel. It was going to continue in the new year, but not with Bridget. One of the regular swimming instructors would be teaching, and the club was even going to pay her for her time. Wally the Weasel was ready to choke on the thought. Every time Bridget was near him, she heard him muttering about budgets, but he was easy to ignore. Bridget knew she'd gone from being someone he just tolerated to someone he actively disliked, but what could he do about it? She was just relieved that he hadn't been able to end the program as she thought he'd been trying to at the start.

Mike didn't go to the club anymore, and Bridget was glad of that. Really. She didn't want him thinking she was trying to bother him. And life was easier now that she wasn't heading downtown every day. Sure, things were quiet since she was no longer teaching her children's class, but it was natural to find things a little flat with winter weather grabbing hold. It was December, after all. She put all of her focus into coaching her swim team instead. She had researched, tried some new out-of-the-pool exercises to help their conditioning, and it was paying off. Two of her swimmers, Annabelle and Austin, were really improving. She called them her A-team. Life became a little less gray as she helped them get better and better.

MIKE WAS FINALLY cleared to play again at the start of December, and now, a couple of games in, he was feeling good. The first game back had been a test. The team looked to be out of playoff contention at this point, and Mike's goaltending might be the only way to save the season. Was he going to come back as the Iceman, or was he going to wash out the way he had last spring?

The start was a little shaky. Practices couldn't replace game time, and Mike was rusty. The Blaze were down two-zip at the end of the first, but the first goal had been scored on a power play, and the other had been well screened. Mike stopped a breakaway at the beginning of the second, and fans started to hope.

The game went to overtime, but Mike held on and the Blaze won. It wasn't just the win, though that was also important. This had been a solid performance for Mike. Toronto had been outshot almost two to one, and there had been good scoring chances. Mike hadn't just scraped through, despite the scoreboard. He'd bailed out the team. The Iceman was back.

He was playing the way he knew he could. But the team would have to claw their way back to playoff contention if he wanted to discover if he was all the way back. He took time to go to the club one day after practice, to let Wally know that Bridget's class could swim in peace now.

He didn't expect to see Bridget, and he didn't want to run into her when he wasn't quite sure what he felt about her. He missed their morning workouts. He missed talking to her. He found himself thinking of things he wanted to tell her. Were they friends? Their last interaction after the game had been awkward. He hadn't reached out to her, in case she was upset, and as time passed, it grew more awkward to think of what to say.

He wasn't sure if he wanted to be a friend, and anything more was out of the question.

Bridget was fun, but she was also a competitor, and she understood his competitive drive better than any other woman he'd known, and even most men. He couldn't see a way for them to just hang out without risking misleading her about wanting more from a relationship, which wouldn't be fair right now. He didn't get involved during hockey.

Wally—Walter—was in his office, and more than thrilled to see him. He wasn't as thrilled to hear that Mike wasn't coming back to swim. And it wasn't just because the Weasel liked to annoy Bridget. As he told Mike, her experimental class was over.

"Fortunately, there weren't any incidents, but they're starting another class in the new year." He sniffed.

"It's nice of Bridget to offer her time," Mike responded.

"Oh, she's not spending her time now, no. They're paying extra to the regular swim instructor to teach the class. It's really going to add pressure to the budget," Walter fussed. Mike was a little surprised at the depth of dislike in Walter's voice, and he wondered if Walter didn't like women who challenged him.

"Maybe you can help me with something Wall-ter," Mike corrected. Bridget and her nicknames. Mike had almost said "Turdchenko" the other day when the backup had been especially annoying.

Walter gave Mike an exasperated look when Mike stumbled over his name.

"Anything," Walter assured him.

"Bridget and her family were very helpful while I was laid up. I wanted to thank them, and wondered if you had any suggestions?"

Mike had just thought of that. He didn't really think Wally would be that helpful, but he'd worked with Bridget for more than a year now so he might know something.

The man looked wary. "Were you wanting to give them a membership here? We have a strict policy—"

"No, no. Nothing like that. I don't think they want to join an athletic club, even this one."

Walter didn't try to hide his relief. "I don't think this is their sort of place."

Mike didn't either, but not in the way Walter meant. The O'Reillys were more interested in hockey than racquetball or curling. They were a blue-collar clan.

"Why do you say that?" Mike asked, making himself unclench his fists.

"I don't know anything about Bridget's family, of course." *Of course*, thought Mike. "But, Bridget already has access to many of the club facilities, and socially of course… well, we don't really have anything for people like her."

Mike kept his face blank with an effort. Wally had such disdain in his voice. Didn't he realize Mike had been one of those people? Did he think everyone looked down on people who weren't rich?

But Wally was continuing. "I mean, socially, there are women here who'd be happy to spend time with you. If you let me know, I could arrange a racquetball game with one. But there's no one here for Bridget."

"No single men?" Mike asked, trying to make Wally spit it out.

Wally tittered. "No, no, we have single men. But we don't have single women interested in other single women."

It took Mike a minute to understand that. Bridget was gay?

"So, while she's a lovely girl, I'm sure she'd be happier socializing somewhere with other people like her."

"Really?" he asked, feeling confused, and wondering why he didn't want to accept what Wally was saying.

"Oh, yes, I know for a fact. And of course, we don't discriminate here, but…" He allowed his voice to trail off, letting Mike fill in the blanks. Mike would have liked to explain the definition of discrimination to him, but was afraid he'd end up explaining it with his fists.

Instead, he got up and left. He was disgusted with Walter, but he was taken aback by the news of Bridget. It was an obvious answer. It explained why his relationship with her was so different. But he was disappointed. He *had* been interested in her. He'd been telling himself otherwise, but if he were honest with himself, he'd wanted to explore that option with her. Not now, with hockey on, of course, but maybe later? Still, it was for the best. Hockey and relationships did not work when Mike was involved. He had to remember that. Look what had happened last time.

"I DIDN'T MEAN to say anything till we were past sixteen weeks, but I can't help it. I am so sick every morning," Jee gloated.

It was the annual Christmas cookie bake for the O'Reilly women. The daughters-in-law and Bridget gathered at O'Reilly Central and made cookies and other necessary Christmas treats, while the O'Reilly grandparents and sons and grandkids went skating.

Baking was delayed as everyone congratulated Jee. It would be a summer baby, if all went well. Bridget hugged her warmly, knowing more than the others how important this was for her friend. It was nice to know that when it was her turn someday, if she had a turn, she'd be part of this same supportive group of women. Bridget often spent more time with her brothers than their wives, but she appreciated the girl power they provided when needed.

The talk focused on pregnancy stories, as each sister-in-law was free to talk to Jee now that she was in "the club." Bridget's attention wandered. Starting a family looked to be a long way off for her. Unfortunately, her mind drifted in the direction of the Toronto Blaze goalie, and she was replaying that last conversation they had when she suddenly became aware of everyone staring at her.

"What?" she asked.

"Bridget, you've beaten those eggs into concrete. What were you thinking about?"

Bridget looked down at the mixing bowl. She had overdone the eggs, a lot. She flushed, embarrassed.

"Pooh, she's blushing. Must be a guy," teased Karen.

Jill looked up from her phone, where she was checking for a text from middle brother David. "It's Connor, right? That swimmer?" Connor had been discussed in the past. Bridget did not want to discuss him again.

Karen looked at Bridget. She was married to Liam, the second oldest brother. "No, can't be him. Bridget won't see him again until that conference in Atlanta."

"I bet it's that goalie—Mike, right? Bridget was seeing him almost every day. Patrick thinks he's a good guy, and you know Bridget, she never goes for the cubicle type." That was Nancy, Patrick's wife.

Bridget's heated cheeks betrayed her.

"Oh, I remember," said Jill. "Do you like him, Bridget?"

Jee had been trying to get an answer to that question, but Bridget had been avoiding her tactful enquiries. Jill, mostly oblivious to anything that didn't involve her baby, avoided tact and asked directly.

Bridget looked around at the circle of faces, all expressing concern for her. She felt foolish, but they wouldn't judge her.

"Maybe a bit," she admitted.

"He's not interested?" Karen asked.

"Of course not," Bridget answered. She held up a hand to stop any contradictions. "You guys have seen that *Hockey Wives* show. Am I anything like the women on there?"

"Nope," said Jill. Blunt but honest.

"And he's got hockey to focus on, and I've got my swimming. Have I told you guys how well Annabelle and Austin are doing? I'm sure they're going to do great at the city finals— maybe even make the provincial championships."

This wasn't as noteworthy a topic for the sisters, but they allowed themselves to be diverted while Bridget dug into the fridge for some fresh eggs.

After baking, the women and the kids decorated the tree while the guys put up the outside lights. It was now officially Christmas for the O'Reillys. Bridget always loved the way the house changed once the tree was up. The whole place smelled of cinnamon and gingerbread and evergreen, and the air was thick with secrets and anticipation. They'd ordered a massive amount of pizza and the atmosphere was buzzing with excitement, arcing from kids to adults.

Jee sat by her and gave her a hug. "Sorry, B. Brian says he's a good guy. He told them he's tied up with team stuff now, but wants to come by over the holidays. Should I give you a heads-up when he's coming?"

Bridget felt a pang. Mike was keeping up with her brothers, but she hadn't heard from him.

"Don't worry, Jee. You just stay healthy with that baby."

Since this was the O'Reilly home, a hockey game was put on TV after everyone had gorged themselves on pizza and the "defective" Christmas baking that wasn't being saved for the big day. Bridget looked around at her brothers and their wives, all at least appearing to be happily paired up and with children either present or arriving soon. She and Cormack were the only singles in the group, and for the first time, she felt left out. She excused herself and went to her apartment downstairs.

She hadn't been able to face watching the Blaze play and imagining all her sisters-in-law watching her when Mike was on. And she didn't like feeling like a fifth wheel in her own family circle.

She shook her head. She really didn't like this self-pitying mood she was in. She was not going to be that girl, the one who was so hung up on a guy who wasn't interested in her that she was no good to herself or anyone else. That was it. No more moping over Mike Reimer. She had many wonderful things in her life and she was going to focus on them.

CHRISTMAS ARRIVED WITHOUT any Mike, and Bridget congratulated herself on her success. The family had their usual chaotic get-together, with families coming and going throughout the day. There was an incredible amount of food, and Bridget spent a lot of the day in the kitchen cleaning up. Still, she felt more like herself again. She knew Jee would let her know if Mike was supposed to come around, and she was doing well with the "out of sight, out of mind" approach.

Jee did give her warning, but Bridget didn't get it. On Boxing Day all the O'Reillys who were at home or not tied up with commitments with their wives' families, and any friends who wanted to, would show up for a road hockey game. This wasn't the usual pickup game, but had full teams and was no-holds-barred. Bridget didn't have her phone on her as there was too great a risk of damage. She was, as usual, the only girl playing, and she neither asked nor gave quarter with the guys. She was arguing a call with Cormack when she noticed things had gotten quiet. She turned and saw a Land Rover joining the mass of cars parked on the street. She felt her stomach knot and told herself not to be stupid.

Mike swung out of the vehicle. He was big, and broad, and to her eyes, extremely appealing. She started fidgeting with her helmet strap.

"Mike! Glad you could make it," said Patrick.

"Hey, Merry Christmas!" several voices greeted him.

"Can you use an extra?" Mike asked.

The teams, while competing fiercely, were made up of a hodgepodge of players from Mr. O'Reilly down to his seven-year-old grandson, Bradley. It took some creativity to balance them evenly.

Patrick declared that Mike couldn't be goalie. He remembered the game from earlier in the fall, and was pretty sure any team with Mike on it would win if he was the net minder. So Mike was given a stick and was recruited to be a winger on the team Bridget was playing against.

Bridget played defense. Mike was a distraction for her, but when the ball dropped, she made herself concentrate solely on the game. She was competitive, whether playing Monopoly or hockey, or swimming, and she soon mostly forgot Mike the man, allowing him to blur until he was simply "the enemy."

SHE BUMPED HIM hard a couple of times. Mike found it difficult to be physical with her (he was not used to coed hockey), and Bridget was able to take the ball from him a little too easily. He was razzed for it, and when she started on a breakaway, he grabbed her from behind and swung her around, dropping her facing back toward her own net.

He took a moment to release her. "Penalty!" she cried, a little breathlessly. Mike grinned at her. He held his hands up, looking innocent. "What?"

There was a shout from the other end as seven-year-old Bradley scored. Bridget broke their gaze, and went to congratulate her nephew.

He was in trouble, he thought. He'd hoped, by avoiding her, that he'd stop thinking about her. He'd come to the Boxing Day game because he wanted to drop off his gift for the O'Reillys, and because the holidays tended to be lonely for him. He didn't get enough time off to go see his mother. He no longer had his group of teammates to celebrate with, and the new team still hadn't fully warmed up to him. He wanted to hang out with some people. Regular people, like the Sawatzkys, but since they were no longer available, the O'Reillys were his best bet here in Toronto. And yes, he'd wanted to see Bridget, too.

He was invited to join the family leftover potluck where he met members he hadn't gotten to know yet, spouses of the guys who'd come to watch games with him when he was laid up. He wasn't sure why he was getting such a once-over. If he'd been a prospective date for Bridget, then yes, that would be understandable. But as he'd learned from Wally the Weasel, he wasn't Bridget's type.

It turned out he had at least one fan in Toronto. Seven-year-old Bradley was his shadow. He let the kid's mom take their picture together on her cell phone, and from the look on the kid's face it was Christmas morning all over again.

He didn't see much of Bridget. She was in the kitchen for a while, then seemed to vanish. Had he offended her when he grabbed her? He'd enjoyed wrapping his arms around her, but had he made her uncomfortable? Had she guessed he was interested? Was she trying to give him a hint? He checked the rest of the family, but no one was taking notice of her absence.

He hadn't done this much second-guessing about a woman since Amber. He knew men who mixed hockey and family, but he couldn't do that, so he'd made a conscious decision to keep things light until he was done playing. He'd dated a few women over the years, but it had always been superficial, easy. It was the least he could do for Amber. And selfishly, he had never wanted to be faced again with a choice between hockey and someone he cared for. It had been easy enough, till now. So why did he have to be interested in Bridget?

After the meal, he watched the Canadian team playing at the World Juniors with the family. He enjoyed watching the tournament, remembering how he'd once dreamed of playing as a professional at the top level. In years past, he'd watched with his teammates in Quebec, but he hadn't been invited by anyone in Toronto. He appreciated that the O'Reillys welcomed him, even though he hadn't yet proved himself a success on the ice here. He didn't want to make things awkward with Bridget, but he was enjoying himself with her family.

He managed to leave behind an envelope without being discovered. He hoped they liked it.

THE NEXT MORNING Bridget was awakened by a pounding on her door. Living in the in-law suite in the basement of her parents' house had its advantages—like being able to slip away last night without anyone knowing. She hadn't slept well, and had hoped to sleep in on her final day off, but here was the disadvantage of living in the in-law suite: she was right there.

Cormack was yelling loud enough to wake up the neighbors.

"Come on, Bridge! Get up here. You gotta see what Mike left. Dad says you get first dibs."

Bridget grumbled a few choice epithets under her breath, and dragged on sweats before heading up to the main floor.

Patrick was at the front door when she reached the kitchen. He had Bradley with him. There was a letter and bits of cardboard on the table. Cormack threw the letter almost in her face, and she had to jerk back to make sure he didn't knock off her glasses. She blinked to clear her vision, and read the letter.

The O'Reilly family:
My apologies for the delay. I very much appreciated all your care and assistance while I was injured and going a little stir-crazy. I couldn't swing season tickets, but I was able to get two tickets for each remaining home game. Sorry, Mrs. O'Reilly, this might not be your favorite activity, but from what I've learned of your family, they will enjoy.
Gratefully,

The letter ended with a scrawl. Bridget recognized it as matching the one on the note she'd received when Mike sent the tickets for her class. She'd kept it in her office at the club. He might not get points for originality, but he certainly had read her family. Tickets for home games for either Toronto team were expensive and hard to come by. This was something the O'Reillys would cherish, and then talk about for years to come.

David showed up as she was reading. Apparently everyone was coming to divvy up the tickets. Bradley was almost vibrating, he was so excited. Patrick was vibrating, too.

Bridget had been to two games now, so she thought she would be taking the leftovers, but her father had stepped in. Without Bridget, they wouldn't have met Mike, and Bridget had the most difficult schedule, so she was to have first pick.

Cormack almost pitched a fit when she insisted she had to go get her phone so she could see when she was free for a game. But she usually had team practice till after the games started on weeknights, and about half her weekends had swim meets in the weeks leading up to Finals. No way could she remember when she was free without checking a calendar.

The team had certainly not been considering her when they made up the schedule. Saturday night home games were on the weekends she was tied up. She couldn't plan on a free weekday evening until possibly March. But over the holidays there was only one midday practice for her swim team, so she was available for the first game, which was tomorrow.

She wasn't sure who to ask to go with her. She'd love to take Bradley, but Patrick wanted to go with him to his first game. She could ask Jee, but she knew Brian wanted to go with her, and Jee was only a lukewarm fan. Her mother settled the question by saying her dad would like to go with her. Bridget agreed.

Brian and Liam arrived, and a convoluted system was set up to give everyone a chance to pick a game. Six kids plus Bridget's dad meant that twenty-two tickets were divided among seven with a lottery for the one left over. Bridget got two more dates in March.

She left her family animatedly discussing who they'd see the Blaze play against and with whom they'd go, and went back down to her apartment. She needed more sleep, but it would help if there was less Mike being discussed. She'd just talked herself into being sensible, and then he'd shown up again yesterday. Well, one game this week, and then she could ignore him until March. Who knew? Maybe he'd be gone by then. Depending on how the team did in the next few weeks, there could be a fire sale and players traded away. The way Mike was beginning to play, he'd be the most valuable asset the Blaze had to trade.

She had a smaller swim team to work with at the club over the Christmas break. She had her two standout swimmers who had advanced in leaps and bounds. Annabelle was fourteen, but had become the fastest swimmer in the club. Austin was right behind her. Bridget was proud of how committed they were, and of how they'd improved. They'd all earned PRs over the season. With two months left, they had a chance of being in the provincial championships. Maybe even make it to Nationals. Since the club had had only one swimmer in the city championships before she arrived, she thought she could call the year a success no matter how it ended.

Bridget was looking forward to going to the game with her dad. The seats were good, club level, mid-ice, and this time it would be a normal experience. Going with the kids had been more cat herding than watching the sport she loved. It had been a terrific experience watching a game in the power box with Mike, but that wasn't her world. Going with her dad, wearing her jersey: that was her. Her dad had taught her most of what she knew about hockey, and they'd enjoy the game together.

The following day, after swim team practice, was Bradley's birthday party. Bridget had asked Nancy to send her the shot of Bradley and Mike snapped on Boxing Day, and had taken it to a shop to get it printed on a T-shirt. Bradley was a December baby, so he was smaller than most of his classmates and tended to be a timid kid. Bridget thought having that T-shirt to show that he had met his hockey idol would be something he'd love, and might give him some points at school.

She'd planned to run practice, pick up the shirt and head home to get her dad. They were going to go downtown early, find parking, grab a burger and then head to the game. Her schedule was so weird that she didn't get a lot of time to spend with him. As one of six siblings, one-on-one time with her dad or mom was rare. She often saw her mom midday if she went home, but her schedule didn't sync with her dad's. This should be a precious and fun night.

She was in her office, making notes on her practice schedule, when her phone pinged. She gave it a quick check and caught her breath. It was from Mike. After not hearing from him directly for a month (not that she was counting), he suggested that she and her dad might like to meet him at a sports bar after the game.

While running practice, her brain kept coming up with ideas. Was Mike doing this because he felt obligated? Did he maybe want to see her? Why now? Should she go? Her swimmers didn't say anything if she seemed a little distracted, but they were nice kids. They were focused on the next meet, and were doing well. Fortunately, this wasn't a vital practice.

She detoured by Jee and Brian's on the way home. Brian was out with one of the other brothers.

"What's up Bridget?" Jee asked when Bridget knocked at the door.

"Gotta show you something," Bridget said, and followed her into the house. She sat at the kitchen table and opened the text for Jee.

Jee looked at her sympathetically. "How do you feel? Do you want to meet Mike?"

Bridget sighed. "I do and I don't. I like

being with Mike. That's the problem. When he told me our workout sessions were over, it was just weird, like it was a big deal. I think he suspected I, well, found him attractive. He probably thought that by ignoring me for a month I'd get the hint that he wasn't interested. And I did! But, well, I was so happy to see him on Boxing Day. I might have been a little obvious. That's why I left early. But I can't seem to avoid him. He keeps popping up!"

Jee looked at her strangely. "You haven't heard from him in a month?"

Bridget shook her head. "No."

"Then how did he know you were going to the game tonight?"

Jee and Bridget looked at each other for a moment. "The boys. Someone told him."

"Think your dad knows about this?" Jee asked, nodding at the phone.

"If he doesn't, he will. If one of the boys knows, they all know and someone will tell Dad. He'll want to meet up with him." Bridget sighed. "So I guess we're going. I don't want to tell Dad that I want to skip because I have a crush on Mike."

Jee rubbed Bridget's arm sympathetically.

"You can let your dad do the talking. Just sit back and you'll get through it."

Bridget sighed again. "For one night, okay. But how long is this going to go on? It's almost like he's part of the family now."

Jee sat up. "Well, we can work that out. How much longer is he playing in Toronto?"

Bridget thought. "His contract ends this season. So he's here till the beginning of April, or till the Blaze are out of the playoffs, if they can make it. Probably wouldn't be much longer, sadly."

"Any chance he'd be traded sooner?"

Bridget considered. It was a big contract, so it wouldn't be easy for another team to pay it and fit it under the payroll cap teams had to abide by. But since it was the final year on the contract, the next team would take less of a hit. The new team would only be committed to him till the end of this season.

"We'll know in a month or so. If the Blaze are in contention, it will be because of him, and they won't trade him. If they lose any chance of making the playoffs, they'll try to trade him."

"And this is your busiest time, right?"

"Absolutely. More meets, which means I

have to fill out lots of paperwork for the Weasel."

"So get through tonight. You won't see him at another game, maybe ever if he gets traded. If he shows up at your parents' place, you probably won't be there, and if you are, just say you're busy and go down to your place."

Bridget quickly answered Mike's text, then hugged Jee. "Thanks. I was freaking out. But you're right. I can get through tonight. Dad will be thrilled, and after that there shouldn't be a problem. As long as I can just manage not to make a fool of myself for one night, then I never need to see Mike again."

CHAPTER SIX

"DAD, I DON'T think Mom would be happy about you eating sauerkraut."

Her father had heaped his hot dog with the condiment. Her mother would never let him, said it disagreed with him.

Her dad grinned at her. "So don't tell her. What happens in the arena stays in the arena."

Bridget rolled her eyes, hoping she wouldn't get in trouble for not stopping him. But since she didn't plan to wrestle the hotdog away from him, she had to shrug and figure she'd done what she could.

Her dad was having a great time. He struck up a conversation with any of their seat neighbors who gave him an opportunity. He followed the game keenly and squabbled amicably with her about the play on the ice. Her dad was never one to ask questions about how she was doing and what her long-term plans were. He got that information from her mom. He and Bridget were happy just to hang out together, and every once in a while he'd drop a serious comment. That was how her dad showed affection. Bridget wasn't one to dissect her feelings with others either, so they got along well.

A groan went through the crowd. There had been a defensive breakdown in the second period on the Blaze's part that led to an unnecessary goal. Someone next to Mr. O'Reilly blamed Mike, but her dad argued that the defenseman Troy Green had been out of position, leaving Mike exposed. The other spectator wasn't convinced, but gave up arguing when he realized the O'Reillys were prepared to continue the discussion for a good while if needed.

In the third period, she realized her dad was looking a little pale. He insisted he was fine, and they stayed to see the Blaze get the go-ahead goal in the last couple of minutes to seal a win.

When the game was over and they got up to leave though, he had to confess that the sauerkraut was not agreeing with him.

"Mike will understand we have to go straight home," Bridget said. Privately, she thought this was a great out for her. A part of her was disappointed, but she'd work on beating that part down—hard—once they got home.

"No, that would be rude. Tell him I'll catch him another time, and remind him about that last breakaway—he was out a little far."

"I can text him all that. I need to get you home."

Her father waved her off, saying he could catch one of those Ubers everyone was talking about.

"Dad, you've never taken one. What if you get sick before the ride's over?"

"Bridget, it's not that long a trip. I can handle it."

"I'm sure Mike won't mind. Mom would want me to take care of you."

"Your mother would want you to have manners. The man got us these tickets, and asked to see us after. If you had been the one who wasn't feeling good, I'd have gone. I thought you liked Mike?"

Bridget gave up. She'd go to meet Mike on her own, rather than try to explain her complicated emotions to her dad.

She hoped Mike didn't think she had got rid of her dad to spend time with him alone, or that she and her dad had cooked up the scheme together. The thought made her squirm. She'd just have to be aloof. Cool and aloof. But while she was waiting at the bar, she found there was another problem she hadn't considered. Women didn't go there alone unless they wanted to meet someone new. After repeating that she was waiting for a friend, and getting a skeptical look back several times, she ordered a couple of Cokes. She drank from one, moved it across the table, and tried to look like she was waiting for her date to come back from the men's room. A date who apparently had had the same difficulties as her father with sauerkraut, based on how long he was taking. She was beginning to get annoyed with her fictitious date and considered bailing on him.

She was checking her phone for the umpteenth time when she noticed out of the corner of her eye another guy approaching the table. She looked up, ready to give an earful to whoever was interrupting her, but it was Mike. Her stomach dropped to somewhere in the region of her kneecaps. He looked at the Coke and asked if her father was in the men's.

Bridget sighed. Here came the awkwardness. "No. He overindulged in some sauerkraut at the game and had to go home. He insisted that I should come meet you, and thank you for him. He had a great time, until his stomach started to act up. He didn't want to stand you up, so I'm here as his emissary. You played well." She told herself to stop babbling. She was not going to mention the breakaway.

"Is someone else with you?" he asked, still looking at the partially emptied Coke.

Bridget flushed. "No, but I got tired of saying I was waiting for someone." She quickly switched the glasses so that the one she'd drunk from was in front of her.

Mike dropped into the seat across from her.

"I'm sorry your dad isn't feeling well. Will he be okay?"

"Yes, he made it home by 'the Uber' where Mom is probably taking care of him and scolding him for the sauerkraut. He loves it, but it doesn't love him back." Bridget stopped. She was talking about her father's intestinal issues. How lame was that?

MIKE WATCHED AN annoyed expression cross her face. Was that because she didn't want to be there? Had she picked up that he was interested in her and was afraid he'd make a move? He didn't know how to say "I like you but I know you're gay, so don't worry, I won't bother you." He'd left her alone for a month, thinking that should help. Maybe he shouldn't have asked to meet after the game. But sometimes, you just wanted to unwind with someone. It wasn't easy going from being one hundred percent on for a game to coming back down for normal life. And he'd wanted to see her, if he was being honest. He wasn't sure how much longer he had in Toronto. So what if nothing was going to happen between them? He enjoyed spending time with her. Was that so terrible?

The awkward pause was interrupted when someone swaggered over to their table.

Mike had been later getting out than the other players because he'd been wanted for press interviews. Troy Green, one of the Blaze's top four defensemen, had obviously been at the bar long enough to have had a beer or three. He wasn't drunk, but he'd gotten enough of a buzz to be willing to say things he might regret later.

"So, Iceman. Squeaked out another one. That goal in the second—"

Mike had realized what was up with Troy immediately. Troy and Turchenko were buddies, and Mike expected Turchenko was here, too. Turchenko wasn't happy that Mike had taken over the starter role again—and was doing well with it. It made Turchenko look bad. If their positions were reversed, Mike would have been looking at his own mistakes and working on them, but Turchenko preferred the easier task of sulking. It was not a happy dressing room.

So Mike had looked over at Bridget, planning to do his best to ignore Troy and get him to leave without making a scene. But he quickly realized Bridget wasn't in on that plan. She straightened up and glared at Troy. Really, was her hair moving again? The eyes were definitely flashing.

"Yeah, Green. You were out of position on that play by miles. What were you doing? Checking out the kiss cam? Looking for a date? Peters skated in like he was leading the Ice Capades while you were tripping over your skates. You're lucky you weren't benched for that stupid move."

It took Troy a moment to process that the retaliation he'd been trawling for was coming from the girl on the other side of the table. Mike knew he wasn't used to being called out by a woman.

"Oh, yeah? You think you know so much?"

It was a pretty weak comeback. A lot of the

players were excellent chirpers—they could get under another player's skin with verbal jabs to make the player lose his temper and do something stupid. Troy was not a chirper. Bridget apparently had some talent in that direction. He wasn't surprised.

Bridget smiled at Troy. "Yes. But I don't think you want my comments on that last line change."

Troy flushed. Mike knew the coaches had already been on Troy's case for both of those mistakes. Mike bit his tongue and let Bridget finish Troy up.

The defenseman looked derisively over at Mike. "You think Iceman here is so perfect—"

"Nope," she interrupted him. "He was out of position when Bozman had that rebound, but Carlsson was where he was supposed to be and blocked the shot. You've heard of that play, right? Shot blocking? You could try it sometime."

Troy stared at her, baffled. He had had a bad game tonight, but he normally played well and was a fan favorite. Mike could see his shock at running into a redheaded female hockey fanatic who could analyze the play as well as most coaches. And who had no interest in making him feel good about himself.

"You got women fighting your battles now, Iceman?" Troy spat.

Mike simply shrugged. He didn't need to foster any more tension within the team, but a few home truths might help the guy.

Bridget shook her head. "If I need help, I'm sure Mike will step in."

Troy stared, in what he might have thought was a menacing manner, and then turned and left.

Bridget glared after him. "What a weasel."

Mike smiled at her. "Is that your go-to insult?"

She grinned back at him. "As a coach of young, impressionable minds, I have to keep my insults PG. But what kind of moron makes a boneheaded play like that and then tries to blame it on you?"

Mike shrugged. "It happens. If the puck goes in, it's on me."

"If anyone really thinks that, they don't know what they're talking about. Well, if Bozman had scored, okay, but otherwise…"

"I'll be sure to call you to explain to everyone the next time that happens. Are you ready to talk to the press?"

Bridget shook her head. "No, you don't

want me opening up my mouth to reporters. I'm a disaster."

Mike looked at her. "Didn't you do interviews while you were competing?"

Bridget shrugged. "Some. Nothing like what you have to do. I was awful. I think one interview is still on YouTube. It's something I have to work on, but so far the interest in my swimmers isn't that extensive. The club newsletter isn't really what you'd call hard-hitting journalism."

A couple stopped by their table and congratulated Mike on his game. They wanted a picture. Mike saw how Bridget sat back, letting him do his thing with the fans. Bridget had finished her Coke by the time the couple moved on. He was relieved when she accepted his apology for neglecting her, assuring him it wasn't a problem.

"You get this all the time?"

Mike shrugged. "It used to be a lineup of people telling me I sucked."

Bridget shook her head. "Good thing it's you, not me. And I hope I wasn't out of line with Troy Green."

Mike grinned, feeling more relaxed than he had in a long time. "Honestly, I enjoyed it," he said. "I have to play nice to help the team. You told him what I'd like to, but can't."

Bridget looked at him. Mike could almost see the gears moving in her head. He knew she'd say something he wasn't expecting. "Was it different in Quebec?"

He was right. "A little. I was the golden boy, so I wasn't getting the 'you suck' stuff."

"The team got along better, too?"

Mike nodded. "Last year things had started to change. New coach, new ways of doing things—I don't think we were quite as tight as we had been. But nothing like what we've got here in Toronto."

"It's bad?" Bridget asked.

"It's improved. But when people are asking about the playoffs, even if we scrape our way in, I don't know that this team can go anywhere. There are good players, but the team hasn't got that cohesive identity that winning teams have to have."

"Like in Quebec."

"Not just Quebec. Quebec was pretty extraordinary. An expansion team that really gelled from the beginning. And the coach was more than good. But I've been on World Junior teams, Olympic teams, World Cup teams. Canada can provide a lot of talent. It takes more than that to win."

Bridget nodded. "Sometimes it's hard to get a team, rather than a group of individuals. Not with swimming, so much. Even a relay is mostly an individual thing. I might not like my teammates much, but I wouldn't have a bad swim because they didn't want to pass me the puck or forgot the right play. I had one of my best swims with a woman I absolutely despise."

Mike tried to picture the woman Bridget would despise.

"On the other hand, I've played on beer league teams with my brothers—"

Mike interrupted her. "You play on their teams, on the ice?"

"Yeah."

He was surprised. Road hockey was one thing. At a rink, on ice, the play would be much faster. He hadn't realized she played at that level.

"Anyway, those teams were more for fun, so it didn't matter if I was only there once in a while when they were short a defenseman. But sometimes a guy would have issues with a woman playing, and that really scuttled the

team. It would be something like that, right?"
She tilted her head, awaiting his response.

Mike smiled. "I guess I'm the woman on
the team in that scenario?" He pointed at her
empty glass. "Do you want another?"

Bridget shook her head. "Time to go, I
think." Mike wondered if he'd said the wrong
thing. She stood up quickly.

Mike threw some money on the table for
the tip, and they made their way out. People
nodded to him, and some looked like they
wanted to talk, but he maneuvered Bridget
out the door without interruption.

"Where are you parked?" he asked. "Or are
you taking a cab?"

"I'm a couple blocks away," she said, pointing in the general direction. "I'm fine. You
can go."

Mike started walking in the direction she'd
indicated. He turned to look at her. She raised
her brows. "Really, I'll be fine."

"Unfortunately, there's no guarantee of
'fine.' My mother raised me better than that,
and your brothers would never forgive me for
letting you walk alone."

Bridget gave in, agreeing that her brothers
would do the same.

They went half a block in silence. Mike

tried to think of an innocuous way to ask if he'd offended her.

Bridget spoke up, sounding suspiciously like someone trying to make polite conversation. "Patrick and Bradley, you remember his son? Your number one fan. They're really looking forward—" Then she stopped in place. "Crap, crap, crap and CRAP!"

Mike looked around to spot what had instigated this outburst, but he couldn't see anything. He turned to her, puzzled.

"Anything I can do?"

Bridget resumed walking. "No, it's my problem. I forgot to pick up my gift for Bradley's party tomorrow. What a rotten aunt! Unless you're up for some breaking and entering, I'm going to have to disappoint him. Crap!"

"Can't you give it to him later?" He wasn't sure what could be that vital. Knowing the O'Reillys, it would be a big party, and there would be a lot of presents.

"Of course, but Nancy's planned this party with kids from his class, and he's been bragging about meeting you. They've hassled him about that, not really believing him, so I had the photo from Boxing Day of the two of you blown up and put on a shirt. It would have been good to have that for the party. But they're closed tomorrow, so now I can't get it. Stupid of me."

Mike had come to a stop.

Bridget shook her head. "Don't worry, it's no big deal, really. His mom has the picture on her phone, and we'll back him up."

Mike spoke hesitantly. "Would it help if I showed up?"

Bridget blinked at him. "What?"

Mike wasn't especially vain, but he was a professional hockey player, and that impressed a lot of people, especially kids. "Just for a while. I don't want to monopolize the party, but if his friends think he's lying about knowing me, maybe if I showed up it would give him a boost."

BRIDGET SHOOK HER HEAD. "You've got stuff to do. You can't just wander around being a party favor for an eight-year-old."

"I don't have practice." Mike grinned at her. "Since I didn't get called out by the coaches like some people we spoke to tonight, I'm a free agent tomorrow."

Bridget didn't know what to say. Bradley would be over the moon. But at the same time, she was trying to keep her distance from Mike. If he was going to keep confiding in her and doing nice things with her family she was going to fall—

She flinched back from that thought. That could not happen. What was wrong with her?

"Come on, it'll be fun. What time?" Mike was smiling at her, encouraging her to agree.

Bridget told herself to be strong. Nothing good would come of it for herself—but when she thought about Bradley, like she hadn't this afternoon, she caved. This would be the last time she'd see Mike, at least like this. If he wanted company after any of the other games, it would be her dad or her brothers he could talk to. And four months from now, or sooner, he'd be gone. After that she'd see him on TV, playing, giving interviews, but not in person. Then she could get over this…infatuation.

She sighed. "Two p.m. It's at the local rink. I can text you the address."

"Why don't I pick you up? Then you can get bonus points for bringing me, to make up for being such a horrible aunt that you forgot to get his shirt."

Bridget couldn't help but smile. "Okay. I obviously need the help."

"So where do you live?"

"My parents'." Her voice grew defensive.

"Not *with* them. I have the basement apartment."

Mike raised his eyebrows but didn't comment out loud. "Okay, do we want to be at the rink for two, or a little after?"

Bridget thought about the parents who'd probably want to do the fan thing with Mike if they saw him when they were dropping off their kids.

"After is probably better," she said.

"So I'll pick you up just after two. Where is your car? And was your dad actually willing to drive with you?"

Bridget glared at him. "Who do you think taught me to drive?"

MIKE SHOWED UP promptly at two, in the Rover. He'd filed away that bit of information, that she lived in the basement suite of her parents' place. It explained how she'd slipped away from the group on Boxing Day so easily... and she was apparently embarrassed about living in her parents' basement. That might be useful information someday. Why? He didn't know, but he did know he liked filing away these bits of Bridget trivia.

Bridget was waiting on the front step. As soon as she waved at him, she was moving to meet him. She opened the door almost before he'd come to a halt, and threw her skates and a backpack inside.

"In a hurry?" Mike asked.

"It's cold out, in case you didn't notice. I know, it's probably balmy compared to Quebec, tough guy, but I was getting cold."

"Then why didn't you wait inside?"

"I didn't want to keep you waiting."

Mike looked at her out of the corner of his eye. "Or maybe you actually do live at home and just made up this story about the basement. It's not really that embarrassing."

"I did not!" she sputtered, glaring at him. "Are you going to drive this thing, or just cast aspersions on my integrity?"

"Oh, I'm having lots of fun with the aspersion casting. And I don't know where I'm going, remember?"

Bridget shook her head. "Fine, turn right at the corner."

The rink was a five-minute drive. Mike guessed that the O'Reillys had spent a lot of time there. It wasn't fancy, just a typical community rink, and completely familiar to Mike. Bridget led the way into the lobby, carrying her gear. Mike followed with a hockey bag he'd grabbed from the back of the Rover while Bridget checked to see if everyone had arrived.

There was controlled chaos inside. There were about twenty kids, mostly boys, but some girls as well. They had either laced up their skates and had moved out to the ice, or were being assisted in putting on skates by family members.

Patrick's wife, Nancy, first noticed them. "Thank goodness! Bridget, can you get out there and get them started while we get the rest in skates?" Nancy stopped, staring at Mike. She looked shocked.

The place got quieter as some of the kids and the O'Reilly clan turned and recognized Mike. To the others he was just another adult hanging around. Bridget sat down beside Bradley and started putting on her own skates. Bradley looked at her in awe, and Mike heard the boy whisper, "Did you bring Mike to my party?"

Mike dropped down beside Bridget and pulled skates out of his bag. He leaned over Bridget and whispered back, "Yes, she did."

"Wow," said Bradley. He looked up at his idol in disbelief. "Thank you."

Mike was touched by the gratitude in the

kid's face. "You head on out there, and I'll join you once I lace up."

Bradley shuffled off on his skate guards. The rest of the family were looking at each other, a range of expressions on their faces. He was pretty sure his arrival was a surprise, and hoped it wasn't a problem. He didn't want to steal Bradley's thunder.

"You brought skates?" Bridget hissed out the side of her mouth.

"You said it was a rink party. I threw them in the Rover just in case, and when I saw you had yours…"

Bridget shook her head, then responded to Nancy's entreaty by shrugging off her parka and heading to the ice.

WORD WAS SPREADING among the kids. One skated up to her. "Is that really Mike Reimer?"

Bridget nodded. Every group had one of "those" kids, and she was pretty sure this was the one in this group, just like Tony had been in her swimming class.

"How much do you have to pay to get him for a party?" asked the kid. Bridget didn't like his attitude.

She shrugged. "I don't know. He came

today because he's a friend of Bradley's. You can ask Mike if he hires out for parties, but I doubt it."

She skated away, and pulled out a whistle to get the kids' attention.

Patrick wanted to have a hockey game with the kids, but before they made up teams, they needed to know how well everyone could skate. So Bridget was going to lead them through some games first. The last kids made their way out onto the ice and over to Bridget, and the adults who weren't going to prepare the party food followed.

"Okay guys, it's time for O'Reilly tag. Who's played before?"

Bradley was the only one who raised his hand.

"Here are the rules. First, you cannot run into anyone. If you do, or knock someone over, it's a penalty, in the box." Bridget pointed to the penalty box. The kids looked taken aback. Penalties for them?

"Second, you cannot touch the blue or red lines. You can stay in one section, or jump over the lines, but you cannot skate across them, or again, you go into the penalty box." She pointed again.

"You are safe from being tagged while

squatting, and still moving on the ice, or if you're skating on just one skate, with the other being above ankle height."

Bridget raised her skate to demonstrate.

"We know that your ankle is above your foot, so there should be space between your blade and the ice. Like this. While moving. If you are staying still, you are fair game. To even things up, adults have to skate backward in the neutral zone. Everyone got it?"

Bridget did a quick summary. "No knocking into anyone. No skating on the lines. If you can't skate fast, you can squat on your skates—" Bridget had her brothers demonstrate, and some of the kids joined in "—or stand on one foot with the other lifted up." A couple of kids wobbled as they tried it while standing still. "And as long as you're moving, you're safe. If you're skating normally, or aren't moving, you can be tagged.

"Patrick and I will ref. Mike can start as It."

Mike looked at Bridget while the kids all scrambled away. "Are you serious about this?"

"Definitely. My dad made this up when we were kids. It was a way to do skating drills while having fun. You can bet that we can jump, squat and skate on one blade really well."

"So, can I tag you now?"

Bridget shook her head. "You weren't listening. I'm reffing for now. And if I see you cross a line..."

But Mike was off, catching up to the big Tony-type boy easily. Bridget kept a careful eye on the skaters on one end of the ice, leaving the other to one of her brothers. Twice she had to penalize the kids, and once, one of her brothers, but everyone was catching on and having fun. Brian skated up to her, and said, "I'm taking a break. I'll ref, you're It."

Bridget dashed off after her nephew, gave him a good scare, and kept an eye out for Mike. The kids had tagged him a couple of times, and she suspected that he'd given them a break because none of the adults had touched him. He could drop into a squat with ease, and even jump over a line while squatting. Bridget hadn't realized that goalies had an advantage in this game. Cormack had never been especially good at it.

Her initial instinct was to be the first adult to tag him, but she thought better of it. Instead, she did her best to ignore him. That was easier than it could have been because he was swamped by the kids. But that focus was her undoing. While skating backward through the neutral zone, she ran into someone and went down. She called for a penalty, and then realized it was Mike.

"You cheated!" he said.

She shook her head and smiled. Brian blew the whistle and waved Mike into the box.

Bridget took the opportunity to slip off the ice and get back into regular shoes. She went to the party room, where Nancy and the sisters-in-law were organizing the food. Jee would normally skate, but she was taking precautions with her pregnancy.

When Bridget entered, she was grilled.

"How did you get Mike to come? Why didn't you tell us?" said Nancy.

So Bridget explained. She didn't tell them that she'd forgotten the shirt because she'd been so worried about meeting Mike after the game. That was too pathetic to share.

"I don't know, Bridget. Maybe he just wanted to spend some time with you," Nancy teased.

Bridget had had enough. She knew her sisters-in-law were just trying to be nice, but this wasn't helping her. She was going to make a fool of herself, and she needed them on her side.

"Can everyone just stop with the match-making? Seriously?

"Listen, the guy has my phone number. He knows where I live, and he knows where I work. But he hasn't tried to get in touch, not even once, since we stopped doing those workouts last fall—which Mom pushed him into, you may recall. Last night was supposed to be a meet with Dad and me, not a date. Today, he's helping out a kid. And I think I guilted him into it.

"So either he's still hung up on his wife and is never going to date again—"

"That's not it," said Jill. All eyes turned her way. "What?" she said. "I looked him up online. There were pictures of him in Quebec. He dated some pretty gorgeous women."

Bridget felt a pang. Somehow, it would have been easier to think he wasn't interested in her because he was still in love with a ghost.

"Then he obviously isn't interested in me. So rather than trying to force us together, or make me think there's something there when there's not, let's just be honest and accept the truth. Now, I'm going to walk home." She ignored the protests. "It's not that far, and then I'm going to the club to swim laps. Tell

Bradley Happy Birthday for me, and that I'll get him his present tomorrow. Tell the boys whatever to keep them from worrying, and I'll see you later."

The shirt wouldn't be needed now, really. The school would be buzzing with the story of Mike Reimer, Blaze goalie, being at Bradley's party. Bradley would be a rock star.

She was losing this battle. It would be really helpful if he could do something horrible, or even a bit mean because he just kept wrapping little tendrils around her heart.

CHAPTER SEVEN

MIKE CHECKED HIS PHONE. Good. Tonight Brian and Jee were coming to the game, and were happy to meet up afterward. Mike badly wanted to talk to Jee. He knew she was Bridget's best friend, and she should be the person he could best approach.

He was doing great, professionally. The Blaze were now, at the end of January, within reach of a playoff spot. There was still a gap, but they were no longer considered a long shot. And the reason for the turnaround was Mike. He was back: back as the Iceman, not the failure they'd had last year. That helped the whole team. They could take more risks when they knew there was a goalie behind them who wouldn't let the puck in. They could play less defensively, and as a result, the offense was picking up. They didn't win every game, but they were piling up points.

So things were better with the team's performance, but he hadn't seen Bridget since she left the ice at Bradley's birthday party at the end of December. He'd noticed her leave. When she didn't come back, he'd gone to see if everything was okay. The sisters had told him she had a headache and had gone home, but the way they'd looked at him…he knew something was up. He thought he'd been reasonably discreet, but perhaps Bridget had noticed that he had tracked where she was on the ice too closely. Had that offended her? Maybe agreeing to come to the party had been over the top. But he was developing a soft spot for Bradley. A week ago, Bradley had come to a game with his dad. Mike brought him a puck from the game, and the kid hadn't been able to speak. Sure, he was just a kid, but it was good to bring that kind of joy to someone.

Really, he hadn't offered to come to the party just to spend some time with Bridget, though that had been part of it. He'd like it if they could at least be friends. He'd spent a good while keeping some distance, since there was no point in wanting a woman who wasn't interested in him. But he found her easy to talk to, and that was rare for him. She understood sports and the role they played in his life. She was fun, and completely unpredictable. He loved seeing her temper flash up, even when it was at him. She wasn't conventionally attractive, true, and not especially tactful, but he appreciated her honesty, and he had discovered an attraction to red hair and freckles that he'd never recognized before.

Okay, "friends" might be a stretch. But he wanted her to know he understood that she wasn't interested in him and that he wouldn't push her or make her uncomfortable. He was sure she'd left the party because of him. He liked spending time with her family, but he didn't want her to feel she had to avoid him when he did so. That wouldn't be right. He met some of them after games and liked having someone to talk to after the comedown from playing. But Bridget had never come to another game. Surely they could find some compromise, a middle ground.

A couple of weeks of thinking, and the best idea he'd come up with was to let Jee know he knew about Bridget's orientation (he was sure Bridget would have confided in her, even if she hadn't said anything to her family) and hope that Jee could reassure Bridget that it was safe to be around him.

He entered the bar, and searched through the crowd to find Brian and Jee. It was harder now to make his way through the crowd as he was greeted by more people after each game. That was directly tied to his success on the ice, he knew. With the ease of practice, he was able to interact and keep going until he found the table the two of them had snagged.

They didn't have any beverages in front of them, so he asked what they'd like to drink.

Brian asked for a beer.

"Club soda," Jee said, and blushed.

Mike placed their orders and asked for his favorite beer from a passing waiter, and turned to his guests.

"She's not drinking alcohol," Brian explained. "Pregnant." Brian was smiling, but he also looked a little worried.

Jee rested her hand on her still flat abdomen protectively. *Difficult pregnancy?* Mike wondered. He felt a pang. He remembered Amber and the baby that had died with her, but the stab of guilt wasn't there. He couldn't change the past, and he was finally starting to let it go.

Later, Brian went to the men's room, and that gave Mike the opening he was looking for. He was still slightly on edge; normally by now he'd have come down from the playing high, but tonight, he had something else keeping him tense. Leaning forward, to keep the conversation private amid the noise around them, he said, "Can I ask you something, Jee?"

"Sure," she said, her tone puzzled.

"Is Bridget out?"

Jee's brow furrowed. "Is she out? Tonight? I don't think so. She's usually in bed by now because of practice. They start pretty early, you know."

Mike sighed. "No, not that out. Out-out. I know her family is Catholic, so I wondered—"

Jee's mouth dropped open. "You mean, *out*?"

Mike wanted to kick himself. Maybe Bridget hadn't told Jee? Jee probably shared everything with her husband, Brian.

"You think Bridget is gay?" Jee asked incredulously.

Mike stared at her. "Isn't she?"

Jee shook her head, and spoke angrily. "Just because a woman is an athlete doesn't mean—"

Mike raised a hand. "No, I promise, that's not it. I've worked with women who play hockey professionally. I know they're not all gay. I never would assume anything like that. But I was told—"

Jee narrowed her eyes. "Someone told you Bridget is gay? It wasn't Cormack, was it?"

Surprised, Mike said, "No, no one from the family. That's why I thought she wasn't out officially yet."

Jee considered. "If it wasn't the family, who…" Her eyes widened. "Wally the Weasel?"

Mike felt his cheeks warming. Really, accepting Wally's word on this had been pretty stupid.

"Why would he make that up?" Mike asked.

"Because Bridget wouldn't go out with him," Jee said firmly. "He probably decided she must be gay if she rejected him. He seemed to think she wasn't in a position to turn down offers. Bridget thought that might have been why he fought her about that class so strongly."

Mike pictured grabbing Wally around his weaselly neck.

"What a—a weasel!" Jee sputtered.

"So, she's not gay," Mike repeated.

"No! I should know. We've been friends for years and I even know about her and that stupid swimmer, Connor Treadwell. She's never told the boys about him. She's never been interested in women. Not in that way. She's dated guys, and kissed…" Jee was still a little heated. She looked at Mike speculatively. "Why were you asking?"

And here was the drawback. Mike might not have thought this all the way through. He was losing some objectivity around Bridget. He shrugged. "I was…wondering. I wanted her to know I knew."

"Why?" persisted Jee.

"She vanished at Bradley's party, and well, she disappears when I'm around. I thought I was making her uncomfortable, and if she knew I knew…but I guess I don't know." Jee was looking at him with amusement. "So, she's not gay, and she's not seeing anyone right now, is she? Not that Connor guy?"

Jee smiled. "No. I think she finally got over Connor. She met someone else and she was interested in him, but he didn't seem interested in her."

Mike looked at her. She was beaming at him. Was she sending him a message?

"Really? Maybe they got their wires crossed."

"She's going to kill Wally," Jee said.

"Would you mind not saying anything to her about this? It would be a shame if she was incarcerated right now, even for a justifiable homicide."

BRIDGET WAS SURPRISED the next morning, after she'd wrapped up practice and finished her own workout, to find Mike waiting for her in the lobby. The space was quiet at that time of day. She had to assume he'd come here after his own practice. But why? She hadn't seen him since Bradley's party. She ignored the little flutter in her chest. He patted the bench seat beside him.

"Did you forget something?" she asked.

"Not really. I wanted your help."

Bridget watched him with suspicion. He looked very pleased about something.

She sat down, cautiously. "Okay, what is it?"

He shook his head. "It's nothing scary. I'm not even going to ask you to do any breaking and entering. At least, I don't think so. I want to skate."

Bridget raised her eyebrows. "You're telling me you want to spend more time on the ice? I guess I can understand that. Hockey players get so little time to skate. Do you not practice anymore? Kicked off the team, perhaps?"

"Outside," he continued in unruffled good humor. "I want to skate outside. Where's an outdoor rink that'll be available, and not too congested?"

Bridget relaxed, thinking through the options. "Hmmm. Harbourfront is nice, but there'll be a lot of people there. Same for Nathan Phillips Square." She reviewed the other outdoor rinks she knew of. "Wait, I have a place that might do. It's in the Beaches neighborhood, not far from where I live. There's an outdoor hockey rink near the lake. I don't think it would be very busy, and when you're done you could check out the lake. The Beaches is a nice area."

"Sounds good. So how do you get there? And do you know anyone who'd like to go skating now?"

Bridget looked at him, feeling a smile tugging at one corner of her mouth. "It's not too hard to get there. Shall I ask around the pool here for a skater?"

"I was hoping you might…" Mike looked at her, eyes crinkling.

Bridget considered. She'd been trying to stop thinking about him, had even put an elastic on her wrist, snapping it when she found herself dreaming about him. One of her swimmers had asked if she was trying to quit smoking.

The smart thing to do would be to claim to be busy. But she loved to skate, and well, the elastic wasn't working anyway. She was still picturing those gray eyes way too often.

"Let's see. Laundry and groceries, or skating. Okay, you're on. I'll stop at home to get my skates."

"Why don't I follow you there? Then we can take one car."

She was still on guard. What was he up to? "Can I drive?"

"No. I like breathing."

She glared at him. "I'm not a bad driver."

"I don't like your taste in music anyway. I'll pick you up."

Once in the car, Mike followed her closely, since her shortcuts weren't easy to track. She parked, and when he started to get out she called to him she'd be just a minute before racing to her apartment. She dropped her gym bag by the door. She pulled out some long johns and quickly changed into some warm gear. She grabbed her outdoor wear, and her skates, and was out in less than five minutes.

Bridget threw her bag in the back and climbed into the passenger seat. Mike reversed in the driveway and pulled out. He glanced at Bridget, and after confirming which way to turn, asked, "So, you really do live in the basement apartment?"

"Yes. Why?" Bridget frowned at him.

"I've never seen it. You're always perched on the front steps. You could just be embarrassed about living at home, and trying to cover for that. I mean, that's not the worst thing ever. I wouldn't judge. But I'm wondering if the place even exists, or if you've got bodies hidden in there or something."

Bridget had never seen Mike this lighthearted. He was certainly in a good mood.

"A few goalies buried, nothing much." She shrugged. "Actually, I'm just a lousy housekeeper. My place always looks like a disaster, and the people who have seen it don't usually ask to come back."

"I don't know…I'm having fun imagining. I bet it's full of pink ruffles and lace."

Bridget rolled her eyes. "Yeah, right."

"With dolls. Or stuffed animals. Yes, stuffed

animals. And posters of boy bands on the walls."

Bridget frowned at him. "Brian rented it until he and Jee got married, and she refused to start married life with her in-laws upstairs. So I moved in when I started coaching. There was no pink, and no lace. You've met Brian. Do you think that's likely?"

"So no boy bands?"

"Just a poster of Turchenko," she responded.

Mike laughed. "I'll have to tell him he's got a fan. So, where am I going next?"

It WAS A cool winter afternoon and there were few people in the park. They parked on a side street and took the hike down to the rink. The ice looked like any outdoor hockey rink, except that it was spitting distance from the beach boardwalk and the expanse of Lake Ontario, which looked dark and forbidding today. It was empty, except for a mom and tot who didn't stay long. Then Mike and Bridget had the ice to themselves.

Bridget hadn't been on the ice since Bradley's party, and she took a few moments to warm up. She sped up, hockey-stopped in the corner and then came down the ice backward.

"Definitely a defenseman," said Mike, gliding past her. "No one loves to skate backward more."

Bridget laughed. "My mom tried so hard to push me into figure skating instead of hockey, so I took classes for a couple of years. But I wanted only to play hockey, and she finally gave up. By then I could skate backward pretty well, so defense it was. It was the only opening left on the all-sibling team anyway. I will say, you're not too bad a skater for a goalie."

Mike skated up to her. "Thanks so much. Please, don't strain yourself trying to say something nice."

"Fair is fair," she said. "You did pretty well at the party. I hadn't realized goalies had an advantage jumping on skates."

"I may be a goalie, but I can skate," Mike retorted.

She looked at him skeptically. "Backward?"

"I bet I can skate backward as well as you can."

Bridget's eyes lit up. "You bet? Really? What are the stakes?"

"Cute. I'm not falling for that."

"Bwaack, bwaack, bwaaack..."

Mike stopped. "You want to bet about whether I can skate backward better than you?" he asked.

"Don't talk the talk unless you can walk the walk, or, you know, skate the skate."

Mike grinned down at her. "You O'Reillys are incorrigible. How are we going to test this?"

"Shall we see who's fastest backward?"

Mike raised his eyebrows. "You're on. What are you *not* going to win?"

"Driving the car?" she asked, eyes glowing.

"I believe we already have a bet going on that, so no."

Bridget came perilously close to pouting. "Hmm…how about a jersey? Yeah, I think I'd like a jersey. I have only hand-me-downs, so I'm due. And since Giguère hasn't played in ten years, I think I can let him go now."

Mike shrugged. "Like I said, doesn't matter, since you're going to lose."

"Okay then, what do you want?"

Mike stopped. "I think I'd like to see this mystery apartment of yours. I'm still not convinced there aren't some boy band posters in there."

Bridget shrugged. "Fine. You can maybe peek in the doorway when you bring the jersey."

"So how are we going to do this?" Mike asked.

Bridget looked around, assessing. "We'll start at the entrance. We can change between the inside and outside tracks at the halfway mark. First one back to the entrance—which will be me, goaltender—wins."

"You can stay on the inside the whole way," said Mike. "So you have a chance."

Bridget's eyes sparked. "No, I'll have already changed lanes before you get there."

They skated to the entrance gate, and took their positions, Mike on the outside by the boards. They counted down together and tore off.

Skating backward wasn't easy. Bridget had done it in skating lessons, and continued it when playing with her brothers. However, goalies didn't have to skate very far, and they didn't need to hone that skill. There wasn't much call for a goalie to skate backward at speed, especially around corners.

So Bridget was surprised when Mike pulled ahead of her. The bet had been lighthearted, but Bridget wasn't going to give any quarter. She concentrated, called on her reserves and still lost.

Mike had immediately assumed a relaxed and waiting pose, leaning against the boards as if she'd been minutes behind him instead of seconds. Only the fast rising and falling of his chest and the clouds of his breath in the cold air gave him away.

Bridget skated up to him. "How did you do that? And don't tell me your skating technique. Goalies don't skate backward. They don't skate much at all!"

Mike smiled. "Same story as you. My mom didn't want me to play hockey. Instead of figure skating, I got power skating lessons."

"Apparently you took more than a couple?"

Mike started skating again, forward, and Bridget joined in.

"My mom is pretty determined. But we lived in the basement of a house where a family with four boys lived. They were all hockey mad. Their mom took care of me while my mom worked, so we played hockey. I begged for hockey lessons, but she explained that hockey was expensive and dangerous. She was okay with me learning to skate, but she didn't want me playing hockey."

He grabbed Bridget's gloved hand, swinging her around so they were now skating in the other direction.

"When I came to her with fifty dollars I'd saved up from doing yardwork for neighbors to pay for hockey, she finally caved."

Bridget made as if to pull her hand away, but Mike ignored that, and she stopped tugging.

"The Sawatzky kids always put me in goal because I was the smallest. I wanted to be a forward. But my mom thought goalie would be safer—more protective gear, no checking—so the compromise we came up with was that I could play, if I played in goal. I had to keep up the yard work to cover the extra equipment costs. I thought that was better than nothing. And, turned out I had a talent for it. If she'd let me play any other position, I might have been only average, and never made it as a pro. There's irony. She was never a big hockey fan, but my career is thanks to her."

"So what did you learn in those power skating classes?" Bridget asked. "Can you show me?"

Mike turned to grin at her. "You've lost that bet, fair and square you know. No rematches."

Bridget nodded. "Yes, but there's always the possibility of future ones with my brothers."

Mike shook his head, but agreed.

When they finally unlaced their skates an hour later they had shortened breath and cold noses. Why couldn't she have this much fun with someone like Cormack's friend Bernie, who actually liked her?

"This was a great idea, Mike. Thanks for asking me." Bridget tried to warm her toes with her hands before putting them back in her cold boots.

"Thanks for coming. I had an urge to skate outside. It's been a while. Totally different feeling."

Having put on his boots and gathered up both their skates, Mike asked, "Hungry?"

"Starving," Bridget admitted.

"I'll buy, since I won the bet. Where should we go?"

"Queen Street is just up there. There are lots of places. Let's go see what looks good."

As THEY WALKED back to Mike's Rover to drop off their skates, he asked what restaurant she'd chosen.

She gave him a once-over. "You'd like this place I have in mind. They have good food and lots of snooty beers."

"You think I'm a beer snob?"

"I'd bet on that."

He smiled at her. "You'd win that one."

"I thought that might explain the almost untouched Coors Light my family served you. My dad thinks if he drinks light beer he doesn't have to count them."

After dropping off their skates, Bridget led them to the restaurant she'd chosen. It wasn't too busy this time in the afternoon on a week day, but the server widened her eyes when she recognized Mike. She was discreet, though. Looking for a good tip, Bridget figured. Smart woman.

She asked if it was a party of two and if they wanted a booth or table. Mike agreed to two and asked for a booth. The booths ran along one side of the restaurant, and the waitress led them there.

Bridget found the booth a little more intimate than she'd have liked. She'd indulged herself in this time with Mike, but she was afraid she'd say or do something that would let him know how much she liked him. Then things would get awkward, and she'd probably never hear from him again. Part of her knew that would be a good idea, but that part wasn't having much success today.

Mike picked a nice snooty beer, and Bridget ordered a Guinness.

A customer walked by the booth and Bridget noticed Mike turn his face away, just slightly. Was Mike trying to avoid fans? He normally was a textbook study in public relations, so she wondered what was different. Did he sometimes get tired of putting out that energy to be nice to strangers? Was it hard to keep up the public persona? Bridget thought she'd gotten to know the real Mike underneath, but maybe he'd fooled her as much as anyone else. And having thought it, the words came out.

"Is it hard to have people recognize you everywhere you go?"

Mike caught the more serious tone in her voice. "It doesn't happen everywhere. Believe it or not, there are a lot of places where people don't care about hockey. But, yes, it can be. When I arrived in Quebec City, it was their first playoffs since the team was back in the city, and with the story of Amber's death and then the success we had, I got my picture taken a lot, and so people recognized me. It never really stopped. And then here, in Toronto…"

"I can imagine. No anonymity here for hockey players. You always seem to like the fan thing, though."

"Why do I get paid so much?" he countered.

Bridget blinked at him. It was obvious. "Because you're good."

Mike smiled. He had a lovely smile, Bridget noted, then concentrated on what he was saying.

"Okay, wasn't really fishing for a compliment there. Let me put it this way, where does all that money come from?"

Bridget thought for a moment, and then nodded. "From fans," she said, feeling like a kid in school trying to impress the teacher.

"Right. The people who buy tickets and T-shirts and jerseys. The ones who follow the games and celebrate when we win and mourn when we lose. I had an excellent coach in college. He told us never to forget that—keeping those fans happy is as important to our sport's survival as anything we do on the ice. I guess it took with me."

"But sometimes you want a bit of privacy?"

Mike nodded. "Yeah. Guys from some of the teams in less traditional hockey markets talk about the anonymity they have there, and it sounds good. But I can't really complain. I've been fortunate that most of the time fans have been positive with me."

It was almost uncanny that a couple popped up at the end of their table at that moment.

These were actually Quebec City fans, who apparently didn't realize Mike was no longer popular there. They told Mike they had been season ticket holders in Quebec, and had never forgotten the Cup wins when Mike was with the team. Bridget basked in the reflected glory.

After a few more minutes of gushing, they apologized. "We're so sorry," said the gray-haired woman. "We shouldn't be interrupting your date."

Bridget hit earth with a resounding thump. "Oh, it's not a date," she responded, as much to remind herself as them. And that was all it took. The old man went through all the highlights of Mike's time in Quebec in chronological order. Bridget hadn't known how many shutouts he had his first year there. She'd have been a liar if she'd tried to plead ignorance on almost any stat connected to Mike after that conversation, however. Bridget hoped this evidence that not all the fans in Quebec had forgotten him would help him. She knew there was still some unresolved anger there.

The woman finally hustled her husband away after he'd taken a picture, got his hat autographed and been dissuaded from picking up their tab. The silence they left in their wake was a contrast from the nonstop talking. Mike didn't seem keen to break it, so Bridget bit her tongue and followed his lead. When the bill came and she offered to go Dutch, he snapped out a "no" and she sat back, not sure just what had set him off. His mood had taken a one-eighty.

When they were back in the Rover, she wasn't going to ignore it any longer.

"Did I do something?"

"Not a thing," he replied tersely.

Right. He'd shut down for no reason. She tried to work it out. "Should I have pretended it was a date to get that guy to leave us alone? I was just being honest, but I'll make something up another time if that's what you want." If there was another time. It wasn't really looking promising.

"Don't strain yourself," Mike bit off.

Bridget bristled. "What is your problem? It's not my fault they thought we were together. I thought you'd like that set straight. The hostess was interested in you. Maybe you wanted to get her number, and I was just making it clear you were available."

"Don't do me any favors."

"I won't. Just let me know the game plan beforehand, and I'm good with it. Call it a date, if you want. It's not going to hurt my rep."

"Well, if you're sure it won't cramp your style. I mean, I'm not a swimmer."

Bridget had no idea where that came from. "This is nuts. It's like you thought we really were on a date."

There was a silence in the car.

Bridget's face flushed, and her mouth dropped open. She closed it, swallowed and said in a small voice, "*Was* it a date?"

"I don't think it can qualify as a date unless both people think it is," Mike muttered.

"I don't get it. Why would you want to go out with me?" Bridget was honestly puzzled.

Mike looked at her. "Why do you think?"

"But—you ghost me for weeks, and then suddenly, you're back and we're going on a date? What am I missing?"

Mike leaned back against the seat and sighed. "You're right. I apologize. I was giving mixed signals. I thought I had some good reasons to keep my distance."

Bridget's felt her temper flare. "I'm sure they were very good."

Mike shook his head. "No, they really weren't. One was especially bad. But—I told you about Amber."

Bridget nodded.

"Hockey is my first priority, and relationships don't work well when I'm so focused on my sport. Since her death, I've dated only very casually. That's all I've been willing to commit to. And I didn't think you would do casual. You seem to go all in on everything you do." He smiled at her.

Bridget was still trying to work her mind around the idea that Mike wanted to go out with her. She really hadn't got that vibe. And now he was saying that he did only casual? Where was he going with this?

"I think you have the same focus and drive that I do, and you understand what I'm going through. So maybe being together could work. But, also, I want to spend time with you, so I could just be fooling myself."

"Mike, could you just spell it out for me, really clearly?"

"Bridget O'Reilly, would you go out with me, on a real, mutually agreed-upon date?"

Bridget felt a little glow inside. Mike Reimer was asking her on a date.

Bridget reached over and gave his hand a poke. He was solid, not a figment of her imagination. "Mike, I would love to go out on a real date with you."

Mike smiled. Was that relief she saw in his eyes?

She felt her mood take a serious turn. "Are you sure, Mike?"

"About you? Absolutely. Why don't I take you home now, and then we'll work out when we can set up this real date. Start fresh."

Bridget held in a grin. "Okay."

"And about our bet…" he started.

"Yes. Right. I forgot. So, if you want to come in now…" She trailed off. She tried desperately to remember whether anything deathly embarrassing was lying around. Bras? Tampons? Moldy bread?

"I won't insist on my winnings today, but when I pick you up for this real date, then I'll see this 'basement apartment.'"

CHAPTER EIGHT

BRIDGET WAS STILL floating the next morning. She led her team through practice with a smile.

Annabelle said, as she was heading out of the pool area, "We're doing good, eh?"

Bridget nodded. "You guys are doing excellently."

"I knew we must be when you were smiling all the time," Annabelle declared.

Bridget gave her a quick hug. "You'd make any coach smile. Now go get ready for school."

She found a text on her phone after practice.

Ready to set a date?

She was thrilled and terrified. Which was silly. She'd spent time with Mike before. But it was different now. Before she'd been a bystander. Now she was in the game, and it was win or lose. And she knew that for her the stakes were high.

Got my calendar open.

Her phone rang. Mike.

"Hey," she said, breathlessly.

"Practice over?" he asked.

"Yes."

"Team's doing well?"

"Excellent. You?"

"The same as always. So, when do you have a free evening?" Mike asked, returning to the point.

"Hmm." Bridget checked her calendar. "City Championships this weekend. We'll be tied up till who knows when on Sunday."

"My next week looks bad. Games, a couple of club events."

"Next weekend?"

"Road trip. Hey, how's Wednesday? Two weeks from now?"

Bridget scrolled down. "It's a school PA day. I can do an earlier practice, and be free in the evening."

"Then it's a date, a real date. I'll pick you up at seven."

"Great!" Bridget cringed. Did she sound

too eager? And was she not going to see him for two weeks?

"Okay. I gotta run. Keep me posted on the meet."

Then he clicked off.

Bridget stared at the phone, feeling a goofy look on her face. Just as well she was alone in her office. She had a date with Mike, in two weeks.

Two weeks. He was picking her up. He'd be collecting on that bet to see her place. Could she make it look presentable in that time? And should she dress up? Wear jeans? She sent a text to Jee.

BRIDGET WALKED INTO her place. "Hey, Jee—" Bridget started to say. "Do you know why—"

She stopped, question answered. She had parked on the street, finding it more difficult than she'd expected, since all the family cars seemed to be parked there. Jee had promised to pick up food and meet her in her apartment. She'd wondered what was up with everyone else. Now she knew. All the sisters were sitting at her table. Pizza was spread out, and they'd obviously been talking.

Bridget took a look at the circle of faces. "What's up?" she asked, looking wary.

"Sit down. We're not going to bite you."

Bridget did so, reluctantly. "Why is everyone here?"

"It's an intervention, Bridget," Jill answered.

Bridget choked. "For who, me? I didn't bring the pizza. I normally eat better than you guys."

Jee sighed. "Bridget, it's not about pizza. You asked me to help you pick out something to wear for your date, right?"

Bridget nodded. She took a bite of pepperoni. She was hungry.

"That's what for. You don't have anything to wear. You've got to buy some clothes."

Bridget shook her head. "What are you talking about? I have clothes."

Karen snorted. "Technically, yes, you aren't naked. Were you going to wear yoga pants or get all dressed up in jeans?" she asked.

Bridget flushed. "Okay, I can wear my dress."

Nancy rolled her eyes. "Bridget, how long have you had that dress?"

"Not that long. I don't know. I don't wear it that often."

"You got it for Great-Aunt Maeve's funeral! You were still in competition then," Jill said.

"It's a classic!" Bridget defended.

"Chanel is classic. That dress is not," said Nancy.

Karen added, "Bridget. It's ancient and makes you look like a shapeless blob. Plus, since it's black, it washes you out. So you look like a washed-out shapeless blob."

"Well, thanks, guys. Way to help."

"Bridget, do you think Mike is going to be wearing sweats, or do you think he'll be dressed up? Is he taking you out to a pub? A sports bar?" Karen asked.

Bridget hadn't thought that much about it.

"Don't you want to look good for your date?" asked Jee.

That did it. Bridget did want to look good. She just wasn't sure what they could do with her. It was easier not to try. She exhaled. "Okay, yes, I want to look good. What do I need to do?"

"The first step is admitting you have a problem. Now, let's get the details."

"It's a week from Wednesday."

"That far away?"

Bridget shrugged. "I've got City Championships this weekend. Depending on how the kids do, that could go well into Sunday. My A-team are really looking good, and I think they might end up going as far as Nationals. That's me. Mike's got games and some kind of hockey things on next week."

"Next weekend?"

"He's on the road. Florida, I think."

Jee sighed. "When you were trying to avoid him, it seemed like a good thing that your schedules were so busy. But it's not so good for dating."

Karen suddenly broke in. "Did you suggest Wednesday, or did he?"

"Does it matter?" Bridget asked.

"Just tell me."

"Okay." She reviewed the conversation in her head. "Mike. Once we were past the second weekend he said Wednesday."

Karen looked around. "Do you know what date a week from Wednesday is?"

Everyone reached for their phones.

They looked up. "The 14th. Mike is taking her out on Valentine's Day."

Bridget choked again.

Karen patted Bridget on the back as she walked by. "Hey, this'll be fun. I've wanted to get you to do something with your hair for years."

The sisters-in-law worked out a plan. Karen was the ringleader, pulling apart the minimal conversation she and Mike had had. Dinner. Place unknown, but it was Valentine's Day. She decided a dress was the best bet and made Bridget go shopping with her on the Saturday before the date.

It took two department stores and five boutiques before she found the right thing. A deep bronze dress that brought out Bridget's red hair and green eyes, flattering her complexion. Bridget complained that it emphasized her freckles, but she had to admit the fit made the most of her figure. She turned and twisted in front of the mirror.

"Hey, this does look nice. Nice, and yet a little bit sexy, too."

Bridget was relieved, since she thought they were done. But there was a lot more to come. Undergarments (Karen steered her away from her usual sporty options) and shoes. Jill had a coat to lend her, and Karen made Bridget promise to practice walking in the heels they bought.

Bridget had been dragging as the day wore on, but she gave her sister-in-law a big hug when she dropped her off. She went in and tried on everything together, trying to get the overall affect in her small bathroom mirror.

It just might work. If she could manage not to fall off the shoes.

By Tuesday, the day before the date, she was nervous again. Bridget had had to reveal to the sisters the details of the bet she'd lost to explain why she suddenly had an urge to clean. They promised to help out. When Nancy arrived, Bridget had already started a frenzied cleaning. Nancy gave her a bemused look. The oven was open and partly wiped out, and Bridget had the ceiling light down, washing it in the sink. There was a pile of clothes on the couch, and the dishes weren't done. The place looked like a whirlwind had gone through it—which was the status quo for Bridget.

"What are you doing?" Nancy asked.

"Cleaning."

"The light fixtures and the oven?"

Bridget glanced around at the chaos. "Um, they were dirty?"

"Okay, I don't know about your bet, but is Mike really planning to look inside the oven and do the white glove test on the lights?"

"I don't know. I just thought I'd start with the tough stuff."

"You're hopeless, girl. Why don't you finish

that up while I work on the rest of this place? What is this pile of clothes on the couch?"

"Laundry. It's clean, I just haven't put it away."

"I'm just going to guess where it goes and you can straighten it out later. Are you ready for tomorrow?"

"Never."

"What time are you getting your hair done?"

"Two. What do you think the hairdresser will do to it?"

Nancy gave her a look. "Afraid it'll be too drastic?"

Bridget sagged. "Guess not. It's already short, so it's not like he can do much."

Nancy came over to Bridget. She gave her a quick hug. "Bridget, I've never seen you this wound up. You must really like this guy."

Bridget nodded. "I do." *Too much*, she thought, but didn't say.

"Remember, he's lucky you're going out with him."

Bridget wasn't so sure, but she appreciated the sentiment.

It was Wednesday, February 14th, time for the date. By seven, she was ready. Karen had done her makeup, and done a great job. Her hair had highlights, and had been cut to look like it just fell into place naturally, although Bridget knew from experience that it never did fall into place anything like this. She kept giving it a shake to see if it would still look good. It did, so she decided it was worth what the hairdresser had charged her.

Bridget admitted to herself that she didn't usually try too hard to look good because she was afraid she'd fail. But maybe, maybe, she'd give it a try more often.

There was a knock on the door. Deep breath, adrenaline rushing, but no outlet. The beginning of a race. Showtime.

She opened the door, and Mike was there.

She forgot to breathe for a moment. He was wearing a dark suit under an overcoat that fit him beautifully, accentuating his broad shoulders and tall build. He looked so good.

"Hi," she said, pushing the air out of her lungs.

"Hello." He smiled at her, and she felt better. This was Mike. The Mike she knew. "For you," he said, passing over a bouquet. It was full of golden-yellow roses—more than a dozen, maybe more than two.

She was shocked. "Thanks. They're beautiful. You didn't have to—"

Mike smiled again. "I wanted to."

"Thank you," she repeated. "I'd better do something with these…" She turned and looked for something to put them in. She found an empty jar under the sink and decided it would have to do. She noticed he was still standing in the doorway.

"Oh, come on in."

Bridget turned to the tiny kitchen and set the flowers down beside the sink. She started filling the jar with water. "You won the bet. Enjoy!"

She carefully arranged the flowers inside. It was a tight fit. They were beautiful, and she took a moment to smell them before turning around to place them on the table. Mike had stepped in far enough to drop a bag— chocolates?—on the counter.

"Beautiful," he said.

Bridget looked around at her place. It was looking much better, and her sisters-in-law had added a couple of touches to give the room color and character, but it was still pretty basic. She looked back at Mike, and saw him staring at her, roses still in her hands. She colored as she realized he wasn't talking about her apartment.

"Thanks," she said gruffly, looking determinedly at the roses and cautiously moving to set them down on the table before she dropped them.

Mike wandered around the dining/living space. She didn't have a lot of furniture—the table and chairs, a couch facing a TV. One door led to her small bathroom. He glanced in there, and then into the bedroom.

"So, you really do have your own apartment."

"It's still in my parents' house. But it's nice to know someone keeps an eye on the place when I'm traveling. And I don't disturb anyone when I have to leave early or get back late."

"No Turchenko poster?"

"Jee wouldn't let me."

Mike laughed. "I thought you'd do it anyway."

Bridget smiled, relaxing a bit. "The problem was that I'd then be stuck with a poster of Turchenko, and I decided it wasn't worth it."

"That reminds me. I have something else for you."

He crossed back to the bag he'd brought with him, reached in and pulled out two jerseys: one home, one away.

They weren't generic jerseys, and they weren't the ones cut to fit female figures.

They were large, and not crisp and new. They had "Reimer" on the back.

Bridget flew over and pulled one up in front of her.

She looked up at Mike, eyes sparkling. "Are these yours—like, game jerseys?"

He nodded.

"But I lost the bet," she protested.

"Yes, but it wounds my ego to have you wearing an old Giguère jersey around."

Bridget went to try one of them on, then remembered she was dressed up and stopped abruptly.

"I will definitely wear these. They are awesome. Let me put these in my closet and I'll be right back."

When she returned, Mike had his bag in his hands. "Do you have a garbage for this?"

Bridget asked. "No more goodies in there?"

Mike looked down at the bag. "You were looking for something else?"

"Not really, I thought maybe you had chocolates."

"Er—no. Was I supposed to? I thought it was a little too clichéd."

Bridget agreed. "It would have been. But you did bring flowers."

"True. As long as it's not chocolates I'm okay?"

"And no jewelry," she noted.

Mike laughed. "I've got to hear more about these dates you've had. I think jewelry would have been pushing it, don't you?"

"On top of two jerseys? Yes, definitely. So, have you seen enough?"

Mike gave another glance around and nodded.

"Hope you feel like you got something out of this," Bridget said, following his gaze. "There's not much to this place. I warned you."

"You can learn a lot about a person from where they live. You've seen my place."

Bridget shook her head. She thought about the cold hotel room, with no personal touches beyond Mike's workout equipment. "I don't think a hotel suite really gives you much insight. And I'm not sure what you can learn here. You can learn that I can't decorate, I guess, but that's about the best this place is offering you. You might be mistaken into thinking I can clean, but that would be wrong. I had help."

Mike smiled. "I learned that there aren't

any pink ruffles or boy bands, or even a Turchenko poster."

"I'm sure that was a shock."

Mike merely nodded. "Are you ready? I made reservations."

Bridget felt nervous again. She wanted to ask him if he knew it was Valentine's Day, and if he'd picked the day on purpose. She wanted to know how seriously he was taking this date. But he smiled at her, so warmly that she almost forgot to breathe again, and she stopped thinking.

He took a step toward the door. She followed and opened the closet door for Jill's coat. Mike took it from her and held it up for her. His fingers brushed her neck, and she shivered.

"Cold?"

"I'll be fine."

But she wasn't sure she would be. She'd fallen head over heels for this guy, and she was sure she'd never be the same again.

MIKE DROVE THEM to a tiny place that Bridget had never heard of. It was a family-owned Italian restaurant, warm and intimate. The place was full, except for one table for two that the owner led them to. Surprisingly enough, the place seemed empty of hockey fans; no one gave them a second look. Their waiter was happy to call them by name, but had no apparent idea as to who Mike was.

The waiter took a drink order and then left them to study the menu. Bridget glanced at it, and decided on tortellini, mostly because she could eat it with little chance of spilling on the new dress.

"I hope you like Italian," Mike said.

"Who doesn't?" Bridget answered, picking up a piece of bread. Then she thought maybe she shouldn't, and set it back down without eating a bite. She took a drink of water, and wobbled the glass as she put it down.

"You seem a little nervous," Mike noted.

"You're wrong. I'm not a little nervous, I'm a lot nervous."

The waiter returned with the wine. After the usual wine ritual, he asked if they were ready to order, and left, after subtly indicating they'd selected the best items on offer.

Mike asked for details on the City Championship meet. Bridget had texted him the results, but they hadn't had much chance to talk. Bridget was still thrilled with how the kids had done.

The club as a whole had done better than

they ever had previously. Half the kids had personal bests. Her A-team had won their races in their age group, and four of the kids would be going to the provincial championships. As Bridget went through the details, her words began to tumble over each other, and she scarcely noticed when the waiter brought their salads.

Mike asked, "When are Provincials? Are they here in Toronto?"

Bridget suddenly stopped talking. "I'm sorry. I'm monopolizing the conversation. You must be bored."

"Bridget, it's okay. I'm not bored. How could I be when you're so enthusiastic?"

Bridget looked up at him. "I'm sorry, Mike, but it's our first date—"

"Our first real date," he interrupted, with a smile.

Bridget didn't smile back. "Exactly. I'm talking nonstop about swimming, and it's Valentine's Day, I don't know if you know, and you brought roses and jerseys and we're at this beautiful restaurant and I don't want to do something stupid again. You're right, I'm not good at casual."

Mike reached over with his hand and covered one of hers. It was big, strong and calloused. It felt wonderful. She looked down, afraid to meet his gaze because of what hers could be revealing.

"I know it's Valentine's Day. And I want to be here with you, today, and it's not casual for me," he spoke in a warm tone, reassuring her.

She looked up from their hands, and he nodded.

"To be honest, I don't know what we're doing. I told you about Amber. I don't know how to be with someone while I'm playing. I'd made up my mind that I wasn't going to get seriously involved with anyone till I was done with hockey."

The waiter returned with their main course. Mike let her hand go, and Bridget felt bereft. The waiter fussed over their plates and napkins and wine, and finally left.

Bridget took a bite of her food. She hoped she could swallow it, since her throat was so tight she wasn't sure she could speak right now.

Mike took a bite, and considered before he continued. "After Amber's death, I threw myself into hockey. At first, it kept me busy enough that I didn't grieve too much, and tired enough that I could sleep. And then everything was going great, and as long as I kept that focus on hockey, I could stay on top. I saw a few women, but hockey always came first."

He looked at her, and she nodded. He sounded like he was going somewhere with this, and she desperately needed to know where that was.

"Then last spring something happened to my game. That led to the trade, the playoffs, it was all a disaster. For the first time, I had to actually consider life after hockey, and I was lost. I had no idea what to do. I was terrified."

Mike moved some food around on his plate with his fork. Bridget set her own fork down, since her fingers were unsteady.

"I went to see my college coach. We broached the subject of retirement, but it was still something I couldn't handle. He suggested that even if I could play well again, I needed a more rounded life. But how was I going to do that living as a pariah in Toronto for the next year?"

Bridget twisted her hands in her lap, concentrating on what Mike was saying. This was going to make all the difference to her.

Mike looked at her with a warm smile. "And then, last fall, this redhead dived into the pool beside me and beat me soundly. She kidnapped me and I ended up playing a road ball game with a clan of crazy hockey fans. She helped me work out when I was injured, and I ended up talking to her about things I'd never shared with anyone. I realized she was strong, smart and funny, and I never knew what she'd do next. But maybe most important, she was an athlete, like me. She understood how that worked."

Bridget was afraid to move. Was there a "but" coming? The waiter reappeared, looking in distress at their almost untouched plates. Mike waved him away.

Mike said, "Bridget, what I'd like to do is start spending as much time with you as we can manage with our crazy schedules. But I don't know if that's what you want, and if it is, I want to be fair to you. And I think there's a problem we have to look at."

Bridget froze. Here was the "but." She made her stiff muscles work. "Okay, if I'm on board, what's the problem?" Did she need to be more careful about how she spoke to his teammates? Sign some kind of nondisclosure agreement about the Blaze? Get a new wardrobe for fancy events?

Mike leaned forward. "After I'd talked to Jee that night and found out that I was under some misapprehensions about you, I didn't think things through. I'm not normally impulsive. But I wanted to see you, so I just came to find you at the club."

Bridget had already given him a hard time about the whole gay misunderstanding when he'd finally confessed, and had let Wally know exactly how out of line he had been. "Mike, I think I can understand that hockey is your priority right now. It's the same for me with my coaching."

"I know. I understand that your swimmers need you. That will make things difficult, but if that was all we had to contend with, I wouldn't have any reservations."

Would he ever explain the "but"? She was almost vibrating with tension.

"I can't guarantee that the club is making the playoffs, and if they don't, that removes most of the problem. The team had a chat with my agent. I'm not being traded and they hope to make at least one round of the postseason. I think that's a realistic forecast. I think we can make the playoffs, but that's only if I play my best."

Bridget nodded. She'd had no concerns that he'd be traded anymore. The whole city was tracking how close the Toronto teams were to qualifying for the playoffs. She was pretty sure that chart was on the front page of every sports website. With the way Mike was playing, any rumors about a trade would start a riot. "After that… I don't know if this team can pull together, but we're going places only if I'm doing well, which means I get lots of attention from the press. Lots," he reiterated. "That first playoff series back in Quebec— Amber's death came up over and over. I was under a microscope.

"If I flake out again, I'm going to be the most despised person in this city. I remember the feeling. And that will spread out to anyone I'm connected to. It's not much better when I do well, to be honest. I've been through one brief playoff series here, after several in Quebec. The pressure in Toronto is greater. It will be a constant spotlight. On me, and on anyone around me."

Bridget thought she was getting the picture.

"I want you to know what you're getting into. You've seen what it's like when we've been out together. People recognize me. They want autographs. They want pictures. They want to tell me what I'm doing right, and they'll ream me out for anything they think I'm doing wrong. You'll quite possibly come in for some of that. If you needed to break things off, the press would hound you for how it might affect the team. I don't know how much it might spill over to your family, and your swim team."

Bridget had long dropped all pretense of eating. She hadn't thought beyond being with Mike. That reality still hadn't sunk in, so she hadn't considered what the future would look like. But Mike was looking ahead, and she needed to do the same. Mike wasn't a regular guy, and dating him would be something different as well.

Mike had paused, making sure she was with him. She took a breath.

"And so?" she asked.

"And so the safe play would be to wait till the season's over, but I have no idea when that will be, or what's going to happen then. If it goes wrong, I may have to leave town for a bit. It won't be pretty." Mike's mouth was set grimly, probably remembering last season's ending. He reached for her hand again. Bridget welcomed it, and intertwined her fingers with his.

"So, what do you think, Bridget? Do we take a gamble on this? Do we play it safe and see what happens later? Selfishly, I'd rather have someone going through this with me."

Bridget looked at Mike. His hand was gripping hers, his gaze intense, and she thought, *He's really worried that I might turn him down.*

"So, you're not worried that I might lose my temper and blurt out something I shouldn't?"

Mike shook his head. "I'm not asking you to change who you are. From my perspective, if people don't like what you say, that's their problem. It might even be fun to see you ream out Green or Turchenko to the press. Shake them up a bit."

"That wouldn't help the mood in the dressing room," Bridget noted.

"That ship has sailed. I'm not sure what it would take to make this team gel, but I'm not worrying about that. I'll do my job and they can take care of themselves."

The waiter came out to check again on their main courses, looking anxious.

Bridget withdrew her hand reluctantly and picked up her fork, contemplating her food. She couldn't help but be moved by his concern for her, but she also understood how his guilt about Amber was coloring his viewpoint.

She looked up at Mike. He was concentrating on his dinner. His face was familiar to her now: the gray eyes, the crook in his nose, the firm jaw.

He looked up. Those beautiful eyes were asking a question, and she knew she couldn't say no. How bad could it be, really? If she had Mike with her...

"I bet the Blaze go a lot further than you think. If I'm hanging out with you, think I'd get some good seats?"

His eyes crinkled. "What are we betting?"

Everything, Bridget thought.

CHAPTER NINE

BRIDGET TOOK A look in the mirror. The sisters had been right: she had needed a new dress. Here it was, two weeks later and she was already wearing it again. She thought she was looking good, and she was feeling good as well, thanks to one gray-eyed goalie. She made her way to the hotel lobby with a smile on her face.

It was the last night of the Atlanta swimming conference, with a traditional wrap-up dinner. Except for missing Mike, Bridget had enjoyed the event. She'd learned a lot, as usual, and she'd been able to spend time with the usual suspects: a group of young coaches she didn't run into during her regular season, many of whom she'd competed with. Connor Treadwell was one of those. They were sharing the same table at the dinner.

For once, though, she wasn't dreaming about him. Instead, she'd been checking her phone for messages from Mike. The Blaze were playing tonight, with a chance to clinch a playoff spot, so she was eager to find out how the game went.

If she'd only known all those years ago that ignoring Connor was the best way to get his attention.

She was chatting at the table after the dinner when her phone started playing the *Hockey Night in Canada* theme—Mike's ringtone. She dug into her bag, but as she pulled out her phone, someone reached over her shoulder and grabbed it out of her hand.

Connor held the phone up. "What do you think? Should we check out this guy who keeps calling Bridget?"

Bridget turned and glared at him. He wasn't looking so good to her now. "Give that back!"

Connor instead pressed the answer button. "Bridget's phone. Who's calling please?"

After a pause, Connor responded. "I don't know, Mike. Bridget is busy. And I think we'd all like to know a little more about you. Is it true that you are in fact a professional hockey player, as Bridget claims?"

Bridget flushed. Connor was making it sound like she'd been bragging about Mike. And he made it perfectly apparent that he thought she was lying, too. Had she really been infatuated with this clown?

"Oh," said Connor. "A picture would be lovely." He turned to the crowd around the table, plainly thinking he was being hilarious. "There's going to be a real picture folks. Since Bridget has been so shy with showing us…" He trailed off as the text popped up on the screen. He swiped to the picture.

Connor's mouth tightened, and his cheeks reddened. He tossed the phone to Bridget. "Guy has no sense of humor."

Bridget couldn't help but laugh out loud as soon as she saw Mike's photo.

He had obviously called as soon as the game ended. He was in the locker room, sweaty and wearing only a towel. She thought he looked incredible. Connor was proud of his body, but Mike could give him a run for his money in a best abs contest. There was a defenseman on each side of Mike, similarly appareled. All three were making a rude hand gesture. The coach beside her asked to see, and once Bridget had handed it over, he passed it on until eventually everyone had a look and a laugh. By the time Bridget finally got it back, Connor had left. She escaped to the hallway and dialed Mike back.

"Who was that?" he asked.

"No one important," Bridget answered, glad that it was now true.

"What was his problem?"

"I guess he thought I had an imaginary boyfriend. But I have a real boyfriend, don't I?" she asked, only half joking.

"Not just any boyfriend. One who's in the playoffs."

Bridget fist-pumped, even though she was alone in the hallway.

"Congrats! Was my boyfriend also the first star?"

"Sorry, only second star. Maybe you want to look up that jerk answering your phone now."

Bridget smiled. "Well, he does have an Olympic medal..." she teased.

"What color?"

Bridget laughed. "It doesn't matter. I'm not interested anymore."

"Good. I'd ask more about the jerk but management is throwing a thing to celebrate clinching, so I'd better make an appearance."

Mike said a reluctant farewell, and Bridget returned to her friends. She didn't see Connor again.

THE *HOCKEY NIGHT IN CANADA* ringtone buzzed. Bridget grinned. She and Mike had been trying to meet up in person since she'd come back from Atlanta. They'd talked or texted almost every day, but hadn't been able to actually get in the same room together and there were things she wanted to say in person.

She'd gone to the Provincial championships, and her A-team had qualified for Nationals. That was incredible, but it meant she still had to spend a lot of time at practice. And the Blaze traveled whenever she didn't. But they were finally going to see each other after tonight's game.

"Hey, Mike! Ready for the game?" Bridget was so excited she wanted to jump up and down, but since she was in her cubicle at the pool, that wasn't a good plan. She leaned back in her chair, hoping he could talk for a while, even if she was going to see him in a few hours.

"Actually, I was wondering if you'd maybe pass your tickets on to someone else."

Bridget sat up, on the alert. "Why? What's happened?"

"Stop by after your practice. Come straight in when you get here. We'll order in and watch the game here since I'm not playing. I'll explain when you arrive."

Toronto was starting a home-and-home with Quebec, and Bridget knew how important this game was to Mike. If he could stare down his former team, there would be very little left to question in his game. Something was up if Mike wasn't playing.

Something big.

BRIDGET DROPPED HER tickets with her mom; she was sure Cormack could go with her dad. If not, one of the other guys would jump at the chance. Fortunately, her mother didn't know hockey and didn't press her with questions.

If Mike wasn't playing, and wasn't going to be at the arena, there was a big problem. He should still be on the bench, even if he wasn't starting. He had to step in if something happened to Turchenko. If Mike wasn't at the arena, that meant the team had had to call someone up from the farm team to be backup.

What was going on?

Mike couldn't have been traded; the deadline had passed. Was there some loophole? Traded players often sat out to make sure they didn't get injured. They were normally at the games, though, watching from a box.

So was he hurt? And if so, how badly? Would he be able to play again this season? If the team was going to be in Turchenko's hands, their playoffs were over already, in Bridget's opinion.

She'd canceled the second swim practice to be able to attend this important game. She drove over to Mike's hotel, left the car with the valet, and waited impatiently for the elevator. She jabbed the button to Mike's floor repeatedly, trying in vain to speed up the elevator. She swiped the key card, and opened the door. The suite was dark. She started to feel for the switch when she heard Mike's voice. "Leave the lights off, okay? I'm in the living room."

It wasn't the reunion she'd been dreaming of. The curtains were drawn, and the place was dark and quiet. Dim lighting was romantic, pitch black led to stubbed shins and bruises.

"Mike?" she asked. Why would he be in the dark?

"I'm here. On the couch."

"Are you sleeping?"

"Not really. But I'm supposed to stay in the dark."

She had a sinking feeling she knew what

that meant. But she couldn't say it. "What's wrong?"

"Concussion, possibly."

Bridget sank into the first chair she bumped into. "What happened?"

"I had my helmet off for a minute at practice. Got hit in the head by a puck."

"Are you okay?" Most important question first.

"I'm fine. But concussion protocol is strict, so I have to take a couple days off. Can you come over here where I can at least touch you?"

Bridget smiled and felt her way over to the couch. She sat down by his head. He reached for her hand and gave it a kiss. Bridget felt herself unwind, letting her hand stay wrapped in his. He was okay, and she was finally feeling him in person, even if she couldn't see him.

"Welcome home," she said softly.

"Wish I could see you properly. I had planned this moment much better, but I'm not supposed to let myself get excited. This will have to do."

"So you really feel okay?"

"I'm fine. I've had a concussion before and I know what it's like, but head injuries are a big concern. So even though I told them I was good…" Bridget could hear the frustration in his voice.

"Who was the idiot who hit you in the head?"

Mike hesitated.

"Troy Green?"

She could hear Mike's smile in his voice. "Yes. But he's very sorry."

"Did he do it on purpose?"

Mike laughed, reassuring her. "I really don't think so. The whole team reacted in horror at the thought that I was out. The puck hit my head, I lost my balance, and I hit the ice. But it wasn't going fast, and I know my head didn't hit the ground. Still, here I am. They're not taking chances."

"Why didn't you tell me this on the phone?"

"I had people here, fussing around. I didn't want to get into it with you while there was an audience, and I didn't need you to hunt down Green. But I wanted to talk to you privately anyway, so this will work."

Bridget was suspicious. "What do you want to talk about?"

Mike said, "Come closer."

He edged over on the couch and pulled her down beside him. "That's better."

Bridget was tense for a moment, then began to relax. He wasn't going to break up with her like this.

"What were you so tense about?"

"No good ever comes after 'We need to talk.'"

She felt the chuckle rumbling in his chest. "That's not exactly what I said."

"Close enough. So what do you want to talk about?"

"First, tell me about this idiot who answered your phone."

Bridget snorted. "Connor."

"Yes, Connor with the Olympic medal. I have two," Mike responded.

Bridget twisted to try to see his face. "Are you jealous?"

"Why did he have your phone?"

"He took it from me. There was a whole crowd of people—it was after the last dinner. Your ringtone came in, so I knew the game was over. I grabbed my phone—"

"What's my ring?" he asked.

"Hockey Night in Canada."

Bridget felt his chuckle again.

"So you grabbed your phone…"

"And Connor grabbed it from me, and the rest you know."

"Why did he grab your phone?"

"Who knows? He's an idiot."

"Did you two go out?"

Bridget sat up. "A couple of times. No biggie. You *are* jealous."

"I don't know much about your past, Bridget."

"You don't need to be jealous of Connor."

"No? What happened?"

Bridget frowned. "We went out a couple of times. The last time, we went to an arcade, and I beat him in air hockey. He didn't take it well, and the next day he asked out someone else. That was it."

"You beat him at air hockey and he couldn't take it?"

"Seems so."

"Hard to believe."

"That his ego was that fragile?" she questioned.

"That he couldn't beat you at air hockey," Mike teased.

Bridget jabbed him in the ribs.

"Careful, I might have a concussion."

"You're lucky I don't give you one after that. Of course I beat him at air hockey."

"So I don't have anything to worry about?"

Bridget snuggled back down with him. "Not a thing."

He wrapped an arm around her, and Bridget felt she was perfectly happy. It was hard for her to grasp that he might feel just as lucky.

"Oh, another thing happened," she said. This she'd wanted to tell him in person, but she'd been picturing seeing his face while she talked to him.

"Anything to do with Conner?"

"Nope. I met Jonesy." She paused to let that sink in.

"Is this supposed to mean something to me?" Mike asked after a pause.

Bridget sighed. "I guess not. Jonesy is probably the top swim coach in Canada. He's from Australia, and they managed to lure him to Canada about five years ago. He and my coach, the one I worked with before I joined the club—" Bridget felt Mike nod behind her and she continued "—they've been friends for a while. Well, my former coach was in Atlanta of course, and I bumped into him when he was with Jonesy, so he introduced me. The three of us went out for coffee, and had a really good talk. There's so much to learn from them." They'd also been very complimentary about her, but she didn't want to brag.

When Mike still didn't seem to realize what a big deal this was, she continued. "It was a sign that I'm making it. It would be the same as you having a get-together with—" Bridget thought, and then rattled off the names of some hall of famers.

"They're nice guys. Just don't get Patty angry."

She sighed. Of course Mike had already met his idols. He probably had their personal cell phone numbers in his contacts. It reminded her of the gap between his accomplishments and hers. She wasn't done, though. One day she'd be at the top in her field.

"Should I be warning Jonesy not to get you angry?" he teased, tugging on a lock of her hair.

"I don't know what you're talking about," Bridget replied. "I don't have a temper." Deciding to change the topic before he challenged her on that, she asked, "What did you want to talk about?"

Bridget could feel his body tensing, just as hers had. This couldn't be good.

"I'd forgotten about a commitment I made, back before Christmas. It's a team thing."

Bridget knew he had a lot of team commitments, but he didn't discuss them all with her. She waited to hear why they were talking about this one.

"It's kind of a silly event, but it's for Sick Kids Hospital, so we agreed to it."

Bridget kept quiet.

"Certain members of the team are going to be in a kind of, well, fashion show."

Bridget chuckled.

"I hope I get to see pictures."

"I'm sure you will. But we aren't just walking out there on our own. We're each teamed up with someone."

Bridget sensed this was going to be the kicker.

"Some of the guys are walking with their wives or girlfriends," Mike said, and then paused.

She froze. He couldn't possibly want her to... But no, he'd said this had come up months ago. Who was walking with him?

"Since I didn't have anyone then, I'm paired up with a model from the designer who's rigging me out."

Bridget was still.

"Bridget?"

"So you're like, on a date with her for the evening?"

Mike sighed. "No, it's not a date. The only thing we do together is walk down a runway. I did ask if I could get out of it, but apparently, they've been working with the measurements they have for Appollonia and me, and it's too late to change. I'm supposed to go for final fittings this week."

"Appollonia?"

"She's the model."

Of course she is. "You're going for fittings this week? When is this event?"

"Saturday. When you're in Winnipeg for Nationals. I'd rather be there with you, but I can't."

Bridget lay still. Her thoughts were chaotic. This is what it was like to date someone like Mike.

Mike wrapped her a little closer to him. "Bridget, I'm sorry. I wish I hadn't forgotten, but I did. I wanted to tell you in person. It's probably going to be covered by the press, and I didn't want you to come across the pictures without warning. But it's just a publicity thing—I've hardly met this woman."

Bridget nodded. It wasn't Mike's fault. It

wasn't anyone's fault. But still, it made her feel insecure.

"You ready for the next thing?" Mike asked.

"There's more?" Bridget asked, heart sinking.

"There's another team event, a dinner. They dreamed up this one after we clinched a playoff spot. It's another fund-raiser. There's going to be a player at each table. People buy tickets, silent auction, all that stuff. Each player is supposed to have a plus one. I hope you can be mine."

Bridget gave herself a mental hug. He wanted her to be his plus one. Her grin faded. Wait, could she?

"If I can't?" Might as well know the worst up front.

"I'm supposed to show up with someone. If my mother was closer, and her husband wasn't bedridden, I could bring her, and that would be fine. But…" He left it there.

"When is it?"

"A week from Saturday."

Bridget did the math. A week from Saturday, the first weekend after Nationals. Was that the swimming awards?

"I'll have to check and get back to you."

"I'm sorry to dump all this on you. This

wasn't what I'd hoped for when we could finally spend some time together again. It's part of the baggage that comes along with my job."

For a moment, Bridget wished he was a plumber.

Mike had said he was sure he didn't have a concussion, but he still followed doctor's orders. They got room service and ate by candlelight, then listened to the game on the radio, snuggled on the couch. It could have been very romantic. Unfortunately, the game was a disaster.

The loss couldn't just be blamed on Turchenko: the whole team fell apart. It was as if losing Mike meant they'd lost their ability to follow the game plan. It didn't help that the announcers were speculating that Mike wasn't on the ice because he couldn't face his former team. Bridget would have yelled and thrown something if it weren't for Mike's possible head injury. Mike just grew more and more quiet. She imagined all that tension and anger being channeled inside and then coming out on the ice: that was Mike's way. Just as well he didn't play a position where he was checking other players. He might knock them through the glass.

The after-game radio show was more of the same. To change the subject, Bridget asked Mike when he was going to start driving the McLaren.

"Hmm?" he said, still focused on the radio commentators.

"It's your summer car. You should get it out soon, right? I mean, this is March, so technically spring is practically here," she said oh-so-innocently.

It took a moment, but the gears began to turn in Mike's brain.

"No."

Bridget rolled her eyes. "No, you're not getting it out soon?"

He smiled, his teeth glinting in the candlelight. "No, you're not driving it."

"You're not playing fair, you know," she argued. "We have a bet, and I never get a chance to win it."

"I guess I should apologize for spending all my time in net playing for your hockey team then, instead of with you?"

"Can I at least get a ride in it?"

"I'll take that under consideration. Will you promise not to steal the car if we stop somewhere?"

"There's a bet on the table. I'll wait for

that," she said, with more confidence than she felt.

Mike leaned over and kissed her, a light brush of the lips that still sent her pulse racing. "Thanks. You'd better get out of here now. It's late."

SHE MET UP with Jee for one of their usual get-togethers. First they had to discuss how things were going with Jee's pregnancy. She was finally over morning sickness, well into her second trimester, and thought she was starting to show.

Bridget was thrilled for her friend and her brother, but it wasn't unalloyed happiness. Lately it seemed that her emotions were getting much more complicated and confused. Jee had been her friend since they were kids. Things had changed a little when she married Brian, but they'd still kept their friendship intact. But this, having a baby, as much as she was happy for Jee, would change things a lot. Jee wouldn't have the same free time, and she'd have different priorities. Bridget had seen it happen with the other sisters-in-law. Was Bridget going to have her turn? That hadn't been something she'd thought about before. Did her focus on swimming mean she was missing other big things? And would starting to think this way when she and Mike had just started dating mess that up as well?

She told Jee about the fashion show event, and the charity event that she'd promised to get back to Mike about. She wanted another opinion. She was second-guessing herself now, and she wasn't used to that.

"Saturday. But that's the swimming awards," said Jee.

"I know."

"Why didn't you tell him you couldn't go?"

"That's what I'm trying to figure out," Bridget answered.

"Are you worried about who he might take as his date? Are you jealous?"

Bridget creased her brow. "To be honest, I think that's part of it. But that's not the whole thing. If he was going with, I don't know, his great aunt, I think I'd still feel left out. He's been here with the family, but I've never really had a chance to see what his world is like. And sometimes it seems like we can never find time to be together. Plus, hockey is Mike's biggest thing."

Jee nodded. "Yeah, that makes sense."

"I think it's starting to sink in that hockey isn't just games and practices and training. It's dealing with fans, and doing charity events and being recognized where ever you go."

Jee looked troubled. "Wasn't your swimming like that, a bit?"

Bridget shook her head. "Not to the same degree. Nowhere close. And if this is all part of Mike's life, and I want to be part of that life, too, I'd better figure out if I can get used to it."

Jee looked surprised. "So, what are you going to do?"

Bridget shrugged. "I could do a compromise. They give out the awards in the afternoon, and it's just the banquet in the evening. The younger swimmers and their families don't even go to that. So if I'm there in the afternoon, I could go to Mike's thing in the evening. Everyone compromises a little in a relationship, right?"

Jee looked at her seriously. "Well, there's compromise like blow-drying your hair in the bedroom so he can have the bathroom, and you know, watching TV shows on the PVR if he wants to watch hockey. But there are some things that are too big to compromise."

Bridget sighed. "I guess I'll find out, won't I?"

MIKE WAS CLEARED for any concussion the next day, but it was too late to join the team in Quebec. Bridget came back home from swim practice to find Mike's Land Rover parked on the street, but he wasn't waiting at her door. He was upstairs with the family, watching another ugly loss. Bridget sat down on the couch beside Mike. He wrapped his arm around her, and she curled into him, enjoying the feel of his strength, and telling herself that compromise was essential. She'd go to this dinner thing and find out if she could fit in. If she couldn't? For now, she pushed that thought aside.

The next game was at home, and Mike played with his disheartened team. There'd been a lot of unfriendly press about Mike the past week. Bridget had yelled at the radio a few times, but Mike had been cool, calm and completely unrevealing in interviews. During the game, though, that anger was channeled into his play. Bridget was there, and she could see that now. No one was going to score. Not tonight. After a couple of spectacular saves by Mike in the first period, the team started to regroup. They stopped playing fearfully and by the time the horn sounded at the end of the third period, Mike had a win—and a shutout.

Bridget met Mike after the game at what

was becoming their usual bar. She saw some other players at a table, but she and Mike were left alone. Just as well for Troy Green. If he came over again, she'd do more than verbally abuse him.

Bridget grinned at him. "You know it, but it was an incredible game."

Mike smiled briefly. "I needed to show that I was back."

"It's obvious," Bridget said. "You're leading this team, whether they realize it or not. Is it helping in the locker room?"

Mike shook his head. "Not really. They all knew why I missed the games against Quebec, but still, they don't know if they can trust me when it gets down to the playoffs."

Bridget huffed. "And they won't play well unless they know they can trust you."

Mike reached over and grabbed her hand. "Yes, but that's for the coaches to work on. You've got your own coaching to deal with this weekend. How's that going?"

"Pretty good. My A-team is looking strong. Today we had just the morning practice, light workout, and tomorrow we head for Winnipeg. Then we'll see."

"I'm going to miss you."

"You'd better." Bridget didn't mention Appollonia, but she was thinking about her.

THE BUZZER WENT, and the results were posted. Bridget leaped into the air, and then ran to hug Annabelle, wet as the girl was. Her star was shaking, overwrought. This had been her final race. She'd had a false start, so she was hesitant off the blocks, but she made up for it in the stretch and came in a close second. Annabelle hadn't been expected to be one of the final eight, so this was incredible.

Austin had come in fourth in his race, so the club was well represented and had done far beyond expectations. Bridget was thrilled with both of them, and their families were ecstatic. It was a great evening for all. Bridget sent texts to her family, and to Mike. The O'Reillys were all congratulatory. But Mike didn't respond.

Bridget kept checking her phone, bothered by Mike's silence—and by her own worry. She finally muted the phone, and went out for a celebration with her A-team and their families. Jonesy came by their group and added his congratulations. It was almost a perfect night.

No, not almost. She knew, absolutely, that she was doing the right thing.

She told the swimmers to take a week off, celebrate, relax and enjoy, and then they would get back into a summer training schedule: less intense, but keeping them in shape for fall, when the regular season would begin again. They would all feel greater expectations for the upcoming season, but that was months away. Now was the time to enjoy what they'd accomplished.

She fell asleep soon after returning to her hotel room, refusing to check her phone again. So it was the following morning when she found congratulations from Mike. Apparently, he hadn't been able to keep his phone in the pocket of the outfit he wore for the show. Bridget gave herself a stern talking to. She either trusted Mike, or she needed to get out of this relationship. In theory, she did trust him, but in practice it was tough. She had all the confidence in the world when it came to doing things for herself but found it so much more difficult to depend on someone else.

The team landed in Toronto the next day, met at the airport by thrilled family members. Mike couldn't make it, but Jee and Karen had come waving congratulation signs that had clearly come from the graduation section of the dollar store. Some of the other members of her team who hadn't made it to Nationals had come with their parents to cheer their team members. Parents of her swimmers hugged and congratulated her. It was great. She'd taken a big step toward her dream.

MIKE PICKED HER up on Saturday for the charity dinner. He knew she was nervous about it, but he was pleased she was coming with him. These things could be dull, and Bridget was good at adding life to any event. He also hoped that she'd see dinners like this didn't have to be daunting. That way she wouldn't find going to events too strenuous. He had hardly noticed that he was starting to think long-term with Bridget, but somehow, she was there when he looked ahead.

She was wearing the same dress as from their first "real" date, and she looked just as beautiful in it. She normally wore casual clothing, but she cleaned up much better than she realized. He was proud to be taking her with him. He loved watching her, especially the vivid hair, since it could often reflect her mood. He saw the glasses as part of her now, just like the freckles. It all came together in the fascinating package that was Bridget.

He'd thought of a way to help overcome some of her nerves. After going to her door to pick her up, he led her out into the street, where his McLaren was waiting. She actually stopped in her tracks, and turned to look at him with wide eyes.

"I'm driving," he teased.

She let that pass. He held the door for her to get in the car. She paused, and sat carefully, as if afraid to mar the interior. When he got in the driver's side she was staring at the instrument panel. For the first couple of blocks she was quiet, eyes closed, listening to the sound of the engine, but then she started asking questions. They'd arrived at the event before she'd satisfied her curiosity. Once he'd given the keys to the valet and come around to escort her in, he could see the tension returning. She gripped his arm tightly.

"Don't worry," he said. "If Troy Green can do this…"

He could see her straightening up. He should have thought of this sooner. Make it a challenge, and she'd take it. Her chin lifted, her eyes got back their sparkle and even her hair perked up.

Mike knew the team people: players, coaches, management and administrators. Throughout the course of the year he'd been introduced to some of the non-Blaze people in attendance, too. As they wandered around the vestibule, holding on to glasses of cheap champagne passed out by the wait staff, he did his best to help Bridget, introducing her by her swimming credentials and whispering snippets of information into her ear when he could be heard over the string quartet playing in the corner. They avoided Troy and Turchenko. People wanted to talk to Mike, but he kept the conversation light and his arm around Bridget's waist so she wasn't left alone. He didn't want anything to spoil the night.

It was better when they went through to the dining room and were seated for dinner, as Bridget only needed to remember the names of the people at their table. She was quiet, but he didn't think too quiet. At these kinds of affairs he knew he was the center of attention. He followed a familiar script, appearing candid without saying much. He'd learned the trick of this long ago.

After the meal and speeches, and the applause for the funds raised, he was beckoned across the room by the general manager. He turned to Bridget, who smiled at him.

"Go ahead. I'm fine. After all, if Troy Green can do it…"

He relaxed. "I'll make it as quick as I can, then we can get out of here."

HE DID CUT it as short as he could. As a rule, these things didn't run too long; at least, not for the players. Athletes who wanted to maintain their peak abilities couldn't party too late or too often during the season.

He noticed the team captain's wife, Olivia Sandusky, at their table speaking with Bridget. She'd been very pleasant when he'd checked on dress code with her for the event. He'd wanted to make things as smooth as possible for Bridget. Still, he was a little uneasy. Would the group of players' wives be welcoming? He hadn't even considered that.

He observed Bridget carefully when he returned. She was still quiet but didn't look upset. He suggested they head out, and she agreed. He noticed her glance at the car— part of him wanted to pass over the keys just to see her face. He didn't. After all, they still had a bet in play, and he knew she wouldn't appreciate being denied the privilege of triumphing over him. As well, he still remembered the afternoon she'd kidnapped him. It had been a good day, overall, but he hadn't liked watching her fall for his car while ignoring him.

There were a few moments of silence while Mike headed out of the downtown core. Bridget had her head laid back, eyes closed. "Could we maybe just drive around for say, a week or so?"

"Even if I don't let you drive?"

"Even. This car is wonderful."

"That's why I bought it. So, how did your chat with Olivia Sandusky go?" He kept his voice casual.

"Oh, she was very nice." Mike glanced over and saw her grin. "Apparently Troy's dates don't get the welcome mat because they keep changing, but the wives consider me to be a little more…permanent."

Mike felt something open in his chest. Permanent. Permanent sounded good. Was that what Bridget was thinking?

Apparently not. "I need to tell you something, Mike. I should have before. This afternoon was the swimming awards, and tonight was the banquet. I skipped the banquet to come to this dinner with you."

Mike took a moment to process that. Swimming awards and banquet? This was something big in Bridget's world. She and her team would probably have had a place in it. But she hadn't shared it with him.

Mike pulled into an empty parking lot, and turned off the car.

Bridget waited for him to speak.

"Why didn't you tell me?"

"I thought you would have told me to go to my banquet."

Mike nodded. "Why did you not want that to happen?"

"I wanted to go with you tonight. Our schedules have been crazy, so I wanted to spend time with you, and I wanted to see if I could fit in. Maybe I wanted to make this more real by being more public? I didn't analyze it too far, I just knew I wanted to be with you tonight."

"You didn't consider that I might have wanted to be at your event with you?"

Bridget's head tilted. "I guess I didn't. It seemed like a pretty small thing in comparison."

"Did you get an award?"

"Yes, and the club and Annabelle did, too."

"Then it wasn't a small thing. I would never

belittle your accomplishments just because mine might get more headlines."

Bridget said "I appreciate that. But you'd already said you couldn't get out of this thing tonight. And I thought there'd have to be some kind of compromise, so that's what I did."

"Compromise should work both ways. Did you get a trophy?"

He saw a happy smile flit across her face. "A plaque. It'll go up at the club. I'm sure Wally will give it a prominent spot."

Mike took a moment. He had told her he couldn't get out of this, but if he'd known before the date was set, he could have done something. He didn't like the idea of one-sided compromises.

"Okay, I have a plan. Give me your phone."

Bridget dug into her bag and pulled out her phone. She unlocked it and passed it over.

Mike did what he had to do, then passed it back.

"I've shared my calendar with you. You put in your events, and I have mine, and we'll do our best to make sure we have as few sched-uling conflicts as possible, outside of games and swim meets, okay?"

Bridget smiled. Mike turned the key in the ignition and pulled out into traffic. The conversation left him unsettled. He was glad Bridget was trying to accommodate so that they could be together, and he'd been happy to have her with him tonight. He enjoyed it more with her than he would have with anyone else. But that assumption of compromise… He wasn't sure he actually had made any significant compromises so far, and he wasn't sure how much of that he was actually willing to do. He hadn't in the past. The ghost of Amber was still hovering.

BRIDGET HADN'T TOLD Mike the details of her conversation with Olivia. The other woman had been very kind and welcoming, but the conversation had given Bridget reason to think, and she wanted to work out how she felt before she said anything to Mike.

Bridget had been surprised when Olivia had sat in Mike's seat at the dinner after he'd gone to talk to the GM. She was blonde, attractive but not intimidating. She introduced herself, and Bridget had realized her husband was Darren Sandusky, captain of the Blaze team.

Apparently Olivia knew who Bridget was, and had come over because the WAGs—

wives and girlfriends of the players—had been curious about her.

Bridget had raised her eyebrows.

"If we'd known Mike was involved with someone, we'd have been sure to come to see you to welcome you. Mike was single when he got here, though, so we didn't realize. You've kept it quiet. We try to be very supportive, even if our husbands and boyfriends aren't getting along."

"That's very kind of you. We haven't been going out long. I'm pretty new to all of this."

"I can imagine. Many of us have been with our guys since high school or the farm team days, so we came up the ranks with them. It must be a little overwhelming to be just dropped into this when you're not used to it."

Bridget had nodded. So far, her relationship with Mike had been private. Now that was going to change, and she didn't know just how that would affect things between them.

"I just want you to feel free to let us know if there's any way we can help you. It's not always easy dating a professional athlete. We keep in touch with friends on other teams, so if Mike should move on…"

Bridget knew what she meant. As soon as the playoffs were over, Mike would be on the move, and that could be soon. Bridget had been avoiding that thought. Once his contract expired at the end of June, he would be a free agent. And there wasn't much chance he'd be signing again with a Toronto team, considering their respective finances. Bridget had no idea where things were going after that.

"The WAGs can help you find places to stay, reliable movers, help with the paperwork involved…if you're ever in a position to need something like that, we help each other."

Bridget blinked. She hadn't thought that far ahead. "That's very kind of you. Do you help find work as well?" she asked, mostly as a joke.

"What do you do?"

"I'm a swim coach."

"So, you teach swimming lessons?" she asked, with brows creased.

Bridget had come across this response before. Swimming was a sport that only caught the public eye every four years, when the Olympics pulled everyone's attention for a couple of weeks, so it was easy to overlook the constant time and commitment it took to excel. "Not exactly. I work with competitive swimmers—the kind who race, hoping to represent Canada internationally, and maybe even in the Olympics. I used to compete myself, and now I coach. A couple of my kids just placed well at Nationals in Winnipeg last weekend, so we're getting there." Bridget was still pretty pleased about that.

Olivia looked concerned. "Would that not be difficult? I'm sorry, I don't mean to interfere. I just imagine that's a very limited field you work in, and it might not be easy to find openings when—if you moved around. But, then, if you ever plan on a family, you'd probably have to give that up."

Bridget had been a little overwhelmed at how much this was projecting into a future she was unsure about. She appreciated the welcome Olivia was offering, and realized she had a lot to consider. However, a stranger making an assumption like this about Bridget's potential, possible, maybe-but-let's-not-jinx-it future? It made her sit up. "It's not the 1950s anymore. Women are allowed to have a job *and* a family."

Olivia looked at her sympathetically. "Hon, it might not be 1950, but we're talking professional athletes here. It makes a difference. They get traded anytime. Just look at Mike. He had a no-trade clause, and what happened to him? When they get traded, they have to hop on a plane and go. Who's going to pack up, get the kids out of school, sell the house and find a new one? He can't do it. He's committed to playing with the new team." Seeing Bridget's face, she continued. "I'm not trying to scare you, and I know you two haven't been together that long, but that's what's involved when you're with a pro. Take a good look at things before you commit. Have you got your phone with you? I'll put in my number. If you need to talk to someone, I've got a good ear."

Bridget passed over her phone. As she watched Olivia, she wondered why the woman had come to apparently warn her. It was kind, but was there some reason Bridget needed that message in particular?

"This is awfully nice of you. Does everyone get a welcome like this?"

Olivia laughed. "Not necessarily. Troy over there—" she nodded to the far side of the room where Troy's arm was held by a blonde with cleavage threatening to spill from her low-cut neckline "—brings someone new to every event, so we haven't pulled out the welcome wagon yet. Mike is different, but you know that."

Bridget nodded. Mike *was* different, in

many ways. They'd been having difficulties getting their schedules to sync up so they could spend time together, but that wasn't going to be the only bridge to cross. Events like this, possible publicity. Olivia was right, Bridget needed to look at this seriously. The compromise she'd had to make tonight? That was just the beginning, and Bridget wasn't sure where it would end.

TODAY, THOUGH, BRIDGET was in a good mood as she walked into the club. For the next few weeks she had nothing to stress over. She was ready to get to work on the lighter summer training season for her athletes.

She was later than usual entering the building, since there wouldn't be morning practices for a while. But she had some paperwork to clear up and wanted to fine tune the training plan for the off season. There was also some new information on nutrition and performance she wanted to look into. She'd have to see what Wally would do with the award plaque. He wasn't going to want to feature it, but it was a big deal. She was so absorbed in her thoughts as she made her way down the hallway that it wasn't until the door to the pool resisted her push that she noticed the sign. "Closed till further notice."

Bridget frowned. What was this about? She would have been among the first to hear if there was a problem with the pool. Had someone fouled it last night? She pulled her phone out of her bag and checked for messages.

There was nothing from the club, but she did see an email from Annabelle's mother asking about any other swim clubs Bridget would recommend for Annabelle to transfer to. Bridget had a bad feeling and knew exactly where to look for answers. She stalked down the hallway to Wally the Weasel's office.

He wasn't there, so she sat in a chair to wait for him. In the meantime, she started texting.

Monica, the instructor who ran the aqua aerobics classes during the day, responded first. She'd received an email from Wally a week previously that classes were suspended indefinitely. The pool was closed for structural maintenance.

Bridget's temper smoldered as she read the email Monica forwarded. Wally had included everyone but her; that was obviously deliberate. And what was this with the pool and structural maintenance? Surely she would have heard if anyone was having problems with the pool? After the triumph at Nationals, Bridget was looking forward to building on that success. If the program was canceled for any length of time, Annabelle and Austin would switch to another club to keep their training going. She'd lose her best athletes, and swimmers of their caliber were rare. She'd be starting from scratch again.

By the time Wally showed up, Bridget was ready to ignite. More emails and texts had confirmed that Wally had closed the pool down for the duration, probably as soon as Bridget and her team left for Winnipeg. Monica was going to teach aerobics classes in the gym, but Bridget only coached swimming. There was nothing for her to do without a pool. The pool didn't get a lot of use in the summer, since members left on vacation and spent time at clubs with outdoor sports, but the competitive swimming program didn't take a break.

Wally was almost around his desk before he noticed Bridget sitting in one of the visitor chairs.

"Oh, Bridget." He swallowed. "I didn't see you there. I'm kind of busy…" His voice trailed off as Bridget stood up and closed the door firmly.

"So what's going on, Wally?"

"The name is Walter—" He scurried behind his desk as he saw the look on Bridget's face. He swallowed again. "You mean about the pool, I suppose."

"Yes, you suppose right. I'm usually the first person using the pool any given day. Yet, again, you've failed to notify me about something important to my job."

"Oh, dear, did you not get the email? Maybe your server?"

"Cut the crap, Wally," Bridget answered. "Monica forwarded me the email you sent out. I wasn't on the list. In fact, there were a couple of emails, all of them connected to the pool and this problem you'd detected, but I wasn't on any of them. I'm the swim coach, and I was never asked about it, or told that there was an issue."

"I'm not sure I like your attitude—"

Bridget stood up. "And I don't like your crap. You've had it in for me ever since I started that swimming program. First, you spread lies about my personal life, and now you're jeopardizing the entire swimming program here for some kind of petty revenge? What is wrong with you?"

"I don't like these insinuations—"

Bridget's voice was rising. She leaned over his desk, gripping the wooden edge to resist the temptation to grab him around his weaselly neck. "Don't you care that the two most promising swimmers we have are probably going to leave? What if their families leave as well? Is getting back at me worth it? I suppose you didn't know that the Thorpes were talking to me about their granddaughter joining the program. You know the Thorpes, original member family, rich, the kind you toady up to, you sniveling little—"

Bridget's diatribe came to an abrupt halt, not because she'd run out of words but because a pair of arms had suddenly wrapped themselves around her waist. Neither she nor Wally had noticed the door opening behind them.

"Mike Reimer!" Wally said sneeringly. "Now we have the happy couple."

"Mike! What are you doing here?" asked Bridget.

"I got your text and thought I might be needed," Mike responded.

"Is this what you're upset about, Wally?

Because I said no to you but yes to someone else? Is there even a problem with the pool?" Bridget asked.

Wally looked offended. "There certainly was a problem. And summer is when the pool gets the least usage. I'm merely looking out for..." He trailed off as he saw the look Bridget was giving him.

Mike spoke over her shoulder.

"I don't know how much influence I still have here, but I'll certainly let people know that the manager of the club didn't communicate with his staff about major events that impact their programs. I think I'd also want to ask about the timing of this repair work."

Wally's mouth dropped open.

"I wouldn't want Bridget to have an assault charge on her record, since she works with kids, so I'll take her with me now, but remember, that doesn't necessarily apply to hockey players. And, in case you didn't know, she has five older brothers."

With that he swung Bridget around and gave her a little push out the door.

BRIDGET WAS ALMOST shaking with anger as they walked down the hallway and out the door. When she would have continued to her car, Mike steered her to his Land Rover.

"I don't think you're good to drive right now."

Mike was surprised when she let that pass, but she was still focused on Wally and the pool situation. They'd gone a few blocks before she asked where they were going.

"I'm taking you home."

"I need my car!"

"We'll come back for it."

Other than that, Bridget was quiet, but her expression was stormy. When they got to the O'Reillys, she didn't react when he turned off the vehicle.

Mike gave her a moment.

"You've got the keys to the garage, right?"

Bridget came out of the dark place she'd been in and asked, "What do you want from the garage?"

"I'm not going to let you take shots at me without some kind of protection," he answered.

She stared at him, then marched to the garage.

Mike dragged the net down into position, adjusted his stick, and let her start.

For the first ten minutes, Bridget shot without much precision or planning, but with a lot of force. The sound of the ball hitting Mike's pads or gloves echoed in the morning air. Gradually the anger worked through, and he could tell when she started thinking, could almost pinpoint the moment when she remembered their bet about the McLaren. He had to work a lot harder after that.

It took almost an hour, but Bridget finally stood, and pushed her face guard up. She was flushed, and breathing heavily, but the glare was gone from her eyes.

"Thanks," she said.

Mike straightened up from his defensive stance and took off his helmet.

"Feel better now?"

"Yes. I'm still angry, but I probably won't punch him now. Probably. Wait, shouldn't you be at practice?"

"I took a personal day. I can do that once in a while."

"Probably just as well that you did. I was so angry. I'm not sure what I might have said if you hadn't shown up."

"So what I overheard was the censored stuff?"

"I kept getting madder when I realized

just what he'd done." Bridget stopped, jaw clenched.

"Hungry?"

Bridget blinked at him.

"Let's go grab a bite and talk about it."

They packed up the hockey gear and went to a nearby diner, since Mrs. O'Reilly was helping at an event at the church and wasn't around to offer food. Mike let Bridget vent, revealing more than she realized as she spoke about how this would affect her kids and her own prospects. The success of the last month had moved her career timeline up drastically, and this setback could derail things. She'd had strong hopes for Annabelle and Austin, but she couldn't train them without a base, and the other swim clubs already had coaches. Their results at Nationals meant her A-team could transfer into good clubs, and by the time the pool was up and going again at the athletic club, there'd be little motivation for them to move back. And she wouldn't try to hold them back just because she, Bridget, was grounded by Wally. That wouldn't be right.

Mike became aware that he hadn't appreciated how much this meant to Bridget, and how driven she was. He knew they shared a competitive drive, but hadn't fully grasped that she was equally intent on her dream and her passion. Her two As might be difficult to replace, but Mike thought Bridget was just as singular. He wished he could help, but from what he'd gathered from a call this morning to his sponsor at the club, the pool work had started while the team was in Winnipeg, so he couldn't get it reversed at this point. He also knew his influence was not that great. He'd hardly been at the club the past few months, and his contract with Toronto would be expiring soon. And who knew where he'd be then? His threat to Wally had nothing much to back it up.

So he listened, and agreed with her most insulting aspersions on Wally the Weasel, and thought of something that might distract her, and help him as well.

AFTER THAT TALK, Mike asked for a meeting with management and the coach. They agreed to his request, but he noticed the wariness on the faces of the men in the room. He didn't have his agent with him, and he told them from the start that this wasn't about his future.

The atmosphere relaxed. Right now, no one was sure what to do with Mike. He was playing as well as he ever had, but what would happen once the playoffs started? Mike was determined that if he asked for another meeting they'd be the ones looking to negotiate, but he had something else in mind.

"I don't want to sound arrogant, but right now, our playoff hopes rise and fall with me. Agreed?"

There was a murmur, but for the most part, assent. If Mike couldn't play his best, the team wasn't strong enough to compensate.

"The big question is whether I can still perform. Last year I failed. No question. So this year, I'm asking for a favor, one that will help me play better."

Wariness again. Mike laid it out for them. His coach looked skeptical, but management was fine with his request. For them, there was little cost, and if they could get Mike to take the team further into the playoffs, there was a lot of revenue to be made.

BRIDGET MET MIKE after the last game of the regular season. Mike hadn't played. Most of the starters had been rested. This game wouldn't affect the playoff positions, so there was no need to risk an injury. Mike met her at the arena and took her to a smaller bar, but he was still greeted by a lot of people. Most were asking for reassurance about the playoffs. The mood in the city was cautiously optimistic. They'd been here last year, and it hadn't gone well. But the team was playing better, especially the goalie. Mike did his public relations bit with the fans they encountered, and said things looked to be going well, but he knew, and they knew, that it all came down to what happened on the ice next week.

They finally found a seat in a booth, and after a few minutes, had a chance to talk.

"Pressure is ramping up, eh?" said Bridget.

Mike could see that she had to force the smile. She'd reached out to people she knew, both here in Toronto, and anywhere else she had connections, but there was nothing to be done as far as coaching went. No one was looking for a swim coach at Bridget's level of competition. She was under contract at the club until the end of the summer, but there was nothing for her to do. The pool might re-open in a month or two, but her A-team had found new clubs to train with. Annabelle had been able to get a place in the club Bridget claimed was the best in the city, maybe in the country, with Jonesy, the coach she'd met in Atlanta. It was a compliment to Bridget's coaching that the girl was accepted there.

Mike appreciated that while she was proud of her athlete, it was hard to let her go.

Her comment gave him an opening for his idea. It would help him, and by helping him help the Blaze as a whole. And he hoped it would help Bridget, too. It would give her a distraction, and maybe a sense of purpose that was missing at the moment.

"Yes, pressure is definitely on," he agreed.

"If I can help…" she offered, trailing off.

"Actually, you can. It's a lot to ask though."

He'd gotten her attention. Now, he just had to sell this right.

"Hey, if I can help, I'm only too happy to do anything I can." She'd perked up a bit.

He reached across the table and held her hand. She curled her fingers around his and waited.

"Did I ever tell you what it was like to play my first playoffs in Quebec?"

She tilted her head. "You told me some of it."

"When I was called up, management asked very delicately if I thought I was up to it. It was just after Amber died, and they weren't sure how I was going to cope. I wasn't either, but the chance to be busy, not to sit around blaming myself—I told them working would be good therapy."

Bridget nodded.

"So there I was, finally in the big leagues. I was supposed to be a bench warmer. They needed a second goalie and someone to take shots in practice when the starter was resting. But their backup struggled, and when they finally, in desperation, put me in, there were no expectations whatsoever. Quebec was an expansion team, so making the playoffs was a pleasant surprise. But I knew if I could manage not to embarrass myself, maybe the next year I'd have a shot.

"So, little pressure, lots of support. I had an outlet for my anger and guilt, and things went better than anyone had imagined. And from then on, I was golden. No one was more popular in Quebec than I was. And I kept doing well. The team was with me, the city was with me…up until the coach retired."

Bridget was paying close attention. He could see it in her eyes. She knew what had happened after that, and how things had gone downhill.

"So, as you and the hockey world all know, the playoffs here were different. I didn't play well after the trade last year, and there was some doubt about how I'd do in the playoffs against Quebec. While we were preparing for the series, I don't think I'd ever felt more isolated. And things did not go well."

He paused, remembering. His memories were bleak. He felt her fingers tightening around his, giving him unspoken support.

"So, like the saying goes, it's déjà vu all over again. I'm playing well now, and I think I can keep that up, but every time someone looks at me, talks to me, they wonder. They're wondering in the locker room, they're wondering in the press boxes, they're wondering in the owner's box. I'm wondering, too."

"Mike, you're not in the same place as last year. You're going to be great," Bridget reassured him.

Mike looked at her intently, her eyes enlarged behind the big frames. Having her here was helping him stay calm, stay the Iceman. He hoped she would agree to this plan.

"Right now, everyone wants to be sure I'm as fine as I can be. Anything I want, they'll do. And there's one thing I think will help.

"I still am not part of this team, not like I was in Quebec. I'm not part of this city. So I don't have someone to unwind with, someone to spend downtime with, someone to talk to, especially on the road. I'm second-guessing everything I say to the team because I don't want to scare them. I could use someone I can truly relax with.

"I'd like you to come with me. Be that person for me."

He could see her eyes going wide. She hadn't been expecting this.

"I've talked to management. They're on board for anything I want. I want you. And I thought maybe this would work for you, too, a distraction. And it might prolong the time Wally has left to breathe on this planet."

He watched the expressions flash across her face. "What exactly are you asking?"

"To be with me through the playoffs. I can't get you on the team jet for away games. But we'll fly you to each city, and you'll have a room at the hotel while we're there. You'll have a ticket to the game, get to come to practice, and you and I will hang out. For home games, you come to practice, and you'll have a couple of tickets to each game. I just want you to spend time with me. When I'm not playing or practicing or doing press things, I don't want to be sitting in a hotel room getting up in my head. I want company. But not just anyone. I'd like someone who understands, and someone I like to spend time with."

He paused. She opened her mouth, then

closed it again. Bridget wasn't often speechless. He took a breath. He needed to lay it all out there before she decided.

"A downside might be the publicity. But if we get swept in the first round, it will be a pretty short postseason."

She frowned. Mike could almost see the wheels turning in her head.

"I don't want you to answer right away. I'd like you to think about it. Let me know when you decide, and we'll go from there. I can at least get you tickets to home games no matter what."

He didn't press her further. He knew this would be good for him, but she had to choose if it was right for her. Playoff pressure was going to be tougher here in Toronto than any other place he could think of, so having someone on his side would be terrific. But she had her own career and she might need to focus on that. Here was that choice again: hockey versus something else. Selfishly, he hoped she'd choose hockey.

BRIDGET SAT ON her couch with her laptop, but it was hard to be motivated to research and plan when she had no one to coach. She had nothing to do but think, and her thinking wasn't always productive. Short-term, there was Mike's proposition to consider. Long-term, there was what Olivia Sandusky had talked about.

She opened the browser to the playoff schedule and rubbed her forehead.

She and Mike had started dating, knowing that the end game was up in the air. She hadn't been worried at first. She could admit, at least to herself, that she'd fallen in love with Mike and had wanted to spend as much time with him as she could. Now that they were past the trade deadline, she knew Mike was in the city until the Blaze were out of the playoffs and had cleaned out their lockers for the season. That might be in a week and a half, or theoretically, it could be in June, if they went to the Cup finals. Mike's contract expired June 30. And there was very little chance he'd be in Toronto after that.

She looked up the page with the salaries of the players. Mike was in the top grouping. Unless he totally failed, that's the kind of salary he'd be looking at again. She couldn't wish any setback for him. She found the committed salaries for the following seasons for the Toronto teams. They couldn't afford Mike-money if they wanted a competitive roster. Not much chance Mike would be here next year.

And what about her? She wasn't sure where her career was going. After her blowup with Wally the Weasel, she didn't know if she'd even be able to keep her job at the club. They had no reason to get rid of her, based on the results she'd given them, but Wally was pretty weaselly. He'd already shown the lengths to which he'd go. He certainly wasn't going to provide a good reference.

She looked up the club website. The pool was still closed indefinitely. Wally had had to post a piece about how well the competitive swim team had done, but there was very little about the program for next year.

She set the laptop aside. She wasn't sure if she wanted to return there, which meant she'd be back to square one. She needed more time to decide if she was ready to face that again.

If she were to start at someplace new…well, what were the chances that it would be in the same city, or even the same country as Mike? Pretty well nil unless they planned for it. Together. Assuming he wanted to do that.

She stood up, and started pacing. She couldn't ask him to give up his hockey dreams. His wife had. She remembered the pain in his voice when he'd talked about her that first time. She couldn't put him through something like that again. Hockey was too essential to him. It was who he was. Last year, when he'd had to consider life without hockey, he'd been lost.

Swimming was important to her, but she had more in her life if it all went away. For him, hockey was everything. His mother was in Phoenix. He had no other family, no real friends in Toronto. He talked about the Sawatzky family, but only in the past tense. Hockey was his family, his financial success, his sense of worth and value. Hockey was Mike. No wonder he wouldn't deny it, even for his wife. Bridget wasn't sure exactly how he felt about her. They hadn't been together that long, and she knew she couldn't compete with the sport he lived for.

So what did that mean for her, and for them as a couple?

She would never have asked him to sacrifice his hockey in any case; she was an athlete, and she respected what that meant too much to ever consider making such a demand. But because she was an athlete, she had her own drive and her own goals. What would happen when they conflicted with his?

Really, it should be a no-brainer. Assuming Mike wanted to keep this relationship going, he had a career that was established and made big money; she could ride on his coattails, and maybe keep coaching wherever he ended up. Work enough to keep her from being bored, but not enough to impede his career. Could she settle for that?

She dropped back down on the sofa. And what if they got really serious, got married and had kids? Her stomach knotted. She knew the demands kids made, and even if they had paid help, someone had to be the person who took the sick days, went on school outings, took care of business when Mike was busy playing. Two parents with jobs that entailed a lot of travel, with strange hours and lots of pressure? That was a recipe for disaster.

She didn't think Mike would ask her to end her career for him, but if they were going to have a real chance, one of them was going to have to make that sacrifice. And how could that not have a negative effect on their relationship?

Maybe it was fate that she didn't really have a job right now. Maybe the choice was made for her.

She'd say yes. She'd do the playoffs with

him, however long that might be. Try out life as a hockey girlfriend, full-time. See what it was like. Maybe it would be better than trying to start coaching from scratch. Maybe. She pictured those silver-gray eyes looking at her, confiding in her, teasing her…maybe she could do this. She'd never considered it before, but maybe for Mike she could. Call it compromise. How much was she willing to give up?

CHAPTER TEN

FINALLY, IT WAS HERE. The playoffs. Since Toronto had qualified in the last playoff spot, they'd be starting every series on the road. Round one was in Philadelphia. Bridget's flight to Philly was uneventful, and she caught a cab to the hotel and checked in. She scoped out the hotel's pool, and was wandering back through the lobby when she saw the team coming in.

They were all big guys, but Mike was one of the tallest. He was at the back, on his own. Mike had told her about the team dynamics, but it still bothered her. When he saw her, standing near the elevators, he dropped his bag and went to her, ignoring the rest of the team and leaned in for a kiss.

"You made it," he said.

"People are staring," she answered, a little breathlessly.

"Let them. I feel like I haven't seen you for days." Mike grabbed her hand and towed her back to his stuff. A couple of the players nodded at her (she noticed Troy Green ignored her) and she helped Mike pick up his luggage.

Bridget went up to the room with Mike. He had seniority and was a goalie, a breed that often had excessive quirks, so he had his own room. He threw his bag on the bed, and then suggested a late dinner in the hotel dining room, followed by an early night. Visiting team had first practice in the morning, and he wanted her to come along.

In the restaurant, Bridget recognized the head coach and a manager at one table. Mike nodded to them but guided her to a table by themselves.

"I see you didn't shave. Growing the playoff beard?" she teased.

Mike grinned. "Part of the playoffs."

Bridget noticed that he was more…more something. He was never given to extremes, but though he looked calm, she sensed he was wound up. She recognized the feeling from racing—standing in the blocks, poised to start, waiting for the buzzer and controlling the tension enough to avoid a false start. The playoffs were what he lived for. Mike was starting his race.

She had been right. He was hockey, and

this was his chance to reclaim his position as one of the best. For some, this pressure would be paralyzing. For Mike, and for her, and for others who lived to compete, this was what they thrived on.

He asked about her family, how they were doing. They talked about Philadelphia. Bridget had competed here, and Mike was usually here at least once a year. They didn't talk about hockey. And yet, somehow, it was buzzing under everything.

After Mike signed for the meal and they headed out of the restaurant, Bridget finally got close to the *H* word.

"So, what is my schedule?"

Mike asked what floor she was on, and pushed the button on the elevator.

"Can you come to morning practice?"

"Sure, if that's what you want."

"Good." He smiled.

"What?" she asked.

"What, what?"

"You look smug about something."

"I have a surprise for you tomorrow. Don't ask."

Bridget closed her mouth.

"Then I'll work out a bit, get a massage. Nap, meal and head to the rink. You're welcome to join me. You've got a ticket at the desk for the game. You sure you don't want to sit with the other team guests? Or if there's someone you know in the city, I could ask for another."

Bridget shook her head. She'd be fine on her own.

The elevator opened, and Mike walked her to her door. He leaned down, gave her another of those tantalizingly brief kisses, and then strode off. Bridget went to sleep dreaming about the kiss.

In the morning, Mike sent her a text, asking her to meet him for breakfast in the lobby. It was early but she was used to early rising and was already awake. She had time to swim laps before showering and meeting him. He was waiting at a table for her, and she couldn't help smiling at him. The playoff beard was just playoff stubble now, but it looked good.

Some fans from Toronto had made their way to Philly, and Mike was greeted and offered good wishes. An occasional glance was thrown Bridget's way, but the focus was always on Mike.

There was a bus waiting to take the team to the rink, but Mike hailed a cab. He answered her questioning look. "Surprise."

At the rink, he gave her a lanyard with a security pass, and they made their way into the warren of dressing rooms and workout rooms that were off-limits to fans. The rest of the team wasn't there yet, but the trainers, coaches, valets and equipment managers were all at work. Mike directed her to head out toward the ice, saying he'd join her soon.

She made her way through the tunnel the team used to reach the ice, staring up where thousands of rabid fans would soon be filling the seats, yelling, cheering, playing along with their team in spirit. She watched the Zamboni leaving the ice, thinking how quiet the arena was now. A man was standing at the bench, and looked up when she had made her way there.

"Bridget?"

She nodded. She had never seen this man before, so didn't know who he was. But he bent over and straightened back up with a pair of hockey skates.

"You wear a men's eight?"

Puzzled, she nodded again, slowly.

"Try these on."

"Why?" she asked.

"Reimer wants you skating." The tone was

neutral, but Bridget could guess that this was not normal protocol.

She sat down and slid her foot into a skate. "Perfect," she said. She went to lace up the skates, but he laid her foot on his lap and started tightening them for her.

"I can do that," Bridget protested.

"No problem," he said, deftly tying the laces, and then holding out the other skate.

When he was done, Bridget stood up. She moved her feet; they felt good.

The man waved to the ice. Bridget looked at it, unbelievingly. "Really?"

He nodded.

"Thanks…" She paused.

"Jack," he said.

"Thanks so much, Jack," she said, took a deep breath, and stepped out onto the sheet of ice.

It was exhilarating. She hadn't been able to skate much this year, and having the huge ice to herself was a treat. She lapped the boards, skated forward, then back.

She turned around at a sound, and saw Mike arriving from the tunnel. He was wearing his pads and carrying his helmet as well as two sticks, and a bucket of pucks.

Bridget skated over. "This is fantastic! Excellent surprise."

Mike grinned. "Oh, that's not the surprise. I'm giving you a chance to win your bet."

Bridget realized one stick was his goalie stick. The other was a skater's stick, which he passed to her, along with the bucket of pucks. "Let me finish my warm-up and I'll be with you."

Bridget looked at him incredulously. Then she dumped some pucks on the ice and started shooting.

Mike finally finished his stretches and skated to the net. He scuffed the ice in the goalie crease with his skates, tapped the goalposts, did a rotation around the net and then settled into his goalie stance.

"Start from the blue line, anytime."

Bridget grabbed a puck with her stick, and made her way back to the blue line. She stared at the net, considering. Then she chose an angle to one side and made her first attempt.

She wasn't bad, she knew. But there was no denying Mike was not just good: he was the best. He had some ability to sense where she planned to shoot before she did. She didn't give up. Sometime he'd be just a little too slow, and then the McLaren was hers for at least one drive.

It might have been fifteen minutes, then the rest of the team started to arrive. They were startled to see a girl firing pucks at their goalie. Most weren't sure what to say, but Troy Green was always happy to shoot his mouth off.

"Man, even girls are scoring on Reimer."

Troy had found her button. She was moving before she was even aware. She checked into Troy with her hip. He'd bent to grab a puck, so he was off balance, and down he went. Bridget stopped, suddenly concerned that she might have hurt more than Troy's pride.

But Troy was fine and redeemed himself a bit in her eyes by laughing instead of getting angry.

"Okay, I won't rag on your boyfriend when you're around," he said as she gave him a hand up.

Mike called out, "Nah, say what you want about me. Just don't tell her girls can't play hockey." He smiled over at Bridget.

"She's feisty," said Troy. Bridget narrowed her eyes. "Okay, sorry," he said, backing off.

The last players were straggling onto the

ice and the coaches were out, so Bridget skated quickly to the box. Jack was there and helped her take off the skates.

Bridget climbed up to the seats to watch. As both a hockey fan and a coach herself, it was fascinating. The public didn't usually get into team practices, so this was an uncommon opportunity.

The practice ended, and the Zamboni came out to freshen the ice for the home team. Bridget knew she had some time before Mike was ready to go. She made her way down to the bench to thank the head coach for allowing her to be here.

"We don't stand a chance if Mike isn't on his game," he responded. "If anyone asks, I never said that."

"There's not much I can do, but if he thinks my being around helps, then…" She shrugged.

He nodded. "Mike says you're a coach."

"Swimming."

A slight smile pulled at the edges of his mouth. "Any difference?" he asked dryly.

Bridget nodded. "The water here is harder."

GAME ONE, ROUND ONE, the playoffs. Bridget was early, because she'd cabbed over with

Mike. That had made her wonder why he never commuted with the team, though she'd kept that to herself. The seats started filling in. Her jersey wasn't appreciated by the Philly fans but some Toronto fans gave her high fives. A tubby guy in a Philly jersey sat beside her and gave her an assessing look.

"That a game-worn jersey?" he asked.

"Yeah."

"Must be nice to be rich." He scoffed.

Bridget laughed. Yeah she had a great jersey, but she hadn't paid for it.

"What's so funny?" he demanded.

"My dad's a mechanic. I coach a swim team. You're richer than I am if you can afford these seats."

"I won a contest," he mumbled.

"I know the player. I couldn't afford the jersey otherwise."

"Really? He gonna be up to it this year?"

"Unfortunately for you guys, yeah, he's good."

"Crap."

"So how's your goalie?" asked Bridget.

"He's young."

The teams were introduced, the national anthems sung. Then, after the ceremonial puck drop, the real one happened and the game was on.

The game wasn't a pretty one for Toronto. The team was tentative and had little possession time. An early goal on a screened shot for Philly ignited the home crowd and seemed to deflate the Blaze.

But Mike wasn't giving up. Bridget could almost feel his determination from her seat, and soon everyone was aware of it. Philly was taking two or three shots for every Toronto shot, but nothing was getting past Mike. A breakaway had the crowd on their feet, but Mike shut the door. Bridget cheered, as did the other Toronto fans in the crowd.

"You were right. Iceman is on his game," said her neighbor after the first period ended.

"Told ya. Now if the rest of the team…"

Toronto came out for the second period revitalized. Whatever might happen, Mike wasn't going to let them down this game. Philly was still leading, and was able to add a score on a power play.

"Too bad your friend couldn't score as well," said the Philly fan.

"Game's not over yet," said Bridget.

But the Blaze did lose. During the third, Troy Green, of all people, led a two-on-one and was able to cut the Philly lead to one. Toronto pulled Mike for the last couple of minutes of the third but weren't able to capitalize.

"Good game," said her neighbor. "Your friend did good. We might end up with a series."

"Count on it," said Bridget.

MIKE HAD SAID he would meet her after the game, so she wandered around the concourse, looking at Philly jerseys and plaques. Some Philly fans gave her a hard time, but they'd won, so they were in a good mood. Bridget was familiar with trash talk, and gave as good as she got but kept it good-natured. Finally she was alone, except for the staff starting to close up.

"There you are. Ready to go?"

Mike was in the suit that the team was required to wear to and from games. It contrasted with the beard that was filling in, giving him a decidedly scruffy look.

"Sure."

They didn't talk much on the way back to the hotel. Most of the team had gone on the bus. Bridget wasn't sure if Mike was traveling separately on her behalf, or because he didn't feel like part of the team. She hoped it was for her.

They found a corner at the hotel bar, and Mike ordered two beers. Bridget knew he'd drink only some of his. She felt limp and drained. Would alcohol cheer her up, or just depress her further?

Mike glanced at her quizzically. "You look like you're the one that just played a sixty-minute hockey game, Bridget. What's up?"

"How are you so upbeat? In case you missed it, you guys lost."

"One goal. You know it's hard to win in their arena, especially the first game. They're a pretty high-scoring team, and we kept them to two. Their goalie had a good game, but he's beatable. We'll see in two nights."

Bridget frowned. "So it's not getting to you, after last year? I'm sure the press were all over you about that. This is the playoffs, and after the trouble last year, I know they'll be dissecting every play."

Mike answered her seriously. "I hate losing. And for everybody, a win would have been better, but this is different than last year. Back then, I wasn't playing well. I didn't have any confidence. The team wasn't playing all that well either. Tonight, I played a good game. The two goals were good ones. In the circumstances, I don't think they were stoppable. They also were a bit fluky, so Philly can't do the same thing again. And the team was playing a lot better. They had some really good scoring chances, and eventually they'll find the net.

"Being a goalie is a very mental job. You can let yourself get swamped by it, or you can break it down into its simplest parts and focus just on what you can control. Philly played well tonight, and I couldn't have done anything on those two goals. So I just let it go and look for the next save."

"Good. I promised the guy beside me that we'd make a series out of it."

"You know him?" Mike asked.

"No, we just got talking."

Mike grinned. "And then you'll get in a fight with a Toronto fan at home."

"Hey, there are jerks in any group of fans."

As if to prove the point, two men came over to their table. They'd obviously had a few to drink and were upset about the loss. They were rude and obnoxious. Mike reached for Bridget's hand under the table and squeezed lightly, but it was enough to stop her from speaking out. Mike did his Iceman routine and got rid of them without losing his temper.

"I don't know how you do that."

"I know you don't." He grinned. "That's why I stopped you from ripping up at them. There was no point. They were drunk and wouldn't remember in the morning. Why don't we go now?"

Bridget was glad to leave. She'd kept quiet while Mike was holding her hand, but she wasn't sure she could keep it up.

BY DAY THREE, Mike was finding a comfortable routine. He and Bridget would meet for breakfast and then head early to the arena. She was having a blast, skating on the big ice and trying to get the puck by him. She wasn't going to, but he enjoyed the time with her. He knew his own teammates, and he'd seen lots of film on the Philly players, but Bridget was a wild card and kept him on his toes. He stood in his crease now, watching her. She wasn't wearing a helmet, which was a bit risky, but it gave him a better chance of figuring out her next move since he could watch her expression. He could see the moment she made a decision. Instead of skating toward him, she backed up. What was she up to?

Charging the goalie? Really, was that what she was going to try? He had inches and pounds on her, as well as a full set of pads. Maybe she thought he'd back off, but he was just as competitive as she was, and he had his car to protect.

She tried to sneak around him at the last minute, but they both mistimed. He was trying to avoid hurting her, and she was trying to avoid getting hurt, and somehow their skates collided and they both ended up on the ice. Bridget had the breath knocked out of her, but she wasn't hurt. Mike took a minute to move, making sure she was able to get up before he did. She rolled over quickly and looked at him with concern.

"It doesn't count if we all end up in the net together," he said, then grinned at her.

She sat back, relieved, and only then did he realize most of the team had gathered, watching them.

"Perhaps we can get started before Ms. O'Reilly injures anyone," warned the coach. Mike helped Bridget scramble to her feet, and noticed that she left the ice quickly.

Game two. Toronto came out playing hard this game. Philly also wasn't giving any quarter. It was a tough, physical game. Penalties were frequent, and the goalies were hard-pressed.

Mike could feel that special edge returning. Everything seemed to slow down. He had all the time in the world to see the puck approaching and get in front of it. He'd had that feeling before. It was rare, but when it came, he rode it as long as he could. This was being the best, and there was nothing Mike wanted more.

It was a nail-biter for the fans. Once the puck hit the crossbar, once it was called off on replay. Toronto had a goal called back when the Philly net came off its posts.

The final score was 1-0, for Toronto. Mike was first star. The monkey was off his back.

THE SERIES NOW moved back to Toronto for two games. Mike let Bridget know they were still okay to work on the bet, as long as she didn't injure him. He could tell she wanted to tease him about that, but she was a little awed at the opportunity to skate on the ice at the Toronto arena. Bridget had brought her own skates, and Mike wasn't surprised to find her in conversation with Jack, as if they'd been friends from way back. He suspected she was getting advice to help with their bet.

The way he was feeling, it wasn't going to happen. Mike took a moment to watch her when she started skating on the ice, waiting till she noticed he'd arrived. Her eyes and cheeks were glowing. It warmed something inside him.

"This is so awesome."

He smiled back. "Can you manage not to knock me down today?"

She tried to hold back her grin. "I was trying to crash the net."

He snorted. "That ended up being charging the goalie, and that gets you a penalty."

Bridget stuck out her tongue, grabbed her stick and skated to the blue line with a puck.

It felt like no time till the rest of the team showed up. They were obviously getting curious about this special warm-up.

One player spoke out, "What happens if she actually scores?"

Mike caught the puck high glove side; another foiled attempt. "You don't want to know."

Bridget said, "I get to drive the McLaren."

There was a shocked silence. A third line forward—one of the grinders—was near Bridget and spoke in surprise. "But that has a stick."

"Are you saying I can't drive a stick?" Bridget asked. No one had warned him about her buttons.

The grinder started to skate away, slowly, backward. Bridget pressed forward. "I can not only drive a stick, I do so every day. I also change my oil, my tires, my belts and my brake pads, on my own!" She was poking at his chest with every accomplishment, and the grinder, not paying attention, fell over on his back.

His teammates laughed. Bridget flushed.

The grinder scrambled to his feet before Bridget could offer help. She muttered an apology. Mike skated by, saying, "I forgot to warn you she has a thing about women drivers, too."

Bridget skated off the ice. Mike wasn't sure she'd be back. That was three guys she'd knocked over, on game days. The team had been lucky with injuries so far, and no one was wanting to risk that.

The game that night was one of those weird matches that happen once in a while, but not normally in a playoff. Anything could and did happen. Sticks broke, a puck went in the Toronto net off Mike's back; Philly had too many men on the ice for a full minute before anyone noticed. Bridget's grinder, apparently surviving his fall without getting hurt, managed to score his first ever hat trick. Two of those goals went in off his skate in a melee around the Philly net, but they still counted. Mike shook his head at the end, but the final score was 6-5 for Toronto. They were up two games to one in a best of seven series.

Bridget said she couldn't make the next practice. Mike didn't press her. He wasn't sure that his coach wasn't going to put his foot down, in any case. Jack asked if she was okay; the coach, overhearing, just raised his eyebrows and turned away.

The least said about the fourth game, the better. Toronto played as if they'd just come from Junior A and lost, badly. Mike was the best player they had that night, but it wasn't a good game for him, either. The series was now tied up two games to two. There would be at least six games, if not seven, in this best of seven series. This was much better than last year when the team had been swept in four games, but having left Philadelphia with a split, returning there still tied up was a disappointment.

Mike picked Bridget up after the game in the Rover. The arena had mostly emptied by then. He didn't want to see anyone. The whole team was in a foul mood and didn't want to discuss how they'd played. They drove in silence for a while. Eventually Mike pulled into an empty parking lot.

"Not a good game," said Bridget at last.

Mike sighed. "That's an understatement. Not that I had a great game tonight, but, I told you, this team can't go far the way it is. If I let in a soft goal, they think I'm about to fall apart and they tense up, and the game is shot."

"They still don't trust you?" Bridget asked.

"Until we beat Quebec, with me in net, they won't. And even if we win this series, and go on to play Quebec, we can't win until they trust me. It's a catch-22."

"Could you tell them why last year was such a disaster, and why it won't happen again this year?"

Mike looked at her levelly. "Are you sure it wouldn't happen again?"

"I can't be sure Toronto would win, no, but I am sure you wouldn't fall apart again," she said. "Aren't you?"

"Yes," he said, quiet and confident. "But I don't think telling them what happened last year would help. They can't think that I have a weakness like that."

"But if it's over…" Bridget started.

"I can't just tell them that it is, I have to show them, and then we're back in that vicious circle again."

"At least this one can't be blamed on me. I didn't hurt anyone."

Mike looked at her, and then laughed.

Bridget was puzzled. "Are you going to tell me why that was so funny?"

Mike leaned back and sighed. "You know how superstitious athletes can be, right?"

Bridget nodded. "I've heard of goalies who have to hit the goal posts, skate around the net…" she teased.

Mike reached over and grabbed her hand. "Well, Bridget O'Reilly, you've just become a Toronto Blaze superstition."

It made sense, in a weird way. Troy Green had made a crack on the morning of the first game, and Bridget had checked him and knocked him over. Even though the team hadn't won that game, Troy had had a breakaway and scored the only goal for Toronto. The next game day was the one where Bridget had crashed into Mike, and he had a shutout that night. Game three, the grinder had gone down and ended up with his first ever hat trick. Game four, Bridget wasn't at practice, and the team played horribly. So now, they wanted her back.

Bridget shook her head. "Those were flukes. There's no way that anything I do is going to change how they play."

"Granted, but if a player thinks he's going to do well, it can make him play better."

"Yeah. Until one time it doesn't work, and then it's over."

"But will you come back for practice? I was asked to invite you back."

Bridget looked at him. "Seriously? I've had fun, but you don't have to make them do this. I'm still happy to just tag along and have a great seat for every game."

Mike shook his head. "It didn't come from me, I promise. A couple of the guys approached me in the dressing room after the game, and everyone agreed, for once."

"Even the coach? I think he was giving me the stink eye last time."

"He's eminently pragmatic, and if the team thinks you make them play better, he's all for it."

Bridget looked at Mike in the light of the dashboard. "You know it's not real, right?"

He grinned, and after pulling his hand away, started the car up again. "Yep. But if you want to run into me again, I won't stop you."

THE NEXT DAY was a travel day. Bridget arrived after the team, and found Mike waiting for her in the hotel bar. He stood and greeted her with a kiss—not nearly long enough—and asked if she was hungry. As was now their custom, they went to the hotel restaurant, which was becoming a home away from home.

"There's a lot of press about this rookie goalie in Victoria. They're comparing him to the playoff debut of a 'Mike Reimer,'" Bridget said, looking up from her phone at Mike to see how he'd respond.

Mike was more interested in his food. "Unless both teams make the Finals, we'll never meet."

"It would be fun, new Mike Reimer meeting old Mike Reimer," Bridget responded. She looked around the table, and saw there was no milk for her coffee. The table beside them hadn't been cleared, and she jumped up to steal the milk remaining there.

That was when the interruption sauntered up.

Bridget's first thought when she saw the woman was to wonder how early someone had to get up to look like that. She was wearing a low-cut top and a tight short skirt, and she had the body to make that work. She had blond hair, impeccable makeup and six-inch heels. Bridget was in a T-shirt and yoga pants, with runners on. No makeup, and she couldn't remember the last time she'd checked her hair.

The woman had looked around, spotted Mike, and homed in on him like a laser. Bridget sat back down in the seat beside Mike, instead of across from him.

"Mike Reimer," the woman said in a throaty voice. "I'm your biggest fan."

Maybe if you went by cup size, thought Bridget sourly.

"You've been…incredible."

Bridget waved her hand to see if this woman even knew she was there. Mike had no expression on his face.

"I'd do anything, *anything*, to help you and the team." She leaned toward Mike as she said this, giving him a good look at her assets, if he wished. There was no room to doubt what "anything" she was ready, willing and able to do. And Bridget was sitting right there!

Without giving Mike time to respond, Bridget grabbed his arm and snuggled against him, saying, "Sugar bear, we wanted someone to clean your car—it needs a good detailing. And then there's carrying my bags, it's really a pain. And didn't Darren say he needed some babysitting? I was going to help out, but if this nice lady will help…" She looked up at the woman and smiled a big insincere smile. "Then I could have more time with my little love nugget."

The woman gave Bridget the look she'd give a slug trailing slime on her favorite bag. She glanced back at Mike, but he was looking at Bridget.

"Uh, no. I don't do that," she said, and walked away.

Bridget dropped Mike's arm. She waited for his response. Had she been out of line?

Suddenly his arm was around her, and his lips were by her ear. "*Little* love nugget?"

Bridget looked up to see him laughing. "I could have come up with something much worse."

Mike laughed. "Oh, I'm sure you could…"

BRIDGET WAS NERVOUS the next morning. Jack had welcomed her back as if she'd never missed a practice, and she always enjoyed skating on the freshly cleaned rink surface. She'd long ago realized that she would only score on Mike if he made a mistake, and those were rare. So this was just for fun, a unique opportunity. But then the rest of the team started to arrive—surely way earlier than usual?—and she realized she was supposed to do something to knock down one of these players so they'd play better in the game. With the men just coming on the ice, she wasn't even sure who was playing tonight; there would be a couple of guys sitting out. She skated toward the line of players and the bench, where she could leave. They seemed willing to get in her way, but she swerved around them. What was she supposed to do, chase them around the rink? She turned back and found a bunch of the team on her heels.

She waved her hands at them, wanting space. Three guys fell over. One who didn't started to protest that at least one skater had fallen on purpose. Bridget shrugged. "You'll see tonight who really fell." She then turned and left the ice.

This time she sat near the bench instead of avoiding the coach. After the players left the ice, she approached him. He greeted her with a small smile.

"I hope this isn't a problem," she began.

"The good luck routine out there?"

Bridget nodded. "I know I don't have any special power, but I thought it shouldn't hurt, and might help."

The coach nodded. "You 'helped' our defense this morning."

Bridget looked at him. "Maybe I should 'help' some forwards next time?"

The coach looked over the ice. "Might be a good idea."

"Let me know if there's anyone in particular. I have no idea how to keep this up."

The coach gave her a genuine smile. "I'll let you know if there's anyone I think needs special 'help.'"

"Thanks," said Bridget, fervently. "Is this what they need the most? A confidence boost?"

"On or off the record?"

"Off," said Bridget. "I'm sorry if I sound nosey. I'm just a fan, and I'd like to help if I could."

"Off the record, they're not a cohesive unit."

Bridget nodded slowly. "That's what Mike says. He says they won't trust him till he can win against Quebec, and he can't win against Quebec unless they're trusting him and working as a team.

"I know Mike has been spending all his free time with me, but I don't know if he's being considerate for my sake, or if he'd be on his own otherwise, and that's why he wanted me to come along. I hardly ever see the rest of the team."

"It's hard to build that team identity if they don't spend time together—preferably when they aren't under game pressure," the coach agreed.

Bridget grinned. "I'd invite them to my mom's for dinner if we were in Toronto. Then my dad could give them a stern talking to. I have older brothers, so he's had a lot of practice."

The coach nodded, as if she'd made a serious suggestion.

"That's a thought. Not your mother." He shook his head. "I wouldn't do that to her. But, the rest of the team usually meet up after a game for dinner."

Bridget was taken aback. "Oh. Not at the hotel, obviously."

"No. I believe tonight they have a reservation at a place called Vincenzo's. There's bad weather in Toronto, so we're not flying back until tomorrow morning. There should be room for a couple extra."

Bridget opened her mouth to ask if he was really suggesting she and Mike crash the dinner but he had left. She thought back over the conversation. She didn't see Mike pushing himself in where he wasn't wanted. If she did follow that suggestion? If she did, and it backfired, Mike could be justifiably upset with her. But it wouldn't backfire on the coach, and long-term, that was more important.

The defense played very well that night, but the offence was shut down, and Toronto lost, 1-0.

CHAPTER ELEVEN

MIKE MET BRIDGET after the game. After enduring some taunts from lingering Philly fans, Bridget said, "Let's go somewhere other than the hotel. You know we'll just get interrupted there."

Mike looked down at her. His brows creased. "I'm sorry. You must get tired of that."

Bridget felt a stab of guilt. She wrapped an arm around him. "Just not spending enough time with you, but I know that's part of the deal."

"Okay, you pick a place. And we'll hope it's not full of hockey fans."

"I heard about a place called Vincenzo's. Does that sound okay?"

"Sure."

Bridget was nervous. Mike might be angry with her, and justifiably so. The team was his. She was just a girlfriend. But she was a fan of the Blaze, and she wanted them to do well, and she knew Mike really needed a team that was with him. So, since she had the coach's blessing, she'd give it a try.

Vincenzo's was a small steakhouse.

The tables in the place had been grouped into one long row for the only party being hosted that night: the Blaze team.

Mike stiffened beside her. The people at the table turned and stared as if caught skipping practice. They were all guys, and as many were staring at her as were staring at Mike. No one moved. Bridget sighed. Men!

She stalked over to the end of the table and scowled at them. "I get enough of this macho crap with the guys on my beer league team, so let's just clear the air. Yes, I have breasts, and no, I'm not sleeping with any of you. Now can we move on? What's good here?"

As an icebreaker, it sure got attention. After a short pause there was laughter, and a few "Ooh, burn, Reimer" comments. Space was made for them, and a couple of beers appeared.

Bridget had Mike on one side and a veteran defenseman on the other. The defenseman was one of the top four, not one who'd fallen over on the ice that morning. He played solid hockey and didn't get a lot of press. "Ribs are good," he said. "But stay away from the pepper steak."

"Thanks for the tip. And that was a nice check on number eight in the second. I think his ears are still ringing."

That was enough to start a conversation. Not everyone appreciated the plays away from the puck that could change the momentum of a game. Bridget watched defensemen more than most because that was the position she played. So she was soon chatting away with him, and some of the other guys joined in. They'd known her only as Mike's girlfriend, the girl who knocked people over and didn't like to be told she couldn't drive. Now they were finding she had a good grasp of the game and was willing to back her opinions when challenged.

On her other side, Bridget could hear Mike talking over the game with some of the other guys. Her mood lifted a bit. Hopefully, this wasn't a disaster, and maybe it would help the team, and therefore help Mike. Of course, the guys might ban her after this, or Mike might throttle her, but, nothing ventured…

After the meal was cleared, the chance of playing against Quebec came up in conversation. Quebec had just clinched, so the win-ner of this Toronto-Philadelphia series would be playing them next. There was a pause, as memories of last year's sweep surfaced in everyone's minds.

Mike leaned forward on his elbows. All eyes went to him.

"I know you're wondering about me." The entire table was quiet, listening.

"Last year in Quebec, something was wrong with my game. It wasn't anything I'd dealt with before. I went to the coaches and talked to them about it. The next day management asked me to waive my no-trade clause."

Mutters around the table. Bridget froze. Was he following her suggestion?

"I have a reputation for keeping my temper. But, believe me, I can get angry. I didn't even ask where they wanted me to go. I signed the papers and walked out. You got damaged goods. I played like crap. I wasn't sure if I would ever play properly again. Maybe I should have retired, but I wasn't ready to give up on hockey yet."

The silence continued. Bridget thought the other players could relate.

"I've recovered. And there's nothing more I want than to win these next two games, and give back to Quebec City exactly what they gave to me. A kick to the—" Mike paused.

"Balls," finished Bridget.

The guys laughed.

"If we play them," Mike said, deliberately, "I'll be getting a few penalties…unless you guys can screen the linesmen."

"That won't help us much," said a voice from down the table. Bridget suspected that was Troy.

"The way I see it, the first period, they'll be playing like it's last year again. They're going to chirp, they're going to think they can waltz in and score at will. Then, when they realize that that's not working, they'll be looking for a weak spot. They'll be crowding my crease, figuring they can get to me. I think a few guys might have to lose their balance there to remind them of their manners."

Darren, the team captain, looked at him. "Manners are good."

"By the end of the first game they should be remembering much better. Especially when they go down a game."

"Are you promising?"

"You give me two goals, and I'll do the rest. There's some payback due."

The defenseman beside Bridget leaned

over her. "You haven't played them in a year. They've changed some since then."

"And they haven't played me. They think that was because I was afraid. I'm not. We can use that to our advantage. They remember the guy they faced a year ago. That's not who they're facing this year."

"No?"

Mike reached under the table and squeezed Bridget's hand. Not in warning, this time. "No."

"Make sure Bridget knocks you down then," said Troy.

That got some laughs. Conversation became general again, mostly about how to play Quebec, and Mike's opinion was asked for often. Bridget was happy to sink into the background. None of these guys wanted her coaching, and she wasn't vain enough to think she could offer any. If they were talking, more than they had been, it could only help them as a team. Maybe this was way too simple, but she thought it was logical. She thought that was what the coach had been intending. She hoped she'd read it right.

Mike was among the first to leave, and Bridget followed with uncharacteristic meekness. She suspected he'd have a few things to say on the cab ride back. She was right.

They settled in the back seat of the cab, a space between them. Bridget wondered if that was on purpose, and just how much damage she might have done to their relationship.

"You blindsided me."

"Yep," Bridget admitted.

"I was furious when we stepped in the door."

"I expected that."

"You were about as subtle as a wrecking ball."

"Yeah, well, I know all about testosterone face-offs."

Mike grunted. There was silence. Bridget waited to assess his mood. When she was mad, she blazed out. Mike's anger was quiet, and Bridget wasn't sure just how angry he might be.

"So you have breasts?" he finally asked.

Bridget blushed. "I guess that's a little blunt. But I've had to do that routine with guys before who really have a mental block about women. It kinda slipped out before I realized just what I was saying."

"I think I saw every jaw drop. On the other hand, it was very effective. So how did you come up with this dinner idea?"

"It was really the coach."

Mike paused. "He asked you to do this?"

Bridget tilted her head. "I think so. We were talking about the team after practice, and he thinks, off the record, that the team isn't pulling together, and I made an offhand comment, and he ended up telling me where they were going to be tonight. And honestly, I was getting tired of the hotel."

"You didn't do much for my reputation."

"What?" said Bridget, puzzled.

"'I'm not sleeping with anyone here?'"

Bridget sighed. "I didn't even think of that."

"You certainly do the unexpected. Come over here. I should probably be mad at you."

Bridget happily snuggled up against him, relieved he wasn't too angry with her.

"I thought you might be."

"But you went ahead anyway?"

"I couldn't just watch the team go off the rails. And I want you to get your chance at payback with Quebec."

"You think you're ready to take on Quebec? Any secret plans for there?"

Bridget craned her neck to look up at him. "Do you still want me to come?"

"It won't be easy for you, especially if

you're going to sit there in one of my jerseys. There's not a lot of love lost. I didn't give any interviews when I left, so a lot of fans think I'm a traitor."

"Hey, I grew up with five brothers. I can handle myself. If it helps, I'll be there."

"Try not to get into a fistfight, okay? And yes, I want you there. Definitely." And for the remainder of the cab ride, Mike convinced her that yes, he really did want her around.

The team flew back to Toronto early in the morning. Bridget again was too late for that day's practice, but the following day, game day practice, she was on the ice. The coach hadn't mentioned the dinner, but he welcomed her more warmly than he had previously. He gave her a player's name, and on her way off the ice, she managed to turn back for a call "she thought she'd heard," and ran into the player while he was skating backward. He didn't fight too hard for his balance, and went down—and then played well that night. Mike did his part, and the Blaze won. It was going to a game seven, where anything could happen.

The other Toronto hockey team had once been in a game seven, up by three with less than five minutes to play—and lost. So Toronto was in a frenzy, even though the game was in Philadelphia. Philly fans were not much better. Bridget could almost feel the pressure in the air.

Players were heading onto the practice ice earlier, hoping to get knocked over by Bridget. She still thought it was silly, but she did her part. This time her stick tangled in the blade of the selected player, and she was done.

Bridget didn't know what was said in the locker room before the game, but the Blaze came out hard. Philly couldn't match their determination. The team was up by only two as the third period wound down, but Mike was a rock and the score stood. The Philly fans booed and threw whatever was handy on the ice, but the Blaze fans present were going crazy. Since Bridget was wearing Mike's jersey, she was swept into the celebration.

She was able to meet the players as they were loading the bus. Mike grabbed her, spun her around and kissed her on the lips. Bridget heard the team cheering as he put her down. Of course, they'd cheer anything that night.

THERE WERE ONLY three days between series. Bridget still came to practices, but team events were taking more of Mike's time off the ice.

Bridget found it harder back in Toronto than she did on the road; there seemed to be more time to fill on her own. On the road, she saw a lot of Mike. Not in Toronto. He was swarmed anywhere he went. There was still no word on the pool at the club reopening, and she didn't want to talk about it. She'd decided to focus on being a good hockey girlfriend. Thinking about swimming just unsettled her. And there was work to be done on the girlfriend front.

There were some dark circles just starting under Mike's eyes. Even when he should be relaxed, he wore a tense expression. She knew he was feeling the pressure of competing against his old team.

Maybe it was her imagination, but she thought the crowd in Quebec was more wound up for a game one than the fans in Philadelphia had been for game seven. There had always been a rivalry between the two expansion teams, maybe because they had started in the same year. Their paths had gone in radically different directions, but a lot of that came down to Mike. If he was able to

take out Quebec…as a Toronto fan, Bridget
was all in favor of a karmic reset.

Bridget, as usual, was in there early. She
had another terrific seat, close to the glass,
and liked to watch the place fill up, the prep-
arations for the game, the warm-up. That
morning she'd bumped into the team's top
scorer, who had obligingly fallen over. Mike
had asked for two goals, and this was the guy
best equipped to provide them.

The teams were coming out for warm-up
when someone sat beside Bridget. She didn't
pay much attention. She was watching that
her victim of the day was looking ready to
play. He saw her sitting there as he skated by,
and gave her a thumbs up. The yell of "traitor" beside her made her jump.

She turned and found a man pointing at
Mike and yelling. He looked at her, saw the
jersey and said, "Yeah, Reimer is a traitor."

Bridget tried to channel Mike and tamped
down her first response. "That doesn't make
sense."

The man was taken aback. "He left us, for
no good reason."

"Exactly," said Bridget.

He paused, not sure how to respond.

"Here's a top goalie, with the team he's led

to three Cups. He's got one year left on his contract, then he could get one last big deal and retire after playing his whole career with one team. Sounds good, eh? Instead, he decides, hey, why don't I go play for a team that hasn't ever won a Cup in a city that hasn't won for fifty years and has a reputation for killing goalie careers. Yeah, that sounds like a plan."

The man looked at her. "But—he had a no-trade clause."

"And a team can't pressure a player over that? Promise they'll bench him, make him look worthless for his next deal?"

"Ah, you're a fan of his. You're making excuses for him."

"Fine. But maybe think about it before you decide he's a traitor."

When Bridget looked back at the ice, she saw Mike had skated over to the glass. Someone must have told him she was in an argument. Like she couldn't take care of herself. Mike had his helmet up, and was looking at her with some concern.

She was on the aisle, lower bowl, so she ran down to the glass.

"You okay?" he asked.

"Sure."

He raised his brows.

"Okay, he called you a traitor. I just told him some facts."

He smiled at her. "Bridget, it might not be wise to try to run a PR campaign for me here."

"I just asked if it made sense for you to transfer from everything you had here to Toronto of all places. No inside info. It made him think—I think."

Mike shook his head at her. "Don't worry about me."

Bridget countered, "And you don't worry about me. Just worry about your game. I'll be fine. I could take that guy anyway. He's small and out of shape."

Mike looked at her with a smile in his eyes. "Did he say anything about women hockey players?"

Bridget smiled back. "No, but he's thinking it. I can tell."

"Go get him, then."

When Bridget returned to her seat, her seatmate was a little more polite.

"You know Mike?"

"Family friend," she said. No need to get into anything else.

It was enough, apparently, that the man

thought she might know what had actually gone down, so there was no more traitor talk.

A playoff series between two Canadian teams was uncommon. There was only one anthem sung. Hockey fans not attached to either team bemoaned the certainty that there would be one fewer Canadian team to play for the Cup. In the United States, football, baseball and basketball titles were much bigger news, but in Canada, this was the trophy that counted. The Victoria Chinooks were still doing well out west, but Toronto and Quebec were the only other two Canadian teams playing.

This game developed almost exactly like Mike had predicted. At first, Quebec was high on confidence, sure that they would prevail just like they had the previous year. After Toronto scored the first goal, there was a bit of a setback. Activity stepped up around Mike's crease.

In the second period, Quebec was trying to get to Mike. There was a lot of chirping going on, just like Mike had predicted, but Bridget could have told them that wouldn't work. Watching Mike closely, she could see him start to assert his territory. There were a couple of falls. And eventually, Mike was called for a penalty. The Quebec fans cheered.

But Bridget could also see that Mike's teammates weren't panicking about it. They didn't choke up, and they didn't play more defensively. And when Toronto scored short-handed, the arena got a lot quieter. It was sinking in that these weren't the Blaze of last year. This wasn't the goaltender they had walked all over in the last playoffs. This was the goaltender who had won three Cups for them, and was now playing just as hard against them.

The Blaze won. Bridget, in her Reimer jersey, got a lot of glares and jibes, but it was easy to take when your team had just won. And it was a big win. The confidence level in Quebec had dropped, and it was up in Toronto. Way up.

Mike had had a shutout, and was first star of the game. He was in big demand for post-game interviews, and Bridget waited while he patiently answered the often repetitive questions.

The most interesting thing from her perspective was that Mike gave a tease of an answer about the trade last year. He'd never talked about it to the press before.

"Yes, I think the trade did affect my play last year," he was saying. "I was still shocked, and having a hard time adjusting. That's history. This year, I know where I am, and I think I'm playing at a better level. That's what I have to do—play my best, one save at a time."

She also heard him turn down an invitation to join the guys because he had a place he wanted to take her. She wondered if she might now become a liability to the cause of team unity, but Mike was going to join the team for breakfast. No quiet breakfast for the two of them, then, but that was offset by the thought that the team who'd played so well tonight was doing so because they were, maybe, finally starting to gel as a team. She could certainly put the welfare of the team above her desire to spend time with Mike for these playoffs.

MIKE CALLED A CAB. Fortunately the driver wasn't a hockey fan, and paid them no attention.

"Are you sure, Mike? You can go with the team if you want. I'll be fine on my own."

Bridget was worried about being an impediment. Mike wrapped an arm around her.

"No, I wanted to take you somewhere special tonight."

Bridget rested her head against his shoulder. "That sounds lovely. And I wanted to thank you," Bridget said.

"What for?"

"You did what I suggested, and told the team what happened to you last year. That really made me feel...valuable."

He tightened his arm, bringing her in closer to him. "Seeing what you did with your swim team this year, you obviously know how to coach. And it worked out well. The team was with me tonight, and they weren't before."

The cab driver stopped. He dropped them off at a small Italian restaurant.

"This looks familiar," Bridget said, as Mike paid the cabbie.

Mike straightened. "This was one of my places here in Quebec. The place I took you in Toronto belongs to a cousin of the owner." He looked at the facade. "They are pretty similar."

"Now I know how you found that place in Toronto." She grinned, taking his arm.

"I wanted to introduce you to the owners. They're friends."

The owner was happy to see them, even if

the home team had lost, and led them to the best table in the house. He seemed absolutely thrilled that Mike was with someone. Bridget was amused and agreed to let the Gianettis set the menu. Wine was poured, and they were finally free to talk.

Bridget looked down at her jersey and jeans. "I'm not quite dressed for this."

Mike of course was in another suit. His beard was well grown in now, but the whole team was getting that hockey playoff look. Even the rookies in their first playoffs had some kind of scruff on their faces.

"I don't care," he answered, taking off his jacket and tie and rolling up his sleeves. "That's better."

Bridget pulled off the big jersey. "I don't think I need to advertise your presence. Not after that slaughter."

Mike laughed. "Might be as well."

"Congrats. You did exactly what you said you would," Bridget gloated.

Mike grinned. "That felt freaking great. That's a huge weight off."

"Hey, Mikey, good game."

She saw Mike stiffen. A big blond guy had come over to their table. He was a little older than Mike, had a broken nose and was sporting a red-blond beard. Mike rose to meet him. His expression was blank, his countenance unsmiling. This was the Iceman. Bridget didn't see that much.

"Rob," Mike bit out.

The blond reddened.

"Hey, I'm sorry about last year. I didn't have your back. Mom's raked me down for that. It was tough, you know."

Mike nodded slightly.

Bridget stood as well. "Hi, I'm Bridget."

"Bridget O'Reilly, meet Rob Sawatzky," said Mike tersely.

"Playing for Quebec?" she hazarded.

He smiled at her, missing a couple of teeth. Hockey player.

"Yep. Pleased to meet you." He shook her hand with a firm grip. Bridget met him, firm for firm, and dropped his hand quickly.

"My sympathies, Mr. Sawatzky," she offered.

"Call me Rob. A friend of Mike's you know. Yeah, well, when Mikey is on his game, no one stands a chance." There was a pause, awkward, and then Rob said, "Well, congrats again. Nice to meet you, Bridget" and he returned to his table.

Mike sat down.

"Sorry. I forgot some of my old teammates might be here. I wanted us to have some time alone."

Bridget was looking at him with furrowed brow. "Rob Sawatzky—and he called you Mikey. Was he one of the kids you grew up with?"

Mike nodded. Bridget tilted her head. Mike had never mentioned this before, which actually said a lot.

"How long has he played for Quebec?"

"This is his second year. He's on another one-year deal."

"I saw a ring. Married? Kids?"

"Yes and yes."

Bridget looked at him across the table. His face was closed, but she thought this was something important. "Let me guess. Last year when things fell apart for you, he didn't stand up for you. And I bet it's because of you they signed him to begin with."

"Yes, Detective O'Reilly. But I don't really want to spend tonight talking about Robbie."

Bridget considered. Obviously, Rob was a sore spot with Mike, and he wasn't looking happy to talk about him. Bridget took a minute to think over what she knew of his history with the Sawatzkys. Had he seen them since the trade?

"You do realize, don't you, that you have a very different standing than a fourth-liner who can be replaced anytime? I'm pretty sure 'Robbie' wouldn't get to have his wife tag along with the team the way that 'Mikey's' girlfriend can."

Mike looked at her, frowning, his eyes hard. "So that justifies what he did? I didn't even get a call from him asking what went down."

Bridget nodded. Mike had pride, and that would have hurt him. "Probably somewhere, deep down in that part of us we never let anyone see, he was kind of glad to see something go wrong for you."

"You may recall my wife died. That went pretty wrong," Mike retorted.

Bridget nodded again. Despite the time they'd spent together, he'd only talked about his wife a handful of times. And there was the baby... But Mike didn't have many people who were there for him. She knew, from what he'd said about the Sawatzkys that they had played a big role in his life, but he seemed to have cut them off. He was independent, self-contained, but everyone needed support. The team was coming around him, but they were all new. Those long-time relationships were important. She couldn't imagine being without her family, and Jee and the coaches she'd known since she first competed. That gave her a secure base, a stability for when the bad things happened. Mike might not want to recognize it, but he needed the Sawatzkys. At least, he needed to not have this wound festering.

She looked at him intently. "That was horrible. And I'm sure all the Sawatzkys were a big support for you then. But then, that became professional gold for you. You ended up with the Cup. And playoff MVP. And since then, little Mikey has been a superstar while Robbie has just barely survived, right? There was probably a part of him that was jealous, so he was pleased about what happened to you last season, and he was afraid for his own job, so he was a coward. And because of that, he was too embarrassed to call," she concluded.

"You're trying to defend him?"

"Not defend, just understand. He's another weasel, obviously. He did something pretty weak, and I'm sure he's ashamed. I just don't want his bad behavior to impact you. Obviously you're still upset. He knows he's messed up. So maybe, if you cut him some slack, you can let it go."

MIKE HAD HAD ENOUGH. Fortunately, Mr. Gianetti brought their food, and Mrs. Gianetti, who came out to see Mike's girl, kept the conversation going. Mike was angry that Bridget had taken Rob's side, as he saw it. She didn't understand.

As the meal continued, Mike was quiet, while Bridget made friends with the restaurant owners. They loved the story of Bridget abducting Mike to play road ball, and by the time he and Bridget were ready to leave, Mike suspected the Gianettis might welcome Bridget back more warmly than they would him.

Mike had also had time to consider what Bridget had said. She was right that he hadn't looked at Rob's side. The whole thing had happened quickly, and Mike *had* been hurt. He'd thought Rob's loyalty would be to him, but Bridget had a point. Rob had a family to support. Mike had no family, but he'd thought Rob was close to being family for him. It had hurt, hurt a lot, to know he was in an outer circle, so he, Mike, had never reached out to Rob. Rob's desertion, along with everyone else when he hadn't been able to play well, had made things worse. And Mike had continued to play poorly.

What was it with Bridget? She had a way of getting in his head and turning things around. At least her motivation was to try to help. Who knew what she could do if she was trying to create havoc.

Bridget was quiet in the cab on the way back. This cab driver was a hockey fan, and he wanted to tell Mike exactly why Quebec should have won. Mike did his Iceman routine again, and was relieved when they got back to the hotel.

Bridget looked ready to bolt for her room, but he guided her into a corner of the bar. She sighed.

"Okay, I apologize. I shouldn't meddle. It was none of my business, and I should stay out. Rob was a complete rat-weasel, beyond even Wally and deserves a worse fate."

Mike took her hand and traced circles on her palm, searching for words. He could feel her relaxing when she realized he wasn't planning on raking her down.

"So, why are you meddling, Bridget?"

Bridget looked at him seriously. "Mike, you have hockey but not a lot else. When you talk about the Sawatzkys, well, you sound nostalgic. You need people. No." Her brow creased. "I think you need *more* people, and even though Rob's a rat-weasel, he's a rat-weasel you've got history with. I got the feeling you cut yourself off from the whole family, and I thought it would be nice if you still had that relationship."

"And you care about that?"

"Of course I do, I—" Bridget stopped. "I care about you," she said, eyes lowered. Then, as if she'd said too much, she added, "How mad are you?"

"I'm not angry, just processing." He ran his hand through her hair, pausing as he reached the back of her neck. He tugged her forward, and kissed her. "You're lucky that I haven't had anyone to meddle for a long time, so maybe I don't mind it as much as I should."

She looked relieved as they said their good-nights and she went to her room. He needed more time to think about this.

It was true. He hadn't had anyone to fight his battles for a long time. He had an agent to take care of financial and business matters, but not someone who was looking out for him on a personal level. In spite of how she could exasperate him, it felt really good to have someone willing to jump in on his behalf.

He thought he'd been happy to be on his own. When you had no one but yourself to consider, life was simple and decisions easy. There was no compromising to do. But it was also lonely. He hadn't realized how lonely. He wasn't sure now that he could go back, and that was a problem.

CHAPTER TWELVE

MIKE HAD BREAKFAST with the team, so Bridget got room service before going to the arena for the pregame practice routine. There was a goalie on the ice when she got there, and it wasn't Mike.

"Come," said Turchenko. "See if you can score on me."

Turchenko was not the hardest working player on the team. Bridget had to assume that since Mike had demonstrated that he wasn't giving up his position as starter, even against Quebec, Turchenko had realized he needed to work a little harder. Bridget didn't know if Mike was just too good for her to ever score against him, or if she wasn't good enough to ever win this bet. This was the perfect chance to find out.

Turchenko wasn't Mike, but Bridget didn't score either. He was playing very intensely, as if this counted. Maybe he thought this was a competition with Mike. She'd taken only a few shots when she thought she had a chance on a rebound. She skated in, corralled the puck, and then heard Mike. She whirled around, lost her balance, and went down with Turchenko.

Bridget began to think she did have some superpowers. The game that night was chaos. Quebec took run after run on Mike. The coach finally pulled him for his own safety. Turchenko wasn't terrible, but the game was completely out of hand at that point, with Toronto players out to extract revenge on Quebec. The final score was 7-6 for Quebec. It was a deflated team on the bus to the airport that night.

Bridget had a seat by Mike. He had a couple of stitches on his forehead, and she was sure he had some bruises as well.

"That was quite a game," Bridget said. Mike just grunted. He was obviously distracted, so Bridget left him in silence. The coach took a moment to talk to her while she was waiting for her bag to come out from under the bus at the airport.

"Was this morning an accident?"

"Completely. I didn't know Turchenko could show up that early."

"Hmm."

Bridget sighed. She got the message. He didn't want her to do that again. Everyone was buying into this superstition now.

LAST YEAR, THE team had been swept in four games by Quebec. When they came back this year with a split, the city was ecstatic. The fans finally had hope, and most of it was residing in their goalie. There couldn't have been a bigger contrast with last year. The team fed off their fans and won both games in Toronto. They flew back to Quebec with a chance to clinch the series and win their way to the third round. The arena had seats, but they weren't needed that night. The fans were on their feet nonstop. It was a punishing game. No quarter was asked or given by either team. Bridget wasn't sure who all she'd knocked down that morning, but every player was doing his best. The game went to overtime, then another overtime. And finally, Toronto scored, and the game was over.

The team was going crazy. They had a new attitude, brimming with confidence. They'd beaten their biggest rivals, and now, going to the third round of the playoffs, they had exceeded all expectations. Everything was going well. Except with Bridget.

Bridget knew something was wrong. It wasn't with the Blaze. The team was doing awesomely. Making the third round of the playoffs hadn't happened for a team in Toronto since the arrival of smartphones. Bridget was getting to spend time with the team in a way she'd never dreamed would be possible. She was like their mascot, at least in the mind of some of the players. She was with Mike, and that was still something that made her smile to think about. So what was her problem?

She wouldn't admit this to anyone, but a lot of the time now she was bored. She was used to being a participant in events, not a spectator. Thanks in part to her, Mike was now gelling with the team. She made extra effort to be sure not to intrude where she felt she wasn't needed. There were still times she and Mike had together, but they were getting more and more difficult to carve out from among his other commitments. In Toronto, she didn't have a pool to swim in, and though she could go to the club to work out, she was avoiding it, and Wally. She'd started driving for long periods of time as a way to keep herself busy, finding ever better routes to get around Toronto, just to fill her time. Maybe she could start a career as an Uber driver. She was glad Jee was busy with prenatal classes and therefore not as observant, because Bridget didn't want to talk about this. There was nothing to do now but ride out the playoffs.

THE NEW YORK SERIES was another tough one. The first game Toronto lost. Close, but that didn't count in hockey. New York won the second game as well, but Toronto pulled back even at home with two wins.

It was when they were back in NYC for game five that the swim race took place at the hotel pool. Mike wasn't quite sure how this happened. Someone had asked where he'd met Bridget, and the next thing he knew, six people were lining up at the edge of the pool: five guys and Bridget. Someone counted down, and they started.

The results were never in doubt. The guys were fit, and they could swim, but they'd spent their lives training to play hockey. For them, swimming was a way to build cardio so they could skate longer. They thought that their experience, plus being male, would be enough to beat Bridget. Mike knew better. Bridget had spent her life learning how to get through the water as quickly as possible, and it showed.

Halfway through the lap back to the start line, Bridget flipped over and finished in a backstroke, keeping an eye on her competitors. She touched the wall, and hung on to it, a big grin on her face. Mike was grinning, too.

Most of the guys took it well. Turchenko did not. Being beaten by a girl was a slap in the face to his masculine ego. The other players had already pulled themselves out of the pool when he started to yell at Bridget and reached forward to grab her arm. Mike wasn't sure what Turchenko thought he was going to do, but Mike started to rise from his chair. A hand on his shoulder kept him down. Bridget said something to Turchenko; he took a quick step back. Troy Green jumped back in to pull Turchenko away.

Mike looked up and saw the coach, hand on his shoulder. Coach moved his hand and sat down. Mike gave him a questioning look.

"Let her deal with it. She'd rather take care of herself if she can. As you see, she's quite capable."

Mike knew she could handle herself, but he'd had a strong urge to intervene. Coach was right, though. Bridget was happy to fight her own battles.

One of the swimmers came over to Mike and Coach.

"Turchenko doesn't like losing?" the coach asked, with an ironic undertone. Mike thought he probably wished Turchenko felt the same about his hockey games.

The player laughed. "He doesn't like losing to a girl, anyway."

"What did Bridget say that made him back off like that?" the coach continued.

"She told him if he touched her again he'd better be wearing a cup or there wouldn't be a second generation of Turchenkos. She's something else."

Mike and the coach laughed. "She has five older brothers," Mike said.

"That explains a lot," said the coach.

A second race was then set up. Turchenko was convinced he could win over a longer distance. So, eight laps, just Bridget and Turchenko. A couple of players went to the far end to make sure the competitors touched the wall fairly.

Bridget assumed her starting pose, and Turchenko copied her. Someone counted down, and they took off.

This race was different in that it covered four times the distance. Different, also, because Turchenko had the lead. Mike was surprised, and watched closely. Turchenko kept ahead, but Mike would have sworn that Bridget's turn at the wall was deliberately slow.

Turchenko stayed just ahead. He was swimming hard, while Mike was sure Bridget was taking her time. Turchenko kept about a body length lead on Bridget. After the halfway turn, Bridget flipped, got a little closer to Turchenko, and he turned it up a notch to stay ahead of her.

Finally, the last two laps. Mike wondered if she'd decided to let Turchenko win, to help team morale. But he saw he'd been mistaken. She knew exactly what she was doing. She wasn't just going to out-swim Turchenko, she was going to do it by outsmarting him.

Turchenko was struggling. He was starting to flail. Bridget had been pushing him, just enough to keep him swimming all-out to stay in the lead. Bridget's only concern was in hitting the final wall first, but Turchenko wanted to be in front the whole way. She'd known and used that to get him to spend his reserves. In these last two laps, he had nothing left, and Bridget passed him as if he was standing still.

She didn't wait in the pool after hitting the wall this time. She pulled herself up from the water to the sound of cheers from the guys. She flashed a big smile at Mike, and he smiled back, feeling proud, though he knew he'd had no part to play in her victory. But she was his, and she was amazing.

Turchenko offered his hand, and Bridget shook it. Then a couple of the guys wanted to know how to do that turn at the wall, or the butterfly stroke. In a matter of minutes, Bridget was back in the pool, providing an ad hoc coaching session.

Mike turned to his own coach, wondering what he'd think of this.

"She's good," he said. Mike nodded.

"I'd hire her."

Mike was surprised by that.

"If she coached my sport, and I could get management to sign a female coach," he continued. "She's got Green and Turchenko listening to her. That's impressive."

Mike looked back at the coaching session. He'd never seen her with her swim team, he realized, but he was getting a glimpse now. She was very good at this, and she enjoyed it.

Even her hair seemed brighter. Finding a place where you excelled and felt good—that was a special thing. Unfortunately for Bridget, she was just doing this for an afternoon. The club pool still wasn't open. It would be hockey as usual, and Bridget would be back on the sidelines. Mike knew he should do something to help her. Surely, he had some contacts somewhere. Bridget needed this. He swore he'd find a way to help—after the playoffs. These playoffs had lasted longer than he'd expected, longer than anyone had. They were finite, though. For just a bit longer he had to focus on hockey. It was a familiar thought.

Mike stole that game in NYC, and the team was able to pull off a win back home. So Toronto, at long last, was going to be in the finals. They were playing for the Cup. The city was covered in black, red and yellow, and, for now, everyone was a Blaze fan.

BRIDGET WAS AT loose ends, again. It had become a familiar, though unwelcome, feeling, and now there were two more weeks to get through. The team was flying to Victoria for the first game of the finals tomorrow, and she would be flying out, too. The press was making a field day about the young goalie in

Victoria—the new Mike Reimer, meeting the old Mike Reimer. Bridget asked Mike if he needed a cane now.

The joke had been forced. Of course, she was happy for Mike and the team. But today they were doing publicity, and she couldn't sit in her apartment on her own or she'd go crazy, so she decided to drop by the swimming club where Annabelle was now in training. She could torture herself for a bit. That would be a sure way to cheer herself up.

She walked through the doors. This was a top club, maybe *the* top club. The swimming program at the athletic club where Bridget was still technically coach had been improving when it came to their swimming program, but this club already had Olympic swimmers. One day, Bridget promised herself, she'd be working at a club like this, going to the top meets and seeing her swimmers on the podium.

Or had she missed her chance, she wondered dismally. Couldn't she be happy having accomplished what she had, and watching her A-team as they potentially became those podium swimmers? She sighed. She didn't think so.

Bridget arrived a little early to watch practice. She was taking Annabelle for brunch afterward. Maybe she wouldn't have much chance in the future to use it, but she'd try to pick up some more knowledge while she was here and had the opportunity. She'd already incorporated some of the innovations Jonesy had pioneered in conditioning into the program she'd instituted at the club. Not all. She had her own ideas and had been trying some of those also. She thought they'd been working but...

She took in the chlorine smell, the echoing sounds, the humid feel of the air. She breathed deeply, having missed this so much. Then she spotted Annabelle. The girl looked to be doing well. She was talking to her new coach, Jonesy. Annabelle looked up, saw Bridget and waved to her. Bridget waved back. Annabelle said something to the coach, then they both walked over to Bridget.

Jonesy was an ordinary-looking guy. You could pass him on the street and not remember him. Brown hair, medium height and medium build. He was quiet and undemonstrative, which meant he was pretty well the opposite of Bridget. But close to him, you could feel the intensity. He might not be someone you'd notice in a crowd, but he exuded a confidence and charisma when you spoke to him. And he was very observant. Bridget had been surprised that he recognized her in Winnipeg after that short meeting in Atlanta. After all, there were a lot of coaches trying to make it to Jonesy's level. Not only did he remember her name again today, he surprised her by asking if she had a moment to talk. Bridget said of course. He probably had questions about Annabelle. Any time she could spend with him would be of value. She even wondered if by any chance he knew of someplace needing a coach.

Annabelle ran off to change and Bridget followed him to his office. It was bigger than her cubbyhole at her club, and had pictures of his past winners on the walls. She'd have loved to check them out, but he offered her a seat. There was a moment while he seemed to collect his thoughts.

"You've done a good job with Annabelle. She's talked a lot about you. I'm sure you weren't happy to lose her."

Bridget shrugged. "Not happy" was an understatement.

"Do you know when your pool will be open?"

"No date yet." Bridget didn't think Wally

would tell her till it was filled with water again. Maybe not even then.

"How long are you signed with them?"

Bridget liked the trend of these questions. "Through the end of the summer. But since there's no pool, and no date set for it to open, I'm pretty well done now until next season."

Jonesy was pursuing his own line of thought. "I've had a good five years here." Thinking of the results he'd had, including medals in the Olympics, Bridget had to agree. "But my daughter is pregnant."

"Congrats!" said Bridget. She wasn't sure why he was sharing this with her, but maybe he was just making conversation. She was probably reading too much into the questions he'd been asking.

Jonesy smiled. "Thank you. My wife has told me she's moving back to Australia to be a grandmother, and I think I'd be wise to go with her. Still, I have a lot invested here, and I want to leave it in good hands.

"As you know, things change quickly in our sport. I have assistants here who would be happy to keep things going the way I have them now, but if this club is to stay a success, it needs to advance—take risks, try new things, keep on the front line of innovation."

Bridget nodded. Exactly what Jonesy was known for, and which she'd tried to emulate. Annabelle and Austin showed that it could be successful even when done at a more basic level.

"I'm looking for someone to take over here. Someone with a drive for winning, someone innovative and successful. Someone who isn't going to try to be Jonesy Two, but who will make this club over into the way she wants it."

Bridget froze. *She?*

Jonesy nodded. "I've talked to Annabelle, and her parents and some of your other swimmers. Your previous coach sings your praises. I've watched tape of you competing, and your swimmers before and after training with you. I know you're young, but I started young and I've taken risks before. I'd like you to work with me for six months to transition over, and then I can go see my grandchild and feel confident the club is in good hands."

Bridget was almost speechless. "Really? Are you sure?"

"I know it's a lot to take in, and I've hit you out of the blue. Take a bit of time to consider it. It's a demanding job, but I think you could do some good things here. When can you come back so we can discuss this in a little more detail? That is, if you think you might be interested."

Bridget could only nod. Interested? Words couldn't describe how interested.

They set a time to meet again. Bridget had a nice brunch with Annabelle, and listened to her talk about the club with renewed interest. Underneath, the excitement was thrumming. You didn't get your dream handed to you every day.

She had a lot to think about.

She wanted to call Mike, but he was tied up with a team event. So she went home and fidgeted with anything she touched. She should be over the moon, calling everyone she knew, but there were a lot of things to consider, and she wasn't sure Mike was who she should talk to after all. If she mentioned this to him, they'd have to start talking about the future, and it was a bad time for that. She should do what she did when she needed to think: swimming or road hockey. Thanks to Wally, there was no pool, so she went out to the garage to get a net and a ball.

There wasn't much to do but practice her shot on her own. While part of her mind calculated distance and speed, the other part worried over her problem. Word got out, as the day waned and her brothers showed up to join her. Cormack got in net, and Patrick and Brian joined up against the two of them. Brian and Patrick were soon up 3-0.

Cormack called time.

"What's your problem, Bridget? You let Brian right by you."

"Sorry, I'm a little distracted."

"No kidding. What's the matter?"

Bridget sat on the curb, dropping her stick. "I was offered my dream job today."

Brian cocked his head. "So why aren't you celebrating? Isn't that good news?"

"It's excellent news. Really. It's at the club downtown that is basically the best in the country. I've been asked to be head coach." Her stomach dipped. It was good, but scary, too.

"Congrats, Bridgie," said Patrick. "But, yeah, you don't look happy."

"Part of me is. Really. Unless I mess up, I'll be working with the best swimmers in Toronto. I'll get to go to international meets, probably the Olympics. It'll be lots of work, lots of traveling, and I'll get to do the thing I want to do most."

"I can see why that would upset you," Patrick said, ruffling her hair.

Cormack spoke up. "What about Mike?"

There was a pause.

"How serious are you guys, B?" asked Brian.

Bridget shrugged. "I don't know."

Cormack snorted. "How can you not know?"

Bridget glared at him. "I'm not a moron, Cormack. But it's not that easy. We had just started going out when the playoffs began, and since then it's been crazy. I don't know how serious Mike is. We didn't discuss any plans for after the season, but no one thought the Blaze would go this far and that the playoffs would last this long. And I don't think that the start of the Cup finals is the time to ask Mike to sit down and discuss the status of our relationship."

The guys flinched. Obviously not a discussion they were fond of having either.

"Mike isn't going to be here next year," Cormack stated, and the others nodded.

Bridget knew that. The Toronto teams couldn't afford the salary he could ask for now. And realistically, while the city was going crazy for the Blaze, the team could go this far again only if there was another perfect storm of hockey circumstances. It was not likely. There was no future for arguably the best goalie in the league staying in Toronto, even if money wasn't a factor.

"Could you get another coaching job somewhere else, if Mike wanted you to go with him?" Patrick asked. "I mean, if you've got this offer, you're pretty good, right?"

Bridget looked at him. "Sure, I march in to whatever club I like in the city Mike settles on, and ask, totally ignoring whether or not they have a vacancy, if they want to hire me, because I was offered a job here in Toronto but wasn't committed enough to take it? And of course, I'll give notice if my boyfriend goes to another team?"

Brian sat down beside her and gave her a hug. "So it's love or money?"

"Not really," said Cormack. "Mike has lots of money. Love and money or your job?"

"Dream job or dream guy, I guess," said Bridget.

Brian was Bridget's favorite brother for a reason. He looked at her and asked, "Bridget, if Jee had come to you with a question like this, what would you have said?"

Bridget didn't pause. "Job. I'd never tell someone to give up their job for a guy. I mean, who knows what's going to happen with the guy?" She took a moment and thought over what she'd said. She sighed. "I just didn't imagine it would be so difficult. Mike's great." There was longing in her voice.

"Are you sure that's what you want to pick?" Cormack asked. "You have to admit, the perks with Mike are pretty awesome. And he's not a jerk." Cormack had come around since that first road hockey game in the fall.

Patrick raised an eyebrow. "Well, Bridgie?"

Bridget thought about the last month and a half. It had been fun. But as Mike became more integrated with the team, she was doing less, and getting bored. And this was the play-offs. During the regular season, it would be worse. Whatever coaching she might pick up on an ad hoc basis, after having had this offer dangled before her, would drive her crazy. She'd tried being a hockey girlfriend, and it wasn't enough. She needed her dream, too.

Bridget sighed. "I can't settle."

"What are you going to tell Mike?" asked Brian.

"Nothing right now. I have to meet with Jonesy again after the first Victoria trip to formally accept. And I don't think I should say anything to Mike in the middle of this series."

The brothers agreed on that one. No one who called themselves a hockey fan would upset the team in the finals. Bridget stood up again, grabbed a ball, and shot it at Cormack. She played better, since talking to her brothers had brought out into the open what her decision would have to be, but she could see bad times coming, and she wanted to put it off as long as she could.

PHYSICALLY, MIKE WAS feeling good. There was some fatigue, and a lot of sore muscles, but no injuries. These last couple of rounds of hockey had been incredible. He was playing as well as he'd played in his life. He had Bridget and her crazy family around, which gave him a break from hockey when he needed it. It seemed counterintuitive, but as his feelings grew for Bridget, hockey got a little less important but somehow easier. If they'd lost to New York, or if they lost to Victoria, it was, well, not the end of the world. He still loved hockey, but it wasn't so scary to think of it ending someday. He had something else, something big enough to replace hockey eventually. Maybe he could even have his own team of little redheads. He could admit, at least to himself, that he was thinking permanent. He thought Bridget was, too. As soon as the playoffs were over, they were going to have a talk.

The strain was starting to tell on Bridget, he could see. Just trying to "accidentally" bump into someone at practice was a challenge. There were only so many players, and they would pretty well line up like dominos. No one would admit to taking this ritual seriously, but everyone was there, just the same. The players were desperate. They were afraid of any change in their routine at this stage of the game. For this team to be here was a miracle, and they all knew it. They were waiting for the shoe to drop, ending things.

But something was up with Bridget. Finding time alone now was a problem, but he would swear she wasn't trying anymore. Part of him wanted to find out what the problem was, but a bigger part of him preferred to skirt the issue. He could claim he wasn't superstitious, but he didn't want to upset the balance they had, either. He'd almost scared himself once, thinking impatiently that the season needed to be over soon so he could get things settled with Bridget, and that traitorous thought disconcerted him. He couldn't play to win if he was thinking of losing.

The impromptu swim race in New York had made him face some hard facts. Bridget had been a trouper, hanging around to be there for him throughout these playoffs, but this was an anomaly. When he'd seen how she'd come to life at the chance to compete, and to do a bit of coaching, he'd had to realize that she needed that just as much as he needed to play. He'd been shocked when his coach had said he'd hire her. Mike hadn't appreciated how good she was. Not only did she need that outlet, she had too much talent to waste. And if he really loved her...with a jolt, he realized he did.

This wasn't like his relationship with Amber. It had come on slowly, but that had only made it stronger. Somehow, it went deeper. He was older and wiser. He had a better idea of what he needed in a partner, and Bridget was exactly right for him.

So he knew, if they were to have a future together, her career would have to be as big a factor as his. And that complicated things.

At this point, it didn't much matter if the Blaze won the Cup or not; Mike was going to be the hottest property in free agency. He'd have his pick of teams and would be offered a lot of money. He could go for the cash, or go to a team that would be a Cup competitor for the next several years. He knew the Blaze's position this year was a fluke, but there were teams that would be a strong contender with him. He had once thought he'd retire after spending his career with just one team in Quebec. Now, his options were wide open, and that was exciting. His agent was getting "hypothetical" offers, since Mike was still under contract. Mike had asked him to research competitive swimming potential in any city that was making serious "hypotheticals."

He wanted to talk to Bridget about this, but it would have to be a private discussion, and really, he should keep that talk aside till the playoffs were over. There was a reason players didn't sign contracts during the playoffs. They couldn't afford the distraction. But this worry about Bridget was taking his mind off the game. He needed to let her know he saw a future with her, and to do that they needed to talk it out. There were teams he'd prefer to sign with, but only if Bridget was on board. He could compromise, maybe quite a bit. He felt rather magnanimous, admitting that.

He also wanted to take her to meet his mother after the playoffs. He figured they could visit her before the July 1 free agency started, and maybe visit some of these prospective destinations. Check out coaching situations at swim clubs, as well as hockey possibilities.

He knew it would be smart to wait till the playoffs were over. But when he came out for practice, before game five, he saw Bridget skating. Something about her expression disturbed him. He wanted reassurance, so he found himself asking, impulsively, "Hey, Bridget, how would you feel about flying out to Phoenix?"

"Phoenix?" She glided to a halt, looking perplexed.

"Yeah. I usually head out to see my mother at the end of the season. I'd like you to meet her."

Bridget stared at him, eyes wide. He wondered what was up. He'd met her family; didn't it follow that she would meet his?

"It's a little premature, right? I mean, we should wait till the series is over, and who knows how long things could take?" she asked.

Mike straightened. Something was wrong. "I wasn't talking about tomorrow. I didn't have a definite date, but win or lose, we'll be done in a week and I'll be free. Unless the pool's opening?"

Bridget shook her head. "Not that I've heard," she said, but she wouldn't look at him.

He laid his stick on the net, and skated over to the faceoff circle where she was focusing on a skate lace.

"Bridget," he said.

She looked up at him, and he was startled to see tears in her eyes. "We should talk later, okay? Big game tonight."

A fist was squeezing his chest. Why didn't she want to make plans with him? She couldn't just be afraid of meeting his mother. "Bridget. What's up?"

"Can't we—" she started.

"No. I don't need the distraction of worrying about this. Let's lay it all out in the open."

Bridget straightened slowly and chipped at the ice with the toe of her skate. "Um, I kind of have plans."

Plans. Plans she hadn't mentioned to him. Plans that apparently didn't include him. The fist squeezed tighter.

He waited.

"I went to see Annabelle at her new club." He knew the club. Best in the city, maybe best in the country, she'd said. That Aussie coach, Jonesy, she'd been so excited to meet in Atlanta. And great swimmers. He nodded that he was following her.

"They offered me a job. My dream job. Head coach."

Mike was about to congratulate her when it struck him. Bridget had made her decision, and she hadn't included him. And it meant she wasn't moving anywhere. She was going to be in Toronto for a long time.

She finally looked up at him. "Mike, I know how much hockey means to you. I would never ask you to give it up. But it turns out this is pretty much the same for me. I know you can't stay in Toronto, and I can't leave now. I just wanted to wait till you won the Cup to tell you."

Mike couldn't speak. He couldn't breathe.

"I tried, Mike. I really tried to be who you need. But I'm just not the right kind of person. I can't let this coaching thing go, and you deserve someone who can put you first."

She looked at him, at her eyes pleading for understanding. He wanted to say something, say the right thing, but then the team was jumping onto the ice, whooping and hollering at the excitement of starting game five in the Cup finals, tied up, a chance to win it all.

Mike had been feeling pretty much the same thing until five minutes ago. But he'd give it all up if he could just start over with Bridget. She headed straight for the exit, hardly noticing a rookie fall on his butt while he got out of her path. One minute she was there, then she'd skated away. And Mike stood there, immobile, trying to get air into his lungs, watching her go.

BRIDGET ALMOST TORE off her skates and ran out of the rink. She sped down the sidewalk, not looking where she was going. This had gone so, so wrong. What was her problem, blurting it out like that? Why couldn't she have just smiled and said "sure"? There were two, three games left, maximum. All she had to do was pretend for less than a week, but she couldn't. She'd had to give up playing poker with her brothers because they busted her every time. She could never bluff. How had she thought she could pull this off?

And the look on Mike's face… Bridget was walking down the sidewalk so fast people were giving her odd looks. She needed a good game of road ball, but she wasn't going to find that in downtown Victoria. Her other option? A swim. That she could do. The hotel had a pool.

She'd walked a fair piece away from the rink and she hadn't been sure where she was. By the time she got back, she had a moment of panic. What if Mike was there? She couldn't face him. But no, he would still be at practice. He couldn't throw away a practice for the finals on game day. She could swim for maybe an hour, and hopefully by then she'd be ready to face him again. That was, if he was still speaking to her. She wasn't sure if he'd want her to leave immediately, or to stay around for the team for the last few games. It was going to be difficult either way. Her stomach knotted.

She went through the hotel lobby and caught an elevator with some Toronto fans. Fortunately she'd never gotten much publicity, so she slipped off on her floor unremarked. She slid the card in the lock and headed over to the stand where she'd left her suitcase with her swimsuit. Then she saw him. Still wearing his hockey uniform. He was sitting in a chair waiting.

"We need to talk," he said, in a tight voice.

MIKE HAD NEVER left a practice. He was a professional, and he behaved that way. He was proud of it. The day Bridget got had her alter-cation with Wally when the pool closed, he'd sent in his excuse before practice started, and that was as close as he'd ever come to ignor-ing his commitments. But walk off the ice like he'd just done? Never.

And yet he'd marched off the ice today, ig-noring the questions thrown at him, made his way to the dressing room where he pulled off his skates and pads to put on shoes and then headed out. He was terrified Bridget might just leave. In that moment, he knew straight-ening things out with her was more impor-tant than anything else in his life.

He was sure he'd looked a sight tromping down the sidewalk in his Blaze uniform, but he needed to find Bridget, and the only place he could think to start was her hotel room. She'd have to pick up her stuff, and he wanted to get there before she could leave.

Whether it was the uniform, knowing who he was or the determination in his face, some-how he was able to get the maid to let him into her room. Some of the tension left his body when he saw her things still inside. She hadn't left. He'd just wait until she showed up.

He saw himself in a mirror. He looked ri-diculous. He sat and started to pull off the re-

maining pads and protective gear that were
out of place when he was off the ice. He realized that, suddenly, all those questions
he'd been debating about what to do were
resolved. He was going to do whatever it took
to be with Bridget.

He had time to straighten out his thoughts
before he heard her at the door. She stopped
when she saw him, looking almost scared. He
didn't like that. But there were a few things
he didn't like, and the only way to work them
out was to talk.

"We need to talk," he said. He tried not to
sound angry or hurt, but he was. He'd like to
block the door and tell her she wasn't leaving till things were worked out, and worked
out right, but he had a pretty good idea how
that would go. He'd prefer to see her angry,
not sad and fearful, but this wasn't the time
to provoke her.

She smiled tremulously. "Nothing good
ever comes after 'We need to talk,'" she
echoed from an earlier conversation.

"Let's make an exception to that. Could
you sit? I'd rather you didn't run away before
we can work through this."

That made her chin go up. "I'm not going

to run. I just didn't expect to find you here. Shouldn't you be at practice?"

"Yes," he said baldly.

"Then?"

"This is more important."

She stared. And sat.

"So what happened with Jonesy?" Mike asked.

Bridget fidgeted with her cuff. "He's retiring. New grandchild. He's offered me a six-month lead-in to take over his position."

"That's certainly a step up from coaching at your current club. You deserve it. Congratulations. When did this happen?"

Bridget stared at her cuff. "I went to see Annabelle just before the Victoria series, and he asked to talk to me."

"And you accepted?"

She nodded, biting her lip. "Day before yesterday."

Mike was silent, and Bridget looked up, blinking behind her glasses. "It was the most difficult decision I've ever made."

Mike asked. "Why? It's your dream job, isn't it?"

She nodded. "It is, but there's nothing for you in Toronto."

Mike hoped that wasn't true, but didn't say it out loud.

"Why didn't you tell me?" This was the part that tore at him. It was the part that would let him know if he had a chance.

Bridget sighed. "We're in the finals. It wasn't really the time to ask where you thought our relationship was headed. If you didn't think there was any future for us, it didn't matter. And if you did—" She broke off for a moment. "If you did, then we'd be faced with deciding between my career here and your career elsewhere. When I got that offer, I wanted it so badly. And I just couldn't see any way to have that and have us. This job involves traveling—not just in North America but around the world. We had a hard enough time finding time together when we were both in Toronto. And if we wanted to have a family—" Bridget stopped.

A sliver of hope there. She'd thought about them having a family. Good.

Mike spoke softly. "You thought you'd save me having to choose between the woman I love and hockey again."

Bridget's head shot up.

Mike nodded. "But it turns out that having

the choice made for me is even worse. Tell me, what do you want, Bridget?"

She looked at him. "Well, the Blaze to win the Cup."

He shook his head. "No, the real stuff. What do you most want in your life?"

She went back to her cuff. "My job, obviously. My family. You." Her cheeks flushed.

"Okay. Ask me what I want."

"I know you want—"

Mike shook his head. "Ask me."

"Okay, Mike. What do you want?"

He waited till she looked up. She stilled, staring at him so intently through those crazy big glasses. He hoped she could see he meant what he was saying.

"You."

There was a pause. The silence was loud. She opened her mouth, but he went on, "No, that's it. When you left. I didn't care who won the hockey game, I didn't care who was starter, I just wanted to make sure I hadn't lost you."

Bridget didn't seem to be able to speak.

"It wasn't always that way. For a long time, I thought I didn't have anything if I didn't have hockey. But really, hockey wasn't that much. I'd got the money, the accolades, and at the end of the day, I was going home to a hotel room, alone.

"That changed after I met you. I don't want to go back. I won't go back. I don't know how to make this work, but I'm going to find a way. I love you. You're my top priority."

Bridget looked at him, eyes serious behind the lenses. "Mike, I love you, too, but I won't make you choose."

"You don't have to. I've already chosen."

BRIDGET DIDN'T GIVE him much time before she insisted he call the team and let them know he was fine. Mike expected he'd be benched, but at this point, the team needed to win more than they needed to enforce rules, so Mike would start after all.

Bridget was down at the glass for warm-ups, and the whole team saluted her. The coaches had some questions about what had happened this morning, but Mike knew he was fine to play. He'd never felt better in his life. Tonight, he couldn't lose.

And he was right. This game did come down to the two goalies, but the "old" Mike Reimer had never been better. It took two overtime periods for someone to score, but the Blaze shut out the Victoria Chinooks to go up in the series, 3-2. It was a big win, and the whole team could feel it. Two nights later, playing back in Toronto, Mike knew that they'd broken the Chinooks after that grueling overtime win. Victoria pulled their goalie in the closing minutes, but Mike was in his zone, and shut the door.

The Blaze won the Cup.

There was a moment when the arena was frozen. Mike could feel the people in the arena, collectively, coming to terms with this. Toronto, the hockey crazy city with two hockey teams that hadn't managed to claim the prize in more than fifty years, had won the Cup. The upstart Blaze had finally, finally brought the Cup home. The place exploded.

Only a few people noticed the redhead in the Reimer jersey run toward the tunnel where the team entered. A couple of team assistants helped her over the glass. Mike saw her running toward him. He had no idea how she'd gotten there, since he'd been the center of an ecstatic group of hockey players, but they cleared a path and she leaped into his arms, knocking him down. He wrapped his arms around her, knowing he'd won a prize more valuable than the silver trophy about to be paraded around the ice. He stared into the happy, vivid face above him, and ignoring the rest of the team, the crowd and the cameras, he kissed Bridget, kissed her with all the love and excitement and joy he was feeling in that moment. And her response let him know that he'd made the right choice.

That kiss was the photo on the front page of every Canadian paper the next day.

EPILOGUE

MIKE PULLED THE McLaren to a stop by the O'Reillys' home. He looked over at Bridget, sitting in the passenger seat.

"Ready?"

Eyes sparkling, she nodded. The tip of her nose was a little pink, and her freckles were in full force. The Phoenix sun had been a challenge to her fair skin.

"You're sure about this?"

"Completely."

When Mike had talked about being free a week after the Cup finals, he'd been a little optimistic. Toronto had gone completely crazy with joy, and full credit had been given to Mike for his work. There had been interviews, a parade, and endless celebrations for the team. No one wanted to call it over. It had been two weeks before Mike and Bridget had been able to escape to Phoenix to visit Mike's mother. It didn't surprise him that she and Bridget got along. His mother admired strong women, and she was pleased to hear that Mike wasn't getting his own way with his girlfriend.

Now, a month after that last big game, and the entire O'Reilly family was packed in the backyard of the family home. They had come to share Mike's Cup Day. Every player who won hockey's ultimate prize got to spend a day with the actual trophy. Mike had been through this three times before. The first time he'd gone back to Saskatchewan with the Sawatzkys and his old coaches and team-mates. The next two times had been in Ottawa, mostly doing charity events. This time, spending the day with the O'Reillys was a no-brainer. He couldn't imagine a more perfect scenario.

THE FAMILY HADN'T seen Mike and Bridget since they left for Phoenix, so there was chaos for a while as they entered with the Cup and its keepers in their wake. Mike kept firmly by Bridget's side, arm wrapped around her waist. Bridget was wearing a white sundress and sandals, and he thought she looked beautiful. He was in white as well. He was tanned and happy. The playoff beard was gone.

Once the keepers had the Cup set up just

so, he stood by it to say a few words, Bridget still close by his side. He looked at her, and she nodded back. She put a hand into his back pocket, unnoticed, and pulled something out and slipped it on her finger. He looked out at the happy faces, and felt a warmth inside that even a fourth Cup win couldn't match.

"Thanks to everyone for coming here today. It's great to share this with you. It's not my first day with the Cup, but I think this will be the one I remember best.

"This isn't official yet, so please don't spread the news, but I've accepted a three-year deal with the Blaze." He'd agreed to a hometown discount on his salary so that the team could still sign some of the young guys. Three years, and then Mike was going to retire, and see how he did as a dad while Bridget kept coaching. Bridget was arguing that one, but he was confident he'd get his way.

There were cheers from the family.

Mike looked down at Bridget. "The fact that Bridget is going to be coaching here in Toronto has of course had everything to do with that decision."

He looked out at the family again. "The Cup has done some interesting things in its long life, traveling around the world with the players who've won it. This may be a first though." Mike paused, nervous for a moment. Would the family approve of this as well?

Bridget held up her left hand. It sparkled. There was a diamond, and it was on her ring finger. There was a shocked silence and Mike rushed on before bedlam broke out again.

"We have something else to do—Father James?" Mike called.

The family priest came through the gate. Mrs. O'Reilly gasped and sat on her chair with a thump.

"We're getting married!" Bridget shouted.

Then the family erupted. The women converged on Bridget, the men gathered around Mike. Fortunately, they were mostly congratulatory. Mike faced Mr. O'Reilly.

"Sorry, sir, I wanted to ask for your permission but Bridget started making comments on how many sheep I was willing to pay for her. But if you have any questions, or concerns…"

Mr. O'Reilly looked at him levelly. Even though he had to look up to meet Mike's eyes, Mike was the one feeling small.

Bridget's dad held out his hand. "Welcome to the family, Mike. I appreciate that you're willing to stay here for Bridget. Be good to her."

Mike swallowed a lump. "I will, sir."

Mike had been anticipating a big ceremony, but Bridget hadn't wanted a fuss. She'd been through four weddings for her brothers, and she wasn't interested in that hassle. "Been there, done that, bought the dresses I'll never wear again."

So, here in the backyard, they had a quick and simple ceremony, and the family potluck was all they needed for a wedding banquet. Mike and Bridget had brought champagne, and they toasted with the Cup.

In a quiet moment, Mike pulled Bridget aside. She turned to him, smiling widely. "This was a fantastic wedding. You didn't really want the big fancy ceremony, did you?"

Mike agreed. It would have been a circus, after the Cup win, but he would have happily gone through it if that had been Bridget's desire.

"I haven't given you your gift yet," he said.

Bridget's forehead creased. "I didn't think we were doing presents. I don't need anything!"

Mike smiled in anticipation. He pulled out

his key ring. "This isn't wrapped…" he said as he pulled off the fob to the McLaren.

Bridget stared at the keys, speechless. Mike dropped the fob in her hand and wrapped her fingers around it.

"But, the bet…" she said, looking up at him.

"Now that we're going to be living together, I don't want to spend my time in fear of you setting up some trick to score on me. I'm playing it safe," he teased. In reality, he just wanted to see the look on her face, the one he was seeing now.

"Mike, you've done so much for me already. You're staying in Toronto, you're going to spend the summer hanging around here while I start working with Jonesy, you've promised to coach Cormack—and I didn't get you anything." She looked distressed.

Mike gazed around the backyard. A year ago, he'd been questioning his future, his own worth, alone and lonely. Now he had Bridget, a big crazy family, and even though he was back on top, he had a future that didn't depend on hockey.

He looked at her. "You've given me more than you know," he said and kissed her.

Suddenly Jee cried out. Brian raced to her

She was in her ninth month, and finally conspicuously pregnant.

"I think—I think my water broke," Jee said, in shock.

The backyard emptied as Brian picked Jee up and carried her out. The rest of the family quickly followed.

Bridget looked at Mike, grinning. "My family. I should go to the hospital. What do you want to do with that?" she asked, indicating the silver Cup, now looking forlorn with only its tenders to keep it company.

"Let's bring it with us. Babies usually take a while, don't they? Maybe someone at the hospital would like to see it."

"And I can drive!" Bridget gloated.

She leaned up to kiss Mike. The Cup keepers had to clear their throats a few times before the couple stopped and gave them directions.

Mike swore that the drive over gave him his first gray hair. They were a long time getting to the hospital, but they arrived in time for the day's second addition to the O'Reilly family.

* * * * *

Get 2 Free Books,
Plus 2 Free Gifts—
just for trying the Reader Service!

Love Inspired. SUSPENSE

HOME *on the* RANCH

YES! Please send me the **Home on the Ranch Collection** in Larger Print. This collection begins with 3 FREE books and 2 FREE gifts in the first shipment. Along with my 3 free books, I'll also get the next 4 books from the Home on the Ranch Collection, in LARGER PRINT, which I may either return and owe nothing, or keep for the low price of $5.24 U.S./ $5.89 CDN each plus $2.99 for shipping and handling per shipment*. If I decide to continue, about once a month for 8 months I will get 6 or 7 more books, but will only need to pay for 4. That means 2 or 3 books in every shipment will be FREE! If I decide to keep the entire collection, I'll have paid for only 32 books because 19 books are FREE! I understand that accepting the 3 free books and gifts places me under no obligation to buy anything. I can always return a shipment and cancel at any time. My free books and gifts are mine to keep no matter what I decide.

268 HCN 3760 468 HCN 3760

Name _____ (PLEASE PRINT) _____

Address _____ Apt. # _____

City _____ State/Prov. _____ Zip/Postal Code _____

Signature (if under 18, a parent or guardian must sign) _____

Mail to the **Reader Service:**
IN U.S.A.: P.O. Box 1867, Buffalo, NY. 14240-1867
IN CANADA: P.O. Box 609, Fort Erie, Ontario L2A 5X3

Get 2 Free Books,
Plus 2 Free Gifts –
just for trying the *Reader Service!*